SOME REVIEWS

Is this book completely fictional? The readers will actually ask themselves if perhaps much of what is written by Wayne Frye could be the truth. Starting with the 1986 assassination of one of the giants of peace, Frye weaves a harrowing tale of "what ifs" and "maybes" that drives at the heart of a world where the powerful, mighty and rich rule with absolute impunity. This is heavy stuff.

Library Review

This is an Aaron Adams adventure yarn like no other. Canadian mystery lovers have enjoyed reading about the exploits of Wayne Frye's champion of the downtrodden who refuses to bend before the winds of tyranny. This time, he introduces a woman named Jasmine, who is every bit Aaron Adams' equal when it comes to tackling the ills of a world where the mighty rule with the iron fist of repression. Together, these two go in search of a terrorist who is in service, not to the usual militants, but to the C.I.A. He is a menace who has unleashed horror after horror all over the world in what his handlers call "the defence of freedom." Aaron and Jasmine know the truth, and they will not rest until the truth is exposed and this menace to humanity is destroyed.

Cue Magazine

The ending will haunt you for days. This is a mystery of great magnitude, but, above all, it is a love story about two unlikely souls in search of compassion in a world filled with despair.

The International Herald

The Girl Who Stirred Up The Whirlwind

Some Thoughts Dear
To The Girl Who Stirred Up the Whirlwind

In some countries, every few years the oppressed are allowed to think they are democratically picking someone to lead them. The truth is that they are only electing their new oppressor.

People are not interested in knowing the truth of their own enslavement. Most people have been captured by the propagandists who spew out a steady diet of lies. The human race has made great strides in many areas, but the masses are still psychologically imprisoned by their manipulators.

When people are denied the basics of life, they should become outlaws. Unfortunately, too few of us realize that those at the top of the economic ladder are denying the rest of us that to which we are entitled.

Stortorget Square in Stockholm, Where the Orders for Olaf Palme's Assassination Were Given And Jasmine Alexander's Life Was Changed Forever

J. Wayne Frye

THE GIRL WHO STIRRED UP THE WHIRLWIND

By
J. Wayne Frye

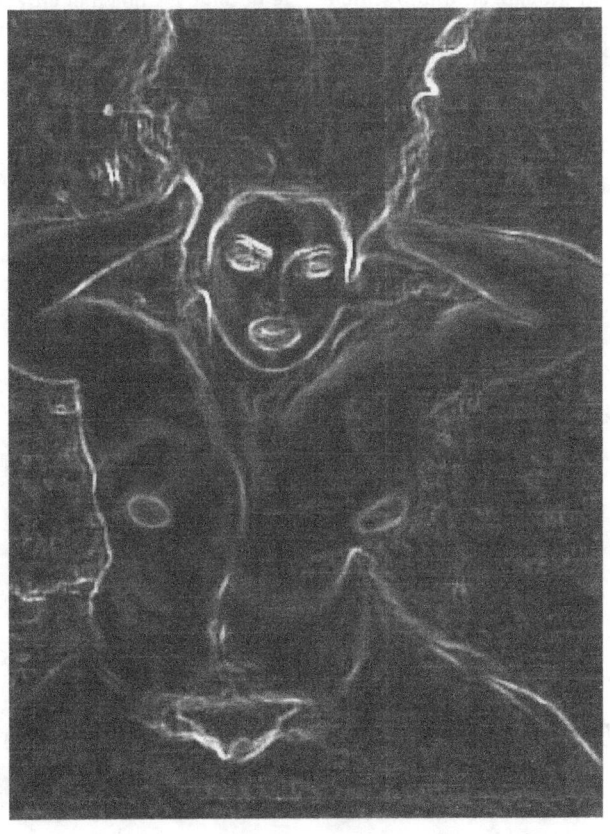

The Author

Wayne Frye's Aaron Adams series has been popular among Canadian mystery lovers since first appearing in 2005. He provides satirical political commentary to many Canadian newspapers, and his books on politics have created a great deal of controversy. He has written marketing/advertising textbooks, been a successful U.S. university hockey coach, professor, university president and served as a marketing consultant to hockey teams and motion picture companies. He has been cited for his work with inner-city gang children in the Los Angeles area and been active in the anti-globalization movement. He became a Canadian citizen in 2003 and lives with his wife, Jasmine, in Ladysmith, British Columbia.

Other Books by J. Wayne Frye

Guide to Local Radio and Television Copywriting
Something Evil in the Darkness at Hopkins House
How Hockey Saved a Jew From the Holocaust:
The Rudi Ball Story
The Catastrophic Calamities of a Village Idiot
Fighting for Justice in the Land of Hypocrisy
Guide to Alternative Education (13 Editions)
Cataclysmic Dreams in Black and White
Mastering Marketing Research
Introduction to Advertising
Marketing Plan Work Book
Public Relations Workbook
Fall From Apocalypse
Advertising Lab Manual
Promotions Workbook
Advertising Design
Armageddon Now
Worth
When Jesus Came to Jersey as the Son of Thunder

Books by J. Wayne Frye with Jasmine Falling Rain Frye

Canadian Angels of Mercy – Nurses in Times of Peril
Points of Rebellion: Aboriginals Who Fought for Justice

TABLE OF CONTENTS

The Girl Who Stirred Up The Whirlwind

TO: My dear wife Jasmine, for whom I honourably named the protagonist in this story. I also, through clandestine subterfuge, found the photograph of her that the publisher willingly used for the back cover design. She may kill me, but I did it anyway, because she represents much more than physical beauty. She is the epitome of the beauty of soul that soars to the heights of understanding in a world where there is far too little compassion for those who are the victims of the culture of greed that rules supreme. *JWF*

Catalogue Number: 20126196110

ISBN: 978-0-9879728-4-2

Fireside Books – Victoria, British Columbia

The Girl Who Stirred Up The Whirlwind

PROLOGUE
HOW MANY HAS HE KILLED?

The man code-named *"The Whirlwind"* had been waiting all his life for this moment. Trained by the best intelligence agency in the world since he was a teenager, the Director of the C.I.A. had personally shaken his hand in the dark corridors of the Langley, Virginia headquarters in March of 1976. The head of the agency decided it was time to make a field operative out of the 23 year assassin protégé.

The South African Police were eager to work with the C.I.A. to help in the battle against communism. The *Whirlwind* would assist in the fight against the African National Congress that was trying to end Apartheid. With Cuba supplying forces to help the nearby Angolan Liberation Front in their battle against totalitarianism, South Africa, as an arms supplier to that country, was America's best hope to make sure a compliant regime stayed in power there. The *Whirlwind* was ready to do his duty, and his penchant for learning languages made him a vital asset who could roam the world to serve the interests of the USA. Always elusive around a camera, no one had ever been able to get a photo of him. As the years passed, those who spoke of him only whispered the word *whirlwind*, as if saying it out loud might lead to calamitous consequences. He was more than a legend in his own time. Like "Carlos the

Jackal," he was a force to be reckoned with, and the string of deaths that occurred whenever it was believed that he was in an area, just solidified the myth. For years, political assassinations and the mysterious deaths of those who challenged the status quo made the few who knew about the *Whirlwind* whisper softly, "wonder whom he has killed? Wonder how many he has killed?"

CHAPTER 1
STRIKE A BLOW AGAINST HOPE

Olof Palme was truly a man of the people. In Sweden, there was no White House or ostentatious palace for the country's elected leader. As Prime Minister, Olof lived in a small, simple, inconspicuous apartment in downtown Stockholm. Olof's insistence on simplicity would be the overriding factor in making it possible for the W*hirlwind* to serve the interests of the dark forces of evil that were determined to destroy all who stood against the insidious spread of the corporate theocracy that was determined to rule the world. Olof Palme was unaware of the sinister forces that were hovering all about him and were in league with those who sought the enslavement of mankind to the culture of greed.

He had long been a thorn in the West's side because of his opposition to America's covert and counter-insurgency operations throughout the world that kept despots in power, as long as they supported the west and its capitalistic exploitation of the Third World. Ever since Palme had become Tage Erlander's Minister without Portfolio to the Cabinet Office right after the JFK assassination, American and British intelligence agencies had kept a keen eye on him, because Olof was suspected by the British and Americans of not just being a socialist, but perhaps an outright enabler of the world's communist movement that threatened the sanctity of the new world order as promoted by Margaret Thatcher and Ronald Reagan.

During the 1970s, Palme became a hero of those who opposed war and the aggrandizement of greed. Elected Prime Minister in 1969, he became an irritant to the western powers. When the USA resumed its inhumane bombing of North Vietnam over Christmas 1972, Palme denounced it so strongly that the Nixon administration threatened to cut off diplomatic relations with Sweden. When Palme continued his denunciations, it was then that the C.I.A. instituted covert operatives to shadow him. The South African Intelligence Service was used in the surveillance and the *Whirlwind* left Johannesburg and rented an apartment in Stockholm, only a few kilometres from where Olof Palme lived.

The USA, Britain and South Africa worked diligently to assist the opposition parties in defeating Palme. Finally, in 1976, they accomplished their objective and Palme was replaced with a more conservative Prime Minister. Yet, in the September 1982 election, the forces of change rose up in mass, and Palme was overwhelmingly elected once again. This was the beginning of the end, as Palme was viewed as a voice for moderation at a time when Ronald Reagan and Margaret Thatcher were determined to finally eliminate the Soviet Union as a threat to the menacing spread of corporate capitalism throughout the entire world. Standing against the USA was a risk few outside the communist block were willing to take. Olof Palme was a man of principle who saw the innate evils of an economic system based on greed and the continuing subjugation of all humanity in service to the monolithic corporations that the American government and its vaunted military machine served. This stand of conscience would not go unpunished by the forces of darkness.

While the *Whirlwind* waited patiently for orders to carry out assassinations, the Thatcher and Reagan governments were slowly formulating plans for the invasion of Grenada and the Falkland Islands, in order to combat what they saw as the increasing assertiveness of nations to make decisions on their own, rather than deciding things based upon what was in the best interests of Washington and London. The covert activities of the Reagan Administration started almost the first day he was in office. In 1981, U.S. and British intelligence communities coordinated efforts to stop all attempts by nations to throw off the yoke of colonialism or introduce governments that were not capitalistic in nature.

Washington and London were finally in the hands of corporate serving, ideologically driven, hard-line, anti-communist zealots who were willing to use any means possible to make certain that the world was protected for exploitation by the capitalists who owned the politicians in both countries.

With the re-election of Ronald Reagan in 1984, the stage was set for the final showdown between capitalism and communism. Leftists were about to be targeted by the U.S. and British governments that would use any means possible to eliminate the threat to capitalism and the corporate theocracy that was slowly engulfing the entire world in its insidious, strangling grasp. Freedom movements throughout the world were to be mercilessly targeted, as any legitimatization of a government that promoted equality of opportunity by showing disdain for a system of economic servitude was considered a threat to the United States and Great Britain. Standing against this idea that only capitalism offered true hope for humanity was Prime Minister Olof Palme. Sweden, itself, represented a threat, because as a socialist democracy, it was generally considered the most affluent country in the world at the time, with a solid commitment to assure all its citizens equality of opportunity and a social safety net that protected the vulnerable, the old and the economically deprived. This was seen by the USA and Britain as a repudiation of capitalism; consequently, it could not be allowed to stand.

Palme's suggestion for a nuclear-free corridor in Central Europe, in the hope of ending the obscene weapons race between the two super powers, was met with outrage by London and Washington, because they insisted on having weapons of mass destruction all across Europe, so they could destroy the Soviet Union in a matter of minutes.

One of Olof's biggest mistakes was visiting left-wing Nicaragua in 1984. The U.S. government was supplying mercenaries there in an attempt to overthrow the legitimately, democratically elected government, and Olof's visit was viewed by the Reagan Administration as a direct affront to America's interests.

Washington and London were hoping that the September 1985 election would finish off Palme. Since it would soon be followed by one in Denmark, the hope was that social democracy in a nuclear-free Scandinavia would finally be rejected by the voters. The European Workers Party, a right-wing organization with close ties to the C.I.A., started exploiting claims that Palme was a Soviet stooge. Money and material support poured in from American-backed organizations intent on getting Palme out of office. Unfortunately for Olof, who won re-election with the help of the Swedish Communist Party, Washington and London decided that they could not tolerate an election outcome that went counter to their needs.

All this time, the *Whirlwind* kept an apartment in downtown Stockholm. Although he spoke fluent

Swedish, along with 12 other languages, he was like a phantom, rarely venturing out in the daylight hours, and sometimes disappearing for months at a time. He had no friends, and on the few times someone would speak to him, he just lowered his head, pulled down the fedora he wore in a cockeyed manner to cover his face and ignored them. No one ever connected his frequent disappearances from his Stockholm apartment with assassinations that were occurring all across the world at the exact times he was gone. After all, he was a totally non-descript person. It was almost as if he didn't really exist.

The C.I.A. section chief in Stockholm, Susan Altman, was at her desk reviewing some documents when a call came in on the code 1 white phone. Looking up to make sure her door was closed, she picked up the receiver and said, "hello."

The voice on the other end, in a South African accent, said, "I understand there is a message for me and the *Whirlwind* is about to be unleashed."

Susan had received a secret coded message from Washington, indicating that the plot that had been contemplated for so long should be set in motion. Her job was to pass the coded message on to the South African Intelligence Service, which would, in turn, see that the *Whirlwind* received his instructions.

The Girl Who Stirred Up The Whirlwind

Working through the South African Intelligence Service provided an excellent way for the C.I.A., MI-6 and their respective governments to avoid culpability if the plot were to fall apart. Susan and Gerick Coatsee, of the South African Intelligence Service, had worked together before, and they both knew that any mission carried out by the *Whirlwind* would be in the hands of a master assassin. Consequently, there was minimum chance of failure. Neither one of them knew for sure, but the rumour was that the *Whirlwind* had over two dozen political assassinations to his credit. They had never seen him personally, but his reputation made him a venerated figure among those who sanctioned assassinations as a legitimate adjunct to foreign policy. Thus, for his refusal to accede to the wishes of Washington and London, Olaf was about to pay the piper.

Susan simply replied, "the usual place at the usual time," and immediately hung up.

Meeting in a nondescript location, far from any prying eyes, might have seemed smart, but that was not the right way to play the espionage game. A public place was often the best way to avoid detection. Coatsee and Altman knew that it was up to them to give the go-ahead to the *Whirlwind*, and there was a procedure they had to follow in order to do it. As always, Coatsee and Altman were at the Borshuset Building in Stortorget Square at exactly 3:00 PM, according to the clock in the square. Coatsee walked out of the building as Altman was walking in. When they passed one another, Altman simply reached down with her left hand and placed a small piece of paper the size of a coat button into Coatsee's left hand. They never even looked at each other.

The Stockholm Stock Exchange Building was indeed an appropriate place to give the go-ahead for this assassination, as it was the centre for the murder of people's hopes and dreams. How many lives had been destroyed by the nefarious shenanigans of the capitalistic manipulators of a system that let all the good things only flow to those at the top of the economic ladder? Those who dared question the authority of a system of economic servitude for the masses could not be tolerated, even in a socialist democracy like Sweden. Outside forces saw socialistic democracy as a threat to the corporate theocracy that was gradually enslaving the entire world to the bottom line. Olaf Palme was a man who dared question the economic order and that could not be tolerated. If economic fairness gained too strong a foothold in Sweden, it might spread to the rest of Europe and gradually turn the world into a more equalitarian place where the haves might be forced to share their bounty with the have-nots.

Coatsee never looked down at the small paper. He simply put it into his left overcoat pocket and continued to stroll through the square toward the end of the promenade, where he walked to the left and entered the narrow alleyway between two buildings. There were too many people strolling through, so he stopped at the appointed place and leaned his back against the brick building on his right. Reaching behind his back with his right hand, he searched for the lose brick. Finding it, he continued looking to his left and right, waiting for the alley to empty. The steady stream of strollers continued, so he removed the tiny piece of paper from his pocket with his left hand and transferred it unnoticed to his right hand. Then he began to wiggle the brick lose and turn it long ways, so that it gave him room to place the tiny piece of paper inside and then slide the brick back in. He turned and walked away, knowing that the *Whirlwind* came by at appointed intervals to check the brick. One could be assured that the *Whirlwind* was too careful to ever be observed retrieving a message. In fact, in all likelihood, he used a go-between to retrieve the coded orders that were placed there for him. This had been the drop used in Stockholm many times to give the *Whirlwind* his orders. And once he had his orders, nothing could stop him from carrying them out, as when the green light was given, there would be no further communication.

Eventually, the *Whirlwind* would call Altman to let her know he was on the job as ordered. In fact, one day later, she received the call on the white phone and the low, obviously disguised voice simply said, "order received. It will be executed within one month as instructed." The plot was set in motion and as always, the *Whirlwind* would deliver as expected, but there would be one hitch this time that would haunt him and his handlers for almost 20 years. It would not be politicians. It would not be any governmental body. It would not be the military. It would be an 8 year old little girl who would make the high and mighty worry for years that the truth might be revealed.

Little Jasmine Alexander was a shy and studious child who was forced to live on the fringes of society, because her mother made her living by prostitution. Although an equalitarian society where, unlike America, poverty was basically unknown, there were still those who chose to live outside the societal norms that guaranteed everyone food and shelter.

Jasmine's mother, Phyleece, was one who, because of a drug dependency, lived a life of despair in a country where those on the lower rungs of society are always offered a hand up, but she kept slipping back into desperation, because of her need to constantly score drugs. Although Jasmine had already been in two foster homes, the court had allowed her mother custody once again, after she completed a drug rehab program. Yet, Phyleece was now trapped in a downward spiral like she had been so many times before. As her life spun out of control, she desperately tried to make sure that Jasmine was properly cared for. Yet, like so many who are imprisoned by dependencies, she was losing the battle.

Phyleece had spent the day scoring drugs and turning tricks while little Jasmine was forced to sit in their two room apartment, dutifully watching television as her mother had instructed. However, in the next door apartment, there was a man who was preparing to commit murder of the foulest kind, and little Jasmine Alexander was about to run afoul of the U.S. government and, more importantly, an evil entity that represented that government. Her neighbour was none other than the *Whirlwind*, who was preparing to strike a blow against hope.

CHAPTER 2
SANITY AND COMPASSION
LAY IN A POOL OF BLOOD

Craig Wilton was a South African intelligence agent who had worked closely with the *Whirlwind* and the C.I.A. for many years on nefarious plots and deeds all around the world. This assassination, like many others they had coordinated, would need a fall guy, and it was Wilton's job to find one and set him up to take the blame. Like most assassinations, this one would have to be made to appear as the act of a lone malcontent who was outside society's mainstream. And did Wilton have the perfect patsy this time.

Christer Pettersson was a known substance abuser who could always be found wandering about Sveavägen Street near the Grand Cinema where Olaf Palme and his wife liked to go on occasion to take in a movie. The time of the assassination had not been set, but the place had already been picked, because Palme and his wife went to the Sveavägen area frequently, and they often did so without any bodyguards. After all, Sweden was a country, unlike America, where the culture of the gun was not aggrandized; therefore, it was just assumed that there was little to fear from a populace that was not steeped in the violence that was perpetrated by those poor victims lost in a system of economic servitude. Sweden was an equalitarian society, where

J. Wayne Frye

everyone was covered by a social safety net that guaranteed citizens would not be mired in abject poverty and relegated to a life of pleading for crumbs from the table of plenty that was always set for the wealthy and powerful. Olaf Palme had a big part in making sure that Swedes were all afforded equal opportunity and that the rich and powerful paid their fair share. He was determined to tackle the problem of income disparity, not only in Sweden, but all over the world. In doing so, he was making powerful enemies in capitalist countries, and with the Swedish industrialists who saw any attempt at lifting up the working people of the world as an affront to their desire to enslave the masses to the bottom line that ensured them the profits that seemed to be at the core of everything they did.

Palme was one of the foremost leaders of the Socialist International, which was valiantly fighting against the neo-liberal economic lunacy promulgated by Ronald Reagan and Margaret Thatcher. Standing against the might of the USA and Britain was a mistake in a world where those two countries saw themselves as the protectors of the moneyed class.

Into this mix came the former head of the C.I.A., George Herbert Walker Bush, who as Vice-President of the USA, actually had more power than the buffoonish, Ronald Reagan. It was he who was fearful that Palme would go before the

The Girl Who Stirred Up The Whirlwind

United Nations and denounce the way the USA was funnelling arms to the anti-democratic Contra rebels through their proxies in Iran. Palme was a threat, not only to the neo-liberal policies of Thatcher and Reagan, but to George H.W. Bush personally. This could actually keep him from becoming President, which had long been the plan promulgated by his father Prescott, who had freely traded with the Nazis during World War II and was determined that the Bush family ultimately elect one of their own as President in order to secure their rightful place as America's royal family.

Craig Wilton and the *Whirlwind* were determined to serve the interests of those dedicated to the preservation of capitalistic exploitation at all costs. Unwittingly, Christer Pettersson, was about to become a vital component in the most sinister plot undertaken by the C.I.A. since its complacency in the 1963 assassination of American President John Kennedy.

Pettersson grew up in a middle class family in Solna outside of Stockholm and later moved to the suburb Sollentuna. In his youth he attended a theatrical school where he was considered promising as an actor. However, he suffered a head injury from which he never fully recovered. Subsequent to his injury, he began a period of substance abuse which would eventually force him to drop out of school. He began to wander the streets of Stockholm and survived by committing petty crimes, until one day, he graduated to a felonious act. In Sweden, getting hold of a handgun was next to impossible, but Pettersson, had a penchant for knives as a weapon of choice. He traded for a World War II German bayonet and started carrying it in his breast coat pocket for protection from the drug dealers to whom he owed large sums of money.

In 1970, he used the bayonet to slay a drug dealer who, according to him, had threatened him. He was convicted of manslaughter and paroled within a few years. Upon release, he went back to his old ways, and became a familiar figure in the downtown Sveavägen district of Stockholm. Now, Craig Wilton had his patsy. All that remained was to smuggle in the Smith and Wesson .357 Magnum pistol that the *Whirlwind* would use for the kill. That would be accomplished by a circuitous routing from New York City to the Azores Islands, then to Cape Town, South Africa and finally to Stockholm. The plot was unfolding beautifully, and like all operations with the *Whirlwind*, Craig Wilton knew it would be carried out with exacting precision by the master assassin.

However, there was one glitch in the whole process. Wilton did not know it at the time, but a precocious 8 year old girl was about to become the thorn that would prick both he and the *Whirlwind* with doubt about their success in keeping a secret for the first and only time, causing them consternation and worry for many years as they knew there was one person with a semblance of knowledge about what really happened when Olaf Palme was assassinated. Jasmine Alexander was about to become a target of both Wilton and the *Whirlwind*, but she would be unaware of it most of her life.

Secretly photographing and filming Christer Pettersson on the streets of the Sveavägen district, Wilton supplied the *Whirlwind* with information that would help him study Pettersson's mannerisms and duplicate his appearance as nearly as possible. The *Whirlwind* had mastered the art of impersonation to a degree that it was possible for him to not only duplicate looks, but mannerisms and speech patterns as well. He prided himself on practicing subterfuge of the foulest kind. He was convinced that there was no act too despicable when serving one's country. He was a practitioner of that detestable doctrine that would be promulgated by George Bush and Dick Cheney at the dawn of the new century that proclaimed all was permissible in the defence of liberty. This was a forerunner of the idea that using terror to fight terrorism was perfectly legitimate. The *Whirlwind* had no scruples when it came to fighting socialism, which he saw as an attempt to assist those who were not worthy of help. His philosophy was that some people were just born to be victims, and deserved no special consideration in a world meant for the few.

Olaf Palme was preparing to go before the General Assembly of the United Nations in March and lay bare the truth of America's violation of its own Constitution in its determination to see that the socialist regime that was set upon a more equalitarian society in Nicaragua was destroyed. The truth of America's determination to support oppressive regimes to protect corporations would be spelled out in detail by a man who was determined to see that the downtrodden of the world no longer had to bow in supplication to the interests of corporations that were abated in their thievery and avaricious greed by the U.S. government.

On the 25th of February, a telegram was delivered to a Republican confederate of George H.W. Bush who was intricately involved in the illegal weapons trade in the Iran-Iraq War and the subsequent funnelling of weapons to the Contras in Nicaragua. All it said was, "the Swedish tree is about to be felled. Fret no longer."

It was now up to the *Whirlwind* to carry out the dastardly deed that would, indeed, fell the tree that was sprouting too many deadly branches that might fall upon those who were polluting the world with their insidious evil. Olaf Palme had three days to live.

The Girl Who Stirred Up The Whirlwind

No one will ever know just how many people the *Whirlwind* had killed or assisted in killing. He had eliminated many of the most prominent anti-apartheid activists while in South Africa to assure the continued alliance of that government with the USA in the battle against socialism on that continent, and he had roamed the world to carry out assassinations of individuals deemed a threat to the status-quo. Those in the know were well-aware that he had personally committed assassinations that were often blamed on others. His penchant for finding fall guys had always been aided by Craig Wilton.

As the countdown to the assassination of Olaf Palme began, the USA and Britain learned that a large arms consortium made up of most of the defence industry corporate giants were also mulling an assassination of Palme, who was considered a threat to the continued Cold War between the then Soviet Union and the West that was bringing in billions to those who depended on war or the threat of war for their huge profits. There was no attempt made to curtail these efforts, as the C.I.A. and MI-6 saw these attempts as a good cover for their own operation.

So, there were a vast array of lookouts, decoys, and the like skulking around the Swedish capitol during Olaf Palme's last days, while the *Whirlwind* methodically checked on the performance of Palme's bodyguards, who were basically non-existent, as Sweden, unlike the USA, was a society where many of the powerful politicians genuinely felt a kinship with the people and freely mingled with them unafraid of any dire consequences. The C.I.A. and MI-6 decoys consisted of former Swedish Nazis and fascist sympathizers, which would offer more confusion and suspects when the murder would eventually be carried out by the *Whirlwind*. Among these miscreant malcontents were South Africans, who were known by Swedish intelligence to be intensely concerned about Palme's exuberant attacks against the South African apartheid-obsessed regime. The overtly oppressive South African government was clandestinely, but enthusiastically, supported by Ronald Reagan and his band of fascist-like foreign policy advisors who saw no dictatorship or repressive regime they were not willing to support in their obsessive battle against communism.

Palme was a doomed man, because the vast intelligence network of the USA and Britain was arrayed to bring him down, as their governments had decided that he was a detriment to their aims of securing the world for capitalism at all costs. This one respected head of state was daring to take a stand against the evils of an economic system based on greed that was hell-bent on taking the modern world back into the Dark Ages, where everyone would serve the Lords of the Manor. Only now, the Lords of the Manor were the corporate CEO's. If Palme were allowed to stand against this new world order, the people might elect more leaders like him who were dedicated to standing against the USA and Britain in their aims for the economic enslavement of humanity to their corporate benefactors.

Although Ronald Reagan was President, it was George H. W. Bush, his Vice-President and the former head of the C.I.A., who was well aware of the threat to corporate theocracy posed by Olaf Palme. Reagan was usually too busy sleeping through National Security meetings to have any idea of what was really going on. So, a disinterested, inept President was sitting idly by as those about him decided to turn their backs on the machinations of deceit that were about to take down a true defender of the downtrodden.

The world was awash in weapons, courtesy of the USA and its arms manufacturers. And one man, who now had his hands on an untraceable smuggled weapon, was the *Whirlwind*.

On the night of 28 February 1986, Olof Palme and his wife, Lisbet, prepared for an evening at the cinema to see the comedy *Bröderna Mozart*. They would enjoy many laughs, but the evening would end in tragedy for not only the two of them, but for the people of the world who sorely needed a champion like Olaf Palme to stand up for them against the tyranny of the elite.

The Girl Who Stirred Up The Whirlwind

Olaf looked in the mirror as he adjusted his tie, turned to Lisbet and said, "Shall we go, darling?"

She took his hand, smiled up at him and leaned her head on his shoulder. They walked out of their apartment and headed toward the cinema without any bodyguards.

Knowing that Friday nights Palme usually went to the cinema whenever the movie changed, the *Whirlwind* had already decided that Friday, the 28th of February, was the day that Palme would pay for his bold stand against tyranny. Back in his apartment, the *Whirlwind* was preparing himself to look like Christer Pettersson with the help of Craig Wilton. However, there was something happening that would forever haunt them and make them live in fear of discovery the rest of their lives.

Jasmine Alexander often played on the landing above the stairs that led to the Whirlwind's apartment. With her Raggedy Ann doll in her hands, she sat quietly as the two men came out of the apartment. She looked up at them and noticed that the Whirlwind did not have his usual fedora hat on. She smiled and said, "you don't have your hat on. I never noticed your eyes before. Did you know one is brown and the other is brown with some green in it?" Looking at Wilton, she continued, "you have funny eyes, too. You don't have any eyebrows. I could always remember the two of you, because you look so funny."

The Girl Who Stirred Up The Whirlwind

Saying she could remember them was a death sentence for Jasmine Alexander. Yet, as Wilton moved toward Jasmine to strangle the life out of her, the *Whirlwind* placed his left hand on Wilton's right arm and whispered, "not now, we can't risk someone coming up the stairs. It might delay us. I will take care of her and that whore mother of hers when I return."

Jasmine Alexander had received a reprieve from a man who never made mistakes, but this time, letting her live in order not to delay their appointed task would be a critical mistake that would forever play upon the minds of the two killers. Without saying a word to Jasmine, they continued down the stairs. At the door to the street, the two men parted with a knowing nod that they were about to deliver a blow of retribution against a man who had dared to stand against the British and American governments. That was what they lived for.

Having reviewed Christer Pettersson's criminal background, Wilton knew that he would be a perfect fall guy. He had developed a relationship with him over the past week, and arranged a rendezvous with him in an alley near the cinema. Telling him that he knew where they could score some major drugs, it was easy to lure him into a set-up. Meanwhile, the *Whirlwind*, now dressed similar to Pettersson, who always wore the same clothes, stood nondescriptly outside the cinema.

The Girl Who Stirred Up The Whirlwind

The *Whirlwind*, as he stood waiting for Palme to exit the theatre, fingered the smuggled gun in his right coat pocket. He thought back on Jasmine Alexander, and how her precociousness had sealed her fate. He had no problem killing a child. He had done it before. Hey, it was what they called collateral damage. This was a war, and the innocent would often suffer along with the guilty.

There was a light snow falling, as death in the form of a man leaned against a building. The *Whirlwind* tilted his head slightly up, scanning about the area to see if there might be any bodyguards lurking about. He knew that the walls had ears, the doors had eyes and that the voices all about him were conduits for that which was often held secret. He watched and he listened for the unusual. Anything out of place would be a reason to abort.

The snow drifted against the shop windows almost in disappointment that it could not enter the warmth that was inside. Couples lazily strolled about, clutched next to one another as the white drifted all about. The fluttering flakes of snow were almost ghostly in the moonlight. The stars were obscured by clouds as there seemed hollowness in the cold. The wheels of cars and the footsteps of the strolling couples made squeaking sounds on the street, as if crying out for warmth in a world where there was only the cold of want. In the quiet there was no sky or earth, only snow lifting in the wind, frosting the window glass, chilling the air and deadening everything in the city. Something else permeated the air, something sinister. And the people, as they meandered down the street, appeared circumspect, almost as if they sensed an impending doom. And the doom was there, leaning against a wall, waiting to delivery his blow against sanity in a world ruled by the insane barons of greed, arrogance and self-righteousness.

As the snow thickened, drifted and fluttered into the doorways of buildings, almost politely begging for entrance, the *Whirlwind* began to think about Jasmine Alexander and her mother, Phyleece. The little girl he would dispatch quickly out of politeness, not compassion. There was no need to make a child suffer, but her mother was a useless whore whom he would enjoy killing. Most of the people he had dispatched he killed quickly, but there were a few who had found themselves in situations that let him relish with delight the torture that he was able to inflict. Watching them suffer gave him a sense of worth and power. He was a man who enjoyed killing, because he felt that he was a mighty sword of retribution doing the work of the God whom he had been brainwashed into believing had, indeed, ordained his beloved America to be the guiding light of the world. This was a dangerous man, as are all men who believe that God sanctions what they and their countries do in the name of patriotism.

The Girl Who Stirred Up The Whirlwind

Like most of the world, the Swedish people were susceptible to the idea promulgated by the propagandists in the USA that America was a country where democracy reigned supreme and opportunity to reach the heights of success abounded for all. Yet, the 1960's saw leaders like Olaf Palme start to question the hypocrisy of a nation that touted democracy but supported tin-pot dictators all over the world in order to secure markets, raw materials and cheap labour for its corporate conglomerates and insure that the evils of socialism, with a more equitable distribution of the wealth at its core, were never allowed to gain favour with those who had the most to gain from a system that promoted equality of opportunity. It was the *Whirlwind's* duty to protect the world from these misguided do-gooders who wanted the abundance that abounded to be shared, rather than harvested and controlled by the few who charged for what should be free to all.

Many wise men, like Palme, saw the assassination of John Kennedy in 1963 as a masked coup d'état by the rich and powerful interests of America to assure that the agenda of economic fairness promulgated by Kennedy was confined to the dust bin of history, along with his intention to pull American troops out of Vietnam and end an immoral war. Although it could never be proved, the C.I.A. was, no doubt, a willing partner in support of the corporate autocrats who saw assassination as a way to solidify their growing hold on the U.S. government that was there, not to serve the people, but the interests of the ever expanding corporate theocracy.

In order to thoroughly understand what led Olaf Palme to his fate, one has to go all the way back to the 1930's in the United States, when, with the Great Depression raging at full force, the American people turned to Franklin Roosevelt in 1932 to deliver them from the grips of a corporate controlled Republican dynasty that had been in power for 12 years, and, like George W. Bush at the turn of the 21st century, had literally destroyed the economy in order to facilitate the desires of the rich and powerful to satisfy their unquenchable greed. Within a year of FDR's election, the entrenched, elite business establishment was conspiring to overthrow him in favour of a fascist state. It is not within the purview of this book to detail the failed coup attempt that was thwarted by a hand full of men who were dedicated servants of democracy. Rather, our concern is with how all this led to Olaf Palme's eventual sacrifice at the altar of greed.

These same elite watched Hitler tackle the depression by using the Jews as scapegoats and going to war in order to fuel industry. Although they watched Hitler fall victim to overreach, the business elites of America looked at his model, and they decided that the USA's industrial base could be expanded and extravagant profits realized if they set up a system of constant war, but effectively masked it under the guise of battling communism, so that people would have no reason to object to fascist policies that would be deemed necessary in order to battle those who hated America. By using fear, the American people would simply line up in unison to have their invisible shackles put on, so they could all be bound in servitude to the corporate theocracy.

This is the system that was eventually institutionalized after World War II. The enemy this time was not Hitler, but communism. Like the myth of Islamic Fascism, the idea of a commie under every bed was used to make Americans cower in fear of an enemy that was more manufactured than real. This myth was used to control the people for nearly fifty years, and it was actively promoted by the C.I.A. as a willing partner to the business elite who are the real power in America. With operatives in every media outlet in the country, the C.I.A. effectively controlled the dissemination of news and saw to it that the vast majority of the people had no idea that they were spoon fed only approved news that would make them worship at the altar of patriotic servitude.

Into this system of manipulative capitalism walked one of America's elite. The man whose father openly traded with the Nazis until he finally had his bank seized by FDR under the Trading with the Enemies Act. Prescott Bush had reared his son, George Herbert Walker Bush, to take his place among the aristocracy that ruled America. George Herbert Walker Bush was recruited by the C.I.A. in the 1950's. This architect of the 1961 Bay of Pigs invasion became C.I.A. director in 1976, and to protect the agency, he directed the efforts to defeat President Carter successfully through dirty tricks like the sabotage of the Carter rescue mission to Teheran in 1979 and arranged a deal with the Iranians to delay release of the American hostages so that Ronald Reagan would be elected; whereupon, he, knowing Reagan was an incompetent stooge, in effect, became President in all but name. It was he who would promote the mass supplying of arms to despots, and through Iran, to supply the anti-democratic Contra rebels in Nicaragua with arms to overthrow the legitimately elected Sandinistas who had vowed to end the inequity of capitalism.

With Iran though, he had a serious problem, as these deliveries had to be kept secret because Iran had been promoted as an enemy by the U.S. government. So, they approached Olaf Palme to collude with them. Seeing this as just another nefarious attempt to foster corporate domination on the poor of the world, Palme flatly refused and threatened to reveal the whole plot to the world. This valiant stand for justice had sealed Palme's fate. Into this scenario comes the *Whirlwind*, who saw himself as a righteous avenger against those who dared stand against the tyranny of corporate and American dominance of the world. Were Swedish politicians aware of what was about to occur? In all likelihood, there were some privy to the coming firestorm that they hoped would make Sweden an accomplice in the proposed dominance of the world by a corporate elite, because there were those in Sweden who saw equality of opportunity the same way the American elite saw it, as a prescription for fairness aimed at those on the top of the economic ladder.

Ironically, there were no police anywhere in sight. Why had they seemingly disappeared from the Sveavägen district that they generally patrolled incessantly on Friday nights? Oh, the *Whirlwind* knew why. The agency had a mole in the police department who had altered assignments to make sure the area where Palme was would be free of patrols at 11:16 when the movie ended. Still, ever cautious, the *Whirlwind* continued to scan all about, looking for any suspect activity. There were those who disobeyed authority sometimes, and if someone did, that could be fatal to people in the *Whirlwind's* line of work.

As the *Whirlwind* gripped the smuggled Smith and Wesson 357 Magnum in his coat pocket, he felt the power seem to surge through the weapon into his hand and throughout his body. He was an avenging angel prepared to deliver a blow against those who dared question the authority of the USA to determine all countries destinies.

The Girl Who Stirred Up The Whirlwind

Glancing at the green coloured clock tower in the nearby square that was filled with people, the *Whirlwind* watched anticipatorily as the hand jumped to 11:13 and then 11:14. He thought he actually heard the clicking sound it made when the hand jumped, even though he was at least 100 metres from the clock. It was the sound of impending death for Olaf Palme.

From behind the clock tower, he saw Craig Wilton walking with Christer Pettersson. They stopped and both lit up a cigarette. Wilton had his coat lapel turned up high and his hat brim turned way down over his eyes to hide his face, but Pettersson stood there under a bright street lamp with a grey overcoat that had the collar turned down and all the passer-by's could clearly see his pock-marked face. Wilton knew how to do his job. The *Whirlwind* let a little smile creep across his lips as he thought what an idiot Pettersson was, an easy victim for Wilton. He was just one of many who had been tagged for assassinations with which they had absolutely no involvement whatsoever, other than being patsies who fell victim to manipulators. Hell, they led useless lives anyway, so Wilton and the *Whirlwind* just made it possible for them to get some notoriety that they would never have gotten otherwise. Many of them wound up admitting to a crime they never committed, because they actually felt like they were important for the first time in their lives. The clock clicked on 11:15, and Wilton was engaging Pettersson in conversation to keep him there until the movie let out.

In the theatre, after the movie ended, Olaf and Lisbet sat holding hands, waiting for the crowd to thin out before leaving. Outside, the *Whirlwind* intensely scanned the emerging crowd for his target. Glancing across at Wilton, he saw that he was having a difficult time keeping Pettersson engaged in conversation. Obviously, Pettersson was anxious to score some drugs. After all, that was his reason for being there.

Then, the *Whirlwind* saw Palme and his wife emerge with their coats buttoned up snugly around their necks. They were conversing as they strolled past the *Whirlwind*, who looked in Wilton's direction and saw him and Pettersson start to walk away from the clock toward him. As planned, Wilton would stroll a few steps behind, so that Pettersson would be nearby when the shots were fired. No doubt, he would start running out of fear, and many people would think it was he who fired the fatal shots. All was set, and the *Whirlwind* waited patiently, gripping the gun in his pocket as they neared the area where Sveavägen crossed Tunnelgatan and led to the Hötorget subway station. They continued at a brisk pace past the Dekorima shop (renamed Kreatima in the 1990's) and headed for the subway station entrance. At 11:21, half way across Tunnelgatan Gata and only a short distance from the station entrance, the

The Girl Who Stirred Up The Whirlwind

Whirlwind moved within three feet of Palme, took a deep breath of the cold night air, pulled the gun from his pocket and fired one shot into Palme's back. As Palme fell toward the pavement, Lisbet quickly grabbed him around his waist, desperately trying to keep him from falling. As she did, another shot, intended for Palme, was fired by the *Whirlwind*. Because Lisbet had positioned herself slightly behind Palme, the bullet hit her in the upper torso. Olaf fell face forward, mortally wounded, while Lisbet, only slightly wounded, fell on her left side. By this time, the *Whirlwind* had already made a dash toward the nearby steps to Malmskillnadsgatan and continued down David Bagares Gata, never looking back.

In the confusion, Wilton ran in the opposite direction, leaving a mystified and confused Pettersson, for a moment, standing in shock looking down at the two figures lying in the snow. All had gone perfect, as planned. The patsy was standing there in shock.

Lisbet stared up at Pettersson and started screaming, thinking that it was he who had felled her and her husband. It was then that Pettersson made the mistake that sealed his fate. Having no idea who the slain man was, he turned and dashed in the same direction taken by the *Whirlwind*. Several people besides Lisbet managed to get a good look at him, and they, along with her, would identify him as the slayer.

The Girl Who Stirred Up The Whirlwind

Calmly getting on the subway, the *Whirlwind* felt a bet smug. Everything had gone off like clockwork. Wilton would be heading back to his apartment, and the *Whirlwind* would go back to take care of Jasmine and Phyleece. Then, he would pack up and leave Stockholm for good when the heat had died down. The airports would be swarming with cops and the military. He and Wilton would simply lay low for a few days and then quietly slip out of town and prepare for their next assignment.

Still gripping the gun in his pocket, he knew that he could not kill Jasmine and Phyleece with it, because it could be traced to the Palme murder. It had to be disposed of as quickly as possible. He got off the subway, strolled down to the Norrstrom River and tossed it into the dark water below. He decided to walk the four blocks home. He felt exhilarated after a kill, and now, he was going to dispatch two more people who might connect him or Wilton to the Palme assassination, because the girl had seen him and Wilton, and noticed an anomaly that could perhaps get them identified. Nothing could be left to chance. The two had to die.

As the *Whirlwind* made his way toward his next victims, all across Stockholm word spread that near the Grand Cinema, sanity and compassion lay in a pool of blood.

The Girl Who Stirred Up The Whirlwind

The Grand Cinema, Where Olaf and Lisbet Palme
Attended the Movies on the Night
of His Assassination

Square Where Olaf Palme Was Assassinated

CHAPTER 3
CHAMPION OF THE DESPERATE

She was a beautiful thing. Tiny, angelic looking and fragile, eight year old Jasmine Alexander sat on the floor watching her mother inject herself with liquid euphoria. And the *Whirlwind* was going to destroy her and her mother. One could logically ask how could a man be so callous and cruel, but in a world where the few at the top of the economic ladder crush those who toil for crumbs from the table of plenty, why would the death of these two creatures who lived on the fringes of polite society be anything unusual? The cruelty of an economic system based on greed destroyed people like Jasmine and Phyleece every day. To protect himself and the system he revered, the *Whirlwind* felt no more shame than those who, in the boardrooms of corporations, daily destroyed lives without any remorse whatsoever. Jasmine and Phyleece were nothing but collateral damage in service to the greater good of capitalism.

The *Whirlwind* did not even bother to go into his apartment. He had already removed any evidence that might lead authorities to him. He had even worn gloves when he was there to make sure there were never any finger prints left behind. Anyway, there were those in the upper echelons of the Stockholm police who would assist in railroading the wrong man for the assassination, because the tentacles of the C.I.A. were everywhere.

The Girl Who Stirred Up The Whirlwind

All that remained were two useless people who might someday connect the dots, if they were properly interrogated by authorities. There was little chance of that ever happening, but the possibility was there. It was a loose end, and the *Whirlwind* never left any loose ends when doing a job.

Creeping up the stairs, he paused outside Jasmine and Phyleece's apartment, scanning up and down the hall, as he leaned his left ear against the door to see if they were still awake. Killing them in their sleep would be easier, but not nearly as exciting. He relished the thrill of strangling the life out of a person, feeling them go limp and collapse in his grasp. That was power, real power over life and death. Nothing was more exhilarating to the *Whirlwind* than killing up close. Too often, he had to do it from afar, due to circumstances. He was actually going to enjoy this. He had never killed anyone so young before. Well, not too young. He smiled just a bit, almost saying out loud, "yeah, there was that 12 year old kaffir in South Africa who died from three days of torture." He really felt good about that one, because the boy had actually had the audacity to spit in his face, refusing to disclose the whereabouts of his confederates who had the nerve to demonstrate against the pass laws. Just as he had when he prepared to kill Palme, he felt a growing exhilaration as he heard the television. They were still up. Death leaned its shoulder against the door.

The Girl Who Stirred Up The Whirlwind

He gently knocked on the door, waiting for his victims to let him in, so that he could go about his business quietly and methodically. Phyleece would be the first to die. He wanted to strangle her, but perhaps a blow to the head would be best in order to subdue her. Yes, she had to be silenced immediately before little Jasmine could scream. The little girl would be easy, just a quick blow to her face would break her neck. However, the best laid plans, even of pros like the *Whirlwind*, can go awry.

What happened next would forever torment the *Whirlwind* with intense worry. Had he known what had gone on before his arrival, he would have been more cautious, because Phyleece was actually waiting for her pimp, a man who had beaten her that evening for buying drugs with the money she was supposed to turn over to him. Having injected liquid uppers into her body, Phyleece's adrenaline was pumping at a fever pitch as she prepared to do battle with a man whose abuse she was determined to suffer no longer. Reaching behind the sofa, where she kept a fireplace poker, she walked over to the window, quickly pulling Jasmine as she held the poker, and said to her, as she opened the window, "if anything happens to mommy, run down the fire escape as fast as you can. Mommy loves you."

Although only 8, Jasmine had learned, at an early age, how to survive in a world filled with pimps, prostitutes, thieves and other miscreants who led lives of quiet desperation. She was not afraid, and she stood there slightly shivering from the cold breeze that was blowing in the open window.

Phyleece, with the poker raised over her head, reached down with her left hand, took off the night latch and turned the deadbolt. Since the hallway was dark, courtesy of the Whirlwind, who had removed the one bulb over the stairwell, she could not see the *Whirlwind's* face. Assuming it was her pimp, she brought the poker down hard and fast. With no gun, all the *Whirlwind* could do was raise his left hand to ward off the unexpected blow. As he did, he got a huge gash on the outer portion of his left hand and blood gushed out as Jasmine turned, climbed through the window and started to run. Seeing Jasmine flee and knowing time was of the essence, the *Whirlwind* socked Phyleece in the face with his right hand before she could deliver another blow. Falling to the floor, Phyleece took a look backward to see that Jasmine had fled. No longer able to enjoy the slow kill, the *Whirlwind* had to act fast. He put his right foot on Phyleece's face, crushing it under his weight. To make sure she was dead, he stomped on her chest furiously with his left foot while his right was still buried in her face. Taking no pause, he ran toward the window, as he simultaneously grabbed Jasmine's coat that was lying on a chair, wrapping it around the wound to stem the flow of blood.

The Girl Who Stirred Up The Whirlwind

With no gun, he had to catch Jasmine and dispatch her before she got out of the alley onto the street. The chase was fast and furious, as little Jasmine struggled to elude him with her tiny strides, while he bounded down three steps at a time.

Jasmine looked back only once at the *Whirlwind*, immediately recognized him from the time she had seen him and Wilton in the hallway and saw that his left hand was bleeding profusely. In her young mind, she thought to herself, "that man is scarred for life, courtesy of my mother. I will never let anyone abuse me, no matter what I have to do. My mother waited too long and then went after the wrong man. I will not!"

Stumbling into the alley, Jasmine saw the lights of the street only 100 metres ahead of her. Her little legs performed like a well-tuned engine in a race car that was headed toward the finish line. Although out of breath, exhausted and thinking that her little heart was about to explode, she never broke stride. Her aim was the safety of the street, where people would still be out late strolling on Friday night. It was filled with the dregs of society, but they were also mostly people who cared about each other. They were the forgotten of Sweden and the rest of the world, who, without each other, had nothing. There was safety there. She had learned long ago that the police were not the friends of the poor. For all she knew, the man so intent on catching her might well be a policeman, himself. Since she was too focused on the street to look back, she did not realize that the ever careful *Whirlwind* had broken off the chase out of fear that his injury and the chase might arouse too much suspicion on the street. Heading in the opposite direction to avoid detection, by letting Jasmine live, the *Whirlwind* had committed a grave error. He did not often make mistakes, but this one would make him lose many a night's sleep, wondering whatever happened to the little girl who could identify him as the stranger in the next door apartment. He never forgot her, and even though he had been gone from Stockholm nearly twenty years, there was not a night went by that he did not fear a knock on the door and a cadre of officials who would have him extradited back to Sweden to stand trial for the murder of Olaf Palme. As he aged, the fear did not subside, but rather, it became an obsession.

Pettersson was accused of Palme's murder after an extensive investigation by the Swedish police. He was picked out from a police line-up by Lisbet Palme. He admitted to being present at the crime scene, but vehemently denied that he killed Palme. "Anyway," he pleaded, "ask anyone. The knife is my weapon of choice. How could I get the money to buy a Magnum pistol. The cost would have been beyond my ability to pay. I was with a guy named Carlos that night, but he has disappeared. I am an innocent man being railroaded."

The Girl Who Stirred Up The Whirlwind

By 1989, Pettersson had been freed after an appeal court cited lack of evidence, including the missing murder weapon. It also questioned the reliability of Mrs Palme's identification. Pettersson was awarded $50,000 in compensation for defamation by the police and for wrongful imprisonment. He quickly spent the money on alcohol and drugs, all the while pointing out that he, himself, was a member of the Social Democrat Party and liked Olof Palme. On a television show he said, "Why wouldn't I like Palme, as he promised to do the sane thing and legalize drugs. Me killing him simply would not make any sense. This was a man who wanted to help people like me. He, unlike other politicians, actually saw those of us who fought addiction and lived outside the mainstream as human beings, worthy of respect."

As late as 1998, the Swedish Supreme Court rejected a prosecutor's appeal to retry Pettersson, citing that evidence was not strong enough to even place him at the scene of the shooting since witnesses, other than Lisbet Palme, had never been able to categorically identify him. Unlike the USA, Swedish courts placed a high burden of proof from authorities. In Sweden, the poor were not only afforded justice, but there was no cruel and unusual punishment, so there was no death penalty. The American government and the C.I.A. had little trepidation about Pettersson in the beginning, because he would obviously be locked up for the rest of his life. However, since he had been freed in late 1989 by a group of judges who were adamant about protecting the rights of Swedish citizens, even when the death of a Prime Minster was involved, the C.I.A. had wanted to eliminate him, but was reluctant to do so, because of the attention it might attract. It might lead to a renewed call for further investigation into the assassination, which the C.I.A. had been able to keep in abeyance through its influence with the Stockholm police authorities.

Then, on the 14th of September, 2004, the C.I.A. section chief in Stockholm got word through an informant that Christer Pettersson had asked for a meeting with Mårten Palme, Olaf Palme's son, explaining he had something important to tell the family.

It was then that the *Whirlwind* was once again given the green light to kill by the C.I.A. The patsy had become a huge liability. Requesting to see Mårten Palme meant that Pettersson had to die, and who else could do a better job than the *Whirlwind*, and it had to be done as quickly as possible, because the meeting with Palme's son was set for 17 September and there was no telling what Pettersson intended to reveal to Palme. Although he did not know enough to expose the operation, if he got the authorities interested again, even the moles in the Stockholm Police Department could not stop an investigation that would be demanded by the people of Sweden. The Swedish people simply refused to suffer abject malfeasance from their officials without taking to the streets. In America, the authorities harassed and brutalized the populace with fear and intimidation. In Sweden, the politicians feared the people, rather than the people fearing the politicians. Many Swedish governments had been brought down over the years by people who simply refused to cower before authority. Being in New York City, and living under the name Harrison Reed, the *Whirlwind* asked his C.I.A. handler if Craig Wilton could go to Stockholm with him on the mission, so that they could not only eliminate Pettersson, making it look like a natural death to prevent any suspicion, but also take care of Jasmine Alexander, who had always posed a threat to uncovering their identities; and thereby, exposing the whole assassination plot.

Wilton, having been accused of crimes against humanity by torturing blacks in South Africa, had, at the personal request of U.S. Vice President Dick Cheney, been given a job with the U.S. government as an interrogator at the American chamber of horrors in Guantanamo Bay. When requested by the *Whirlwind* as backup, he was immediately put on a private military jet and whisked to New York City within a few hours. Upon hearing of his departure, many of the inmates at Guantanamo rejoiced with relief that one of their worst torturers was gone.

The Girl Who Stirred Up The Whirlwind

Like everywhere else the *Whirlwind* had lived, he maintained basic anonymity in New York. However, as he awaited for the pending arrival of Wilton, in the bowels of a Fifth Avenue building, a C.I.A. book reader, Frank Penderent, was about to discover something that had been hidden for years, something that would make him realize that he had been part of a lie for far too long.

Understanding the mentality of those who work for intelligence agencies defies the laws of logic. Frank, who was 34 years old and was a master at decoding messages, saw his C.I.A. work as nothing more than an opportunity to serve his country while also doing something he enjoyed, reading. Believe it or not, the C.I.A actually pays people to read magazines, newspapers and books in search of anything out of the ordinary that might be a coded message from all those evil doers who want to attack that bulwark of freedom, the USA. Frank spent most of his days reading innocuous novels, searching for coded messages. In his 11 years of work with the C.I.A., he had actually come across only three coded messages in any publications, and those messages were not from foreign agents, but from American criminals sending coded messages in one classified New York City newspaper advertisement, and in two pornographic novels.

As a code searcher, Penderent was sometimes given manuscripts and documents that seemed of no particular importance, but they were often reviewed because they might offer a window to the past that could explain future events. At 9:30 AM on the morning of 15 September, Penderent was given a batch of these types of documents.

Although all the documents appeared rather innocuous, stuck between two stained blue spiral binders was a crumbled and partially shredded note that appeared to have been written in a coded language that was easy for Penderent to decipher with the computerized encryptor. He typed the message in for translation. The translation was: *The Whirlwind felled the Swedish tree on February 28, 1986 but C. P. is now asking to see the son of the tree. C.P. must be eliminated. J.A. has eluded us for 18 years and she can connect him to the crime. W and W are preparing to leave for Stockholm to finally eliminate these two threats of exposure. D.D.*

Penderent immediately knew who D.D. was. It stood for Deputy Director of the C.I.A., so this message, that should have been shredded and deposed of with incineration, had been written by the second highest official in the agency, and, no doubt, approved by the director himself. Cautiously wary of those around him, Penderent carefully prepared to do some research on what happened in Stockholm on 28 February 1986. He was violating protocol. He should go to his boss, but he just couldn't. He wanted to know more.

The Girl Who Stirred Up The Whirlwind

It did not take him long to put together what had occurred on that date and what the initials C.P. (Christer Pettersson) stood for. However, it took him almost an hour researching Stockholm newspapers for that day and a few days afterward that were immediately translated by computer to English to piece together more information on a little girl named Jasmine Alexander who had disappeared on that date when her mother was murdered. Penderent asked himself, were the three events connected? The initials J.A. kept flashing into his mind. Surely, the J.A. was not an eight year old girl? How could she be a danger to exposing the C.I.A. sanctioned assassination of Olaf Palme? She would be a young woman now. Why would they wait so long to eliminate her?

Penderent, unlike most people in the agency, was not a slave to the ideology that sanctioned all acts as permissible when used in defence of liberty. For many years, he had harboured disillusions about his job and how it was an adjunct to the suppression, not the defence, of liberty. Now, he was privy to information that a person who had been set-up as a patsy, and a young woman who was only eight years old at the time of an assassination, were about to be sacrificed at the altar of ideologically driven evil that condoned any act by those deemed the righteous servants of a superior economic system that was, in reality, nothing more than a cover for the enslavement of mankind to a culture of greed that made the many who struggled for survival nothing more that slaves with invisible chains.

Methodical and precise in everything he did, Penderent decided to shred the remains of the note, as he contemplated his next step. He did not see Darryl Manley, the director of the division, peering through his glass enclosed office following every move he was making. Manley never trusted anyone, and he had particular concern about Penderent, as he was a man with a conscious, something dangerous for anyone who worked for an agency that required blind obsequence to the cause.

Should he go to Darryl Manley, and discuss what he had discovered? Manley was a stern, uncompromising man who would simply say that any act was permissible in defence of the USA and its superior way of life. Killing people was a part of what they did, and sometimes innocent people had to die in order to protect America.

As he shredded the note, a small portion fell onto the floor at his feet. Manley took note of it and waited patiently for Penderent to walk away from the shredder. He nonchalantly strolled over, picked up the tiny piece of paper and saw the handwritten *86*. What was Penderent up to, he thought. He was hiding something. He walked over to the desk where Frank was now going over the remaining documents, although he was in such deep thought about what to do with the knowledge that two people were about to be murdered that he did not even notice Manley hovering over him.

Manley said, "Frank, what are you working on?"

Somewhat startled, Frank replied, "Oh, just some documents that came in today. They seem rather innocuous, but you never know."

"Put that aside Frank," Manley curtly barked, as he prepared to get rid of him for a while, so he could get to the bottom of what he was so engrossed in. "I want you to go over to Section-3 and pick up some documents for me.

"Sure chief, on my way."

As Frank left, Manley hurriedly called Section-3, which was on Park Avenue, and told the chief there to give Frank Penderent some documents, any useless documents, to bring to him, as he was running a security check on Frank. Then, Manley proceeded to scan Frank's desk and finally sat down to contemplate just what was going on. He glanced down at the computer that was still on, and immediately ran a browser history check. There it was, Swedish to English. Quickly going over the materials that Frank had researched, it did not take long for Manley to realize that Frank was onto something about the assassination of Olaf Palme, Christer Pettersson and some little girl who had disappeared on the same day that Palme was assassinated.

Although not privy to knowledge of C.I.A. involvement in the assassination, Manley had no doubt that it was the agency that had either carried it out or sanctioned it. Noticing that Frank had also researched the Deputy Director on the computer, he thought that a call to the D.D was definitely in order. No one hid information like this. Frank Penderent was up to something nefarious.

A call to the Deputy Director elicited immediate concern that word of the planned murder of Christer Pettersson might leak out. Although not sharing his knowledge of what was about to occur with Manley, the D.D. warned him to keep an eye on Penderent, because something big was about to occur, and there could be no loose ends. If necessary, he would send a containment team to neutralize Penderent. It was just a circuitous way of saying that, if necessary, Frank Penderent would be killed to protect the integrity of the C.I.A.

Upon returning, the observant and tactile Frank Penderent could tell from the warmth of his chair that someone had been sitting in it. Looking at his computer and the slightly askew binders that had been on his desk, left no doubt in his mind that he was under close scrutiny by Daryl Manley. He knew something he wasn't supposed to know.

The Girl Who Stirred Up The Whirlwind

Frank had worked for the agency long enough to know that certain circumstances foretold of coming calamity. He had the misfortune of seeing workers unceremoniously whisked away because they had supposedly been transferred, but why were they never heard from again? The excuse was that they had gone undercover for an operation of importance to national security. Yet, they were not even field agents. Why would they be selected for operations that required special training? Two others had died under mysterious circumstances. Don Lawton had been Frank's friend, and one day, even though there was no indication of despondency, he was discovered in his apartment, an apparent suicide from an overdose of sleeping pills. Then there was Alice Riel, who worked in the document retrieval section. She was found in an alley off Lorton Street in the Bowery, an apparent victim of rape and robbery, but what was she doing in the Bowery? What business could she have had there, when she lived in uptown Manhattan? All those occurrences were flashing through Frank's mind in a kaleidoscopic array of fear for what might await him. Why had he been so curious? Had he not learned from years with the agency that veering from the norm was like raising a red flag. His curiosity had created a tenuous situation that was rapidly backing him into a corner from which he would be unable to extricate himself. He had to do something drastic to save himself, and to assist two apparently innocent people marked for death.

The Girl Who Stirred Up The Whirlwind

Where could Frank turn? How could he save himself from the cataclysm of misplaced patriotism that justified all in defence of country? He was surrounded by those in service to tyranny of the vilest form. Yet, he knew of one man who had devoted his life to defending those with no hope. There was a man to whom those in desperation turned when all hope had been drowned under a torrent of deceit. His friend and confidant had often told him that he was too good a man to bow in supplication to the evils of a society based on economic and patriotic servitude to the elite. He had told Frank that he was too fine a man to devote his life in service to those who practiced cunning deceitfulness and dupery in service to those who had no moral fibre.

Frank looked at the clock on the wall as it ticked to 12:00 noon. He was going to save himself, Christer Pettersson and Jasmine Alexander. During lunch, he would go to the bank, withdraw the $75,000 in his savings account and disappear, but not before he had contacted the one man who might save him and the others, Aaron Adams, the champion of the desperate.

Christer Pettersson

The man now marked for death by the *Whirlwind*.

CHAPTER 4
PERPERTRATORS OF EVIL

As Frank Penderent left for lunch, he glanced wearily out of the side of his eyes at Daryl Manley. Frank had already decided that his curiosity had sealed his fate, as he was now privy to information that was too secret to allow someone out of the upper echelon to know. He had just made himself expendable. He would not be coming back. Chances were, he thought to himself, even Manley had not been privy to what Frank had discovered. Yet, the powers that be had trust in Manley, because he was a real agency man who would gladly die for the cause. They all knew Frank was just an ordinary guy who did not have the convictions of so many who served the bankrupt idea of American righteousness that had long ago been discarded into a polluted river of mediocrity.

There was something deeply sinister in the way Manley gazed back at him, and Frank noticed that Manley immediately picked up the white crisis phone on his desk as he was leaving. He had to hurry. There was little time left to extricate himself from the city and the death squad that was, no doubt, being assigned the task of eliminating another threat to national security. His heart pounded violently and the blood pumped through his veins like a raging river of cascading water erupting in rage and fury.

J. Wayne Frye

The Girl Who Stirred Up The Whirlwind

Upon exiting the building, Frank scanned all about, expecting to be followed. He was an amateur, and they were professionals, so if they were following him, they were doing a good job. He saw no indications that he was being watched. He went into the bank, withdrew $75,000 in cash, much to the chagrin of the manager who had to approve the withdrawal, and even had the audacity to ask Frank what he was using the money for, and then commented how much better it would be to take the money in a cashier's check, which, of course, the bank would charge a fee to issue. Typical of a banker Frank thought. They think your money is theirs. Just another guy with a golden parachute who is over paid, under worked and looks with disdain on those who have to toil for a living. These were the people who would one day bring down the house of cards they had built by gambling with other people's money, abated and supported by that buffoon in the White House, George W. Bush, who was setting America on a course of destruction that would destroy the middle class and poor. Hey, maybe it was good that Frank had to get out of the USA. After all, it was 2004, and it would only be a matter of time until Bush's wars, tax-cuts for the rich and corporate coddling would create economic calamity that would have to be paid for by the middle class and poor while those at the top continued to be pampered like the royalty they considered themselves. Perhaps, in the right country, Frank could avoid much of this calamity.

The Girl Who Stirred Up The Whirlwind

Exiting the bank, Frank could see no one following him. He looked up above the street and saw a helicopter hovering overhead. He stared at the crosswalks and the web cams above them that scanned the street constantly. America was a nation under surveillance. There was no way to escape the watchful eye of "big brother." Every movement, every thought, every contact a person made was suspect in a nation that lived in fear, and the populace was too stupid to see that they had sacrificed their freedom to protect freedom. American had become a huge gulag of working class slaves to an idea that had been killed by corporate theocracy, religious subterfuge and a government that tolerated no questioning of authority.

How easy it was to manipulate a gullible population that was strolling around with cell-phones in their collective ears, striding about in overpriced sneakers produced by third world peasants, enjoying high priced lattes that they thought made them part of the "smart set," climbing into luxury automobiles they could not afford to drive to homes they struggled to make payments on and watching their big screen televisions that provided mundane entertainment filled with commercials that convinced them the good life could only be obtained by procuring more and more in a society where you were judged by what you had, rather than what the content of your character was.

The Girl Who Stirred Up The Whirlwind

Frank abruptly lost his fear, because he suddenly realized that like 99% of Americans, he was already dead. When you allow yourself to be manipulated and used, you are not alive. You are just existing. Frank was through being afraid. He was genuinely free for the first time in his life. He reared back his shoulders and headed for one of the few phone booths left in downtown Manhattan, as the cell-phone craze had converted the nickel phone call to an $80 a month ear piece that was now a necessity for those who willingly handed over their money to just another corporate entity that saw them as suckers waiting to be fleeced. Frank did not own a cell phone, and he was proud of it. He called Aaron Adams and asked to see him as quickly as possible to discuss something of vital importance, a matter of life and death.

The 60 year old Aaron Adams had known Frank for several years, having met him at a lonely diner one evening where they wound up sharing coffee and conversation into the wee hours of the morning. Although there was a great age difference, Aaron had found him a kindred spirit, as they shared a mutual distrust of those in the seats of power. Aaron had been encouraging him for years to give up his job with the C.I.A. and find something that was genuinely worthy of his efforts, rather than serving the interests of those who kept a nation in the iron grip of servitude to an idea that simply no longer existed.

The Girl Who Stirred Up The Whirlwind

Heading to Aaron's office, he kept glancing upward and noticed the helicopter was still hovering overhead. He started feeling about his clothing, wondering if a tracking device had been planted on him. Nervousness overwhelmed him as he looked cautiously at people in the streets, wondering who might be there to monitor him and see exactly what he was up to that might reflect unfavourably upon America and the C.I.A.

To protect his friend from discovery, he wanted to make sure no one followed him into Aaron's office. He went into the elevator, got off on the fourth floor, then proceeded down the stairs to Aaron's first floor office, making sure there was no one in the hallway as he approached the door.

Aaron had never replaced his secretary B.J., who had disappeared under mysterious circumstances many years ago after turning her back on the C.I.A. to help him with his biggest case that had been chronicled by Wayne Frye in the best-selling book, *Fall from Apocalypse*. He had never gotten over her loss and often seemed only a shell of the man he once was. Yet, he had become a champion of the downtrodden in a society that sanctioned poverty as a necessary adjunct to its economic system that was predicated on the belief that those at the top were to be venerated and worshipped. Many times his refusal to bow before authority had cost him dearly, but he was simply a man who refused to cower before the mighty and exalted.

The Girl Who Stirred Up The Whirlwind

Aaron's office was indeed a curious place. It was a dimly lit, old-fashioned chamber filled with, not fine antiques, but the cheap antiques of a long lost era in the sands of time. They were as utilitarian in their current place as they were back when they were in fashion. They had been of no particular value in their day, and were still nothing more than thrift store cast-offs, but they represented the complete lack of outward pretentiousness that solidified Aaron's reputation as a man who saw through the false grandeur that seemed to be at the heart of a society that had spiralled into a deep socio-economic divide between the classes.

Around the walls stood several oak bookcases, the lower shelves of which were filled with rows of gigantic binders containing information on various cases Aaron had undertaken over the years. The upper shelves had an array of various artefacts given to him by grateful clients who often had little money, but wanted to part with things that would let Aaron know how grateful they were for his help. In the centre of one shelf lay broken cobblestone from an alley where a group of homeless people had lived. They had come to Aaron for help in finding the killer of one of their own, when the authorities simply chalked it up to death from poverty like so many other cases that were ignored when they involved those who lived on the margins of society. Beside that was a folded up corduroy coat given to him by a homeless woman before she left town with the daughter that Aaron had located for her. Row after row of objects represented the compassion of a man who never lost sight of the human equation in everything he did.

Hanging on the wall was a bright red poster of Che Guevara, the true hero of the common man. Under it was the quote, "If you shiver with indignation at every injustice, then you are a comrade of mine." Those words represented who Aaron Adams was. It was almost as if the true spirit of those words hovered all about the quaint old office.

Sitting behind a scratched and worn oak desk with his back to a huge window that had *Aaron Adams, Private Investigations* written on it was a 60 year old man who exuded an air of confidence without being overbearing. His handsome, grizzled features were angular, taut, austere and somewhat intimidating, but there was a quiet serenity about his manner that made anyone immediately aware that, although this was not a man with whom one should trifle, he was also a man who could be depended upon to stand with the righteous in their battle against the forces of evil that permeated a society that had sunk into the quagmire of despair for those forgotten souls struggling to survive in a world of pain promulgated by the few who ruled with complete impunity. Aaron Adams was a champion among men. He was an avenging angel for the downtrodden, for those who felt they had nowhere to turn. That was the reason Frank Penderent was there.

Rising to greet Frank, Aaron clasp his hands, feeling a coldness in them. He had always liked Frank, feeling that like his beloved B.J., he had fallen victim to an organization that used people and then discarded them when they were no longer useful. He had seen what the C.I.A. had done to the woman he loved, and he had seen what it was doing to Frank over the few years he had known him. He was a man who believed in fairness and justice, and he was working for an organization that represented neither. Smiling he said, "Frank, have a seat. It is great to see you."

Frank, easing into a well-worn leather chair by the desk, stared out the window behind Aaron, seemingly fearful that something sinister was out there on the street, and replied, "I am in some big trouble, Aaron. I have made a mistake that is going to cost me my life, but it is also going to cost the lives of two other people and soon. I can't go to the police, because it is the agency that is sanctioning the deaths."

Reaching into his left breast pocket with his right hand, Frank removed the $75,000, placed it on the desk and peeled off $10,000 from the stack. He pushed it over to Aaron and said, "That is

$10,000. If you need more, I will be in touch with you periodically, and then you can let me know how much more you need. I will figure out how to get it to you. You know you can trust me to do the right thing. No one must know where I am going, not even you, because it will be dangerous if you know. I have finally had enough of working for an organization that actually has no moral repugnance about killing women and children in its insane protection of a way of life that you and I both know doesn't really exist anymore in a country that has completely lost its moral compass. I am going to relate to you an appalling story. I am not pleading for you to help me. I know the organization, and I know that I can only escape their wrath for so long, but I beg you, as my friend, to allow me to die knowing that you will do all you can to save an innocent young girl who just happened to be in the wrong place at the wrong time. She and another man in Sweden have been marked for assassination by the greatest assassin this nation has ever produced. I do not know his name, only that his code name is *Whirlwind*. He is assisted by an ex-torturer from the South African Apartheid regime. His name is Craig Wilton, and he has been the head torturer at that abomination to all that is just, Guantanamo Bay, the last several years."

Aaron leaned forward, placing his hands almost prayer like under his chin, looked down at the $10,000 and said, "you're a friend Frank. You don't have to pay me anything to fight for justice. That is something far beyond money."

"Then consider it money for expenses Aaron. I know the kind of man you are. That is why I am here, because I know you let nothing stand in your way when you feel that you are fighting for a just cause. Please protect this young woman. It is the one thing I can do, maybe the only thing I can do to atone for the work I have done for an organization that has no core whatsoever, no redeeming set of values that can ever justify its existence."

As Aaron listened intently to Frank and what had transpired, his indignation grew steadily, because he had dealings with the C.I.A. years ago when his secretary had changed her name and tried to flee from a past that included nefarious deeds of which she was immensely ashamed. She had paid the ultimate price apparently, although her body had never been found. Now, he saw a chance to save someone else. Maybe by doing what he could to atone for his inability to save the one he loved.

When Frank finished the story, Aaron, concerned about his safety, handed him a piece of paper with an address in Lonoke, Arkansas on it. "Go to this place. Don't take a plane. Hitchhike out of the city, get a bus from Englewood Cliffs in New Jersey. Don't take the bus directly to Lonoke.

The Girl Who Stirred Up The Whirlwind

Get off at various places and buy a ticket to another city. This place belongs to a friend. I will alert him that you will be using it."

Frank, seemingly more sanguine after unburdening himself to Aaron said, "so, you will help this Pettersson fellow and also Jasmine Alexander. You will go to Stockholm and see that she is alerted to her impending doom?"

In determined manner, Aaron replied, "what do you think?"

Smiling, Frank, letting out a sigh of relief, said, "I think Aaron Adams is on the case, and Stockholm is in for some trouble. Thank you. I am at peace, now."

Rising from his chair, Aaron came around to Frank, motioned for him to get up and said, "Come with me. You are going out through the alley. Get your ass out of Dodge. Arkansas may not be a place where you would want to live, but it is a great place to hide out for awhile. Give me a couple of days, and I will be in touch with you, and let you know how things are going. I'll keep the ten grand, because you know I am always broke. What I don't use, you'll get back."

So, the adventure was about to begin for Aaron Adams. As always, those who promulgated injustice would come up against the great equalizer who carried compassion in his heart for those who suffered indignity, but death in his hands for the hypocritical, arrogant, self-righteous perpetrators of evil.

In the dark of night, Frank's ultimate destination was Lonoke, Arkansas – a small town where he hoped to fade into obscurity.

CHAPTER 5
A TRAIL OF DEVASTATION
EVERYWHERE HE WENT

As Wilton and the *Whirlwind* boarded a plane for Stockholm, Aaron was leading Frank Penderent out of the alley behind his building. Grabbing Frank's hand, gripping it tightly as he looked up and down the street at the end of the alleyway for any sign that there was surveillance, Aaron whispered, "don't worry, I am headed to Stockholm on the next plane. If Jasmine Alexander is alive, I will find her. Pettersson will be easier to find, and I will warn him of the coming calamity. I have gone up against the government before, and I know how to deal with these sadistic bastards. Take care of yourself. You are a good man, Frank. I am glad you have finally decided to sever your relationship with those who promote deception, deceit and mayhem in the name of liberty. I have fought these captains of mischief and deception all my life. You never win, as there are so many of them and so few of us who take a stand against their evil intentions. Yet, even losing when fighting for justice gives you great satisfaction in knowing that you did not go quietly into the night. We must continue the eternal battle, because if we do not, we are just accomplices in the subjugation of all humanity to the evils of a system that is an abomination for all but the chosen few. Go now, and forever rage against the machine."

The Girl Who Stirred Up The Whirlwind

Frank did not say a word; he just gripped Aaron's hands firmer, smiled, turned and strode out of the darkness of the alley into the sunshine of hope.

Frank felt alive for the first time in years. He was living on a precarious precipice and might fall to his doom any minute, but he was tired of the fear and despair in the shadows of evil. He had done the right thing. He had, perhaps, given two people who were marked for destruction a chance for survival. He felt good. He stuck out his thumb, and breathed a sigh of relief.

Meanwhile, Aaron was hurriedly packing, as there was a flight to London, where he could make a connection for Stockholm. He had just missed the earlier direct flight that Wilton and the *Whirlwind* had taken. He only had an hour to get to the airport and hopefully rescue two people marked for death. He had no idea that the four hours difference in his arrival time to Stockholm would be fatal for one of the two people he was trying to save.

And what about Jasmine Alexander all those years? Understanding that retribution was a common trait among people with whom her mother associated, Jasmine knew, even at eight, that she had to make sure that she disappeared into obscurity. The night of her mother's murder, Jasmine took the first of many aliases that she would use. She feared that anyone she told her real name might connect her to a mother who was obviously on someone's hit list and she knew that, for some reason, the person who killed her mother, also intended to murder her. This was a little girl who was wise far beyond her years, and she would use that wisdom to survive in a series of foster homes until her 19th birthday, while never revealing her real name to anyone. The authorities finally just put in her file, "parentage unknown." Finally freed from foster homes, at the age of 19, she decided to get a job as a waitress in the notorious Tensta district of Stockholm. She assumed that she was safe as long as she made sure no one ever knew her real name, because the one she feared would never recognize her physically, but he might recognize a name connected to a distant pass that had marked her for death.

Although not educated, Jasmine had always been smart. Had she wanted, she could have managed to get a benevolent government to pay for a university education, but she was not sure what she wanted to do with her life. The only thing she was sure of was that she wanted to help people who lived a life of discontent, loneliness and desperation. All her life, she had felt that way about herself, as she had no roots and no one who seemed to genuinely care for her. That was why she had so much compassion for those who lived in despair.

The Girl Who Stirred Up The Whirlwind

She meandered from one flop house to the other, simply having no roots whatsoever. And throughout Stockholm's various poor districts, she went by many different names, never feeling that it was appropriate to let anyone get to know her too well.

She lived a life steeped in fear. All she could remember from that faithful night long ago was that there was someone who wanted to kill her, and that whoever it was would not likely have forgotten that she could identify her mother's killer, but she had no idea that the same man had assassinated the Prime Minister. Ironically, she had made it a point to study the writings of Karl Marx, and the Swede she admired more than any other, Olaf Palme. For some reason she felt a kinship with him, as she thought he had been a fellow sojourner in the quest for a more equalitarian society. She, like him, wanted to help those poor souls who voted against their own self-interests. She knew that the majority of people were not interested in knowing the truth of their own enslavement. Most people had been captured by the propagandists who spewed out a steady diet of lies. She realized that the masses were psychologically imprisoned by their manipulators. She understood that in so-called democracies every few years the oppressed were allowed to think they were democratically picking someone to lead them. Yet, she knew the truth was simply that they were only electing their new oppressor.

The Girl Who Stirred Up The Whirlwind

Jasmine was a woman who believed that when people were denied the basics of life, they should become outlaws and demand fairness from those who refused to share the bounty that was all about. For that reason, she was an outlaw herself. She often stole, but never from the owners of a small business. She only took from the huge corporate owned entities, because she saw a justification for one thief stealing from another thief, and she viewed all corporations as malevolent thieves, preying on those who were too complacent and too uniformed to realize they were malfeasant in their own slavery to those who manipulated and used them.

She took a job as a waitress under the name Felina Jacobssen at a small café on Tenstaganen Gata. It was there; one evening when she was working the late shift, that she met Rose Husby. Rose was not nearly as attractive as Jasmine, but she had an air about her that exuded intense sexuality and many of the men who came into the café would make efforts at getting to know her. Yet, Jasmine noticed that she was always alone, seemingly disinterested in even talking to men, much less going out with one. On the other hand, Jasmine had been sexually active with the opposite sex since she was 13; although, she was not penetrated until she was 15. It was at that age that she realized that using womanly wiles often got you what you wanted in a world where men thought with what was between their legs. Several of the perverted husbands in the foster homes she lived in would prey upon her incessantly, but she saw that as just her lot in life, because she happened to be one of the misfortunate people who lived on the fringes of respectable society.

After about a month coming into the café three or four nights a week, Rose asked Jasmine if she would like to be her roommate. Rose lived alone, and had a sofa bed that Jasmine could use. That way, they could save on rent and enjoy each other's company more than the few times a week that Rose came into the café.

Living in a transient hotel, Jasmine, who had many offers from men to provide accommodations for her, but had found no one she really felt comfortable moving in with, jumped at the chance to share a flat with Rose. They became great friends and often roamed about Tenstaganen Gata into late in the night, talking about their hopes and dreams for the future.

Although Rose was a tattoo artist, who worked at a nearby parlour, she, herself, only had one tattoo on her body. It was a butterfly tattooed on her left hip, but Jasmine was not aware of it, as she had never seen Rose naked. However, one night Rose was wearing hip huggers, and when she bent over to pick up half a kronor that someone had dropped on the sidewalk, Jasmine could not help but smile when she saw the tip of a butterfly wing and realized that Rose must have a tattoo on her hip. Jasmine thought back to an old boyfriend who, at sixteen, would only perform anal sex on her, because he was fearful of getting her pregnant, which she thought was stupid when they lived in a nonreligious country where anonymous abortion was available on demand for any girl, regardless of her age. Yeah, she thought at the time, he wasn't fearful of pregnancy, he just wanted anal sex, and he needed an excuse for it. Little did he know that Jasmine enjoyed it more than he did. She remembered when she put a fake tattoo on her lovely, perfectly shaped ass and it nearly made him go crazy. It was the best pounding she ever got from him. In fact, it was the last one, as she was sent to another foster home a few days later.

One evening Rose and Jasmine decided to go to the movies for the first time together. They meandered through the streets of Stockholm, walking and talking without any real thought about what movie theatre they were headed for. Finally, finding a theatre with a film they thought they might enjoy, they went inside and settled into seats, anticipating an evening of entertainment. Jasmine had an uneasy feeling about the theatre. There was something sinister about it. Looking up at the coffered ceilings, shadows seemed to be bouncing about. With Rose sitting on her left, Jasmine, without moving her head, peered out of the side of her eyes to her right, and there seemed to be a mist around the seat only a few feet away. She squeezed her eyes shut for a few seconds, and then reopened them to see the mist still there. Moving her eyes upward, she felt a feeling of despair, almost wanting to cry. Again, she closed her eyes for a few seconds, blinked a few times and the mist, not evil or foreboding, seemed to be slowly dissipating. Obviously benign, as it slowly disappeared into the blackness, an intense feeling of sadness overcame Jasmine. The theatre was a dark chamber of sorrow. She felt as if she wanted to weep.

Without realizing it, Jasmine reached over and squeezed Rose's hand. Rose tilted her head toward Jasmine, smiled, leaned slightly forward and kissed her on the cheek. Jasmine felt a surge of passion between her thighs, and she sensed the moisture down there building. She almost gasped for breath as her heart raced furiously. She nestled her head against Rose's shoulder and they sat there holding hands in the darkness, both filled with anticipatory delight over the closeness they had just discovered. They were in the ambrosia of serenity.

Leaving, they continued to hold hands without uttering a word as they strolled out of the theatre into the misty night. Stepping onto the sidewalk, they turned to walk down Sveavägen, and behind them, the pink marquee of the theatre, almost like a sign blinking the awakening of intense understanding, flickered brightly through the mist, the name seemed to be crying out for recognition in the darkness: *Grand, Grand, Grand.*

Not realizing they had just been in the theatre where Olaf Palme had spent the last two hours of his life, they continued to stroll down Sveavägen, finally arriving at the Tunnelgatan intersection. Jasmine realized that she had never been to the place before, but instinctively, she pulled Rose to a bronze plague imbedded in the street that read, *Here, Sweden's Prime Minister Olof Palme was murdered on 28 February 1986.* Turning to Rose, Jasmine said softly, "my mother was murdered the same night. I never connected the two events before, but now, I know something I have to share with you."

As they got on the subway, Jasmine began to pour out all the pain from the years of frustration and worry that had made her a mere shell of a human being. Feeling like an unbearable weight had been lifted off her shoulders; Jasmine finally was able to open up to someone about the agony of a life spent in despair. She asked Rose, "should I go to the police? Is it time I told the authorities that the same man who killed my mother, may well have killed Palme, and then there is the man I saw with him, as evil-looking and sinister a man as I have ever seen in my life. I was only a child, but I shall never forget the two faces of evil that have haunted me so long."

Rose, still referring to Jasmine as Felina, said, "No, you cannot go to the police. Who do you know to trust? Wasn't it mysterious the way there were no police on the street in that vicinity the very night Palme was shot? That area was always heavily patrolled except for that one night. Many in our own government believe the police were guilty of direct involvement or at least complacent in his murder. Right or wrong, can you afford to take the chance? No, my dear Felina, you mean too much to me to risk it."

Jasmine savoured those words, "you mean too much to me to risk it." Rose loved her.

Taking Rose's hand, they exited the subway, arm-in-arm, defiantly and proudly walking down the street together. They were unashamed of their affection, and they were about to enter into that special coven of delight reserved for those who are truly sexually liberated. Sweden was an equalitarian society, where people of all sexual orientations were treated with dignity and respect, so the two had no fear of recrimination, and no qualms about what they were about to do.

They walked into the flat, dropped their purses and turned toward one another. They had been waiting all night for this moment. Their eyes met with a deep intensity, glistening and sparkling with lust and a deep emotional bond. They melted into one another's arms as their soft, succulent lips met in a never-ending passionate kiss, their tongues darting about as if they were duelling one another.

Rose pulled back, smiled, turned and walked provocatively away, looking back over her shoulder at Jasmine, dropping articles of clothing on the floor as she made her way to the bedroom.

Jasmine, never before experiencing lust for a woman, took a deep breath and thought, "I do want this, I really do."

Moving into the bedroom and watching Rose undress, she started to feel that tingle between her legs and knew the moisture was building again. She removed her clothes, as Rose, completely naked, lay on the bed; her legs spread wide exposing a smoothly shaved vaginal area that had huge lips that were glistening with moisture.

Rose started to caress her own body, sliding her hands over her perky breasts and began to gently twirl her fingers around her nipples. Jasmine was mesmerized by the beauty of Rose. She had never realized how magnificent her body was.

Jasmine, now completely naked with her huge globe-shaped breasts jutting out like two Himalayan mountain peaks, slowly glided toward Rose. Her rock-hard breasts with their deep brown, pointed, erect nipples bounced up and down provocatively as she moved toward the bed, but Rose's gaze was not concentrated on her breasts but upon the huge patch of dark hair that completely covered the area that Rose longed to taste. She had never seen so much hair on a woman, or even a man for that matter. There was even a mildly thick patch that went all the way up Jasmine's abdomen, finally trailing off into the recesses of her navel. She longed to bury her face in the warmth of the hair and smell the scent of Jasmine's loveliness.

Jasmine, although inexperienced in making love to a woman, seemed to understand exactly what to do. She crawled in bed beside Rose and the two turned to one another, first gently kissing lips, noses, foreheads and cheeks as they ran their hands over each other's bodies. Then, they kissed long, deep, hard and passionately as they ground their bodies into one another, melting into one. The bliss of that evening would fade into the deep recesses of time, but the memories of the magnificent passion they shared would be with them the rest of their lives. After hours of lovemaking, they finally drifted off to sleep in one another's arms, both feeling safe and secure for the first time in their lives.

However, security in the arms of a lover can be a fleeting thing, and unfortunately for these two, the bliss was of only of a transitory nature. Back at the café, Jasmine, or as she was known to her co-workers, Felina, proudly proclaimed her new found love, and everyone was happy for her, as she was a favourite of all, because of her compassionate and caring nature.

One day, she proudly showed up to work, and in the presence of several co-workers and the owner, gently pulled down her blouse enough to expose the top part of her left breast just above the nipple, where Rose had drawn a beautiful tattoo of a rose to signify that Jasmine and her were one. Although at the time, the rose tattoo was nothing more than a curiosity and a symbol of affection, years later; it would prove to be a vital clue that would allow Aaron Adams to locate her in his attempt to save her from annihilation.

For almost a year, things seemed to be going extremely well for the new lovers, and they settled down to a harmonious domestic life together. However, in late 1998, the *Whirlwind*, who had been involved in numerous assassinations since the murder of Olaf Palme, was sent on a mission to Norway, where he was to assassinate a publisher who had been linked to radicals in the Palestinian Liberation Front. Israel's Mossad Intelligence Agency, in collusion with the C.I.A., identified Norwegian, Jorn Helgesen, as a clandestine arms dealer who was trying to make it possible for the Palestinians to purchase rocket launchers to ward off constant Israeli incursions into the Gaza Strip.

The Girl Who Stirred Up The Whirlwind

The *Whirlwind* flew into Oslo, Norway and took the express train to Trondheim in northern Norway, where Helgesen lived with his wife and three children. He was a successful publisher who strongly believed that the USA and Israel were involved in genocide against the Palestinian people. The *Whirlwind* had already planned an escape route after the assassination that would take him through north-eastern Norway, then south to Mota in Sweden, and finally to Stockholm. There, he would catch a plane back to the USA and safety.

The Helgesen assassination is not the subject of this book; consequently, we will only take a look at it in a cursory way as just another example of the callousness of the *Whirlwind* and those who sanctioned what he did. It also connects to another sinister deed that occurred in Stockholm only three days later. In order to make the assassination of Helgesen seem like an accident, the *Whirlwind* managed to set-off a gas explosion in Helgesen's home, killing Helgesen, his wife, his three children, along with an aunt and mother-in-law.

Feeling smug and proud that he had once again brought an enemy of America to justice, the *Whirlwind* made his way to Mota, where he boarded a train for Stockholm. On that train was a young woman named Rose Husby, who had been attending a tattoo artist's convention in the lakeside resort of Mota.

The Girl Who Stirred Up The Whirlwind

What role does chance play in people's lives? What were the odds that these two people would wind up on the same train, even sit in adjoining seats in the club car?

Always cognizant of the need to conceal his identity as much as possible, the *Whirlwind* was nondescript, wearing a fake beard and attaching thick bushy eyebrows. Sitting next to Rose, the now 44 year old could not help but notice her provocative frame. Always a connoisseur of full-figured women, the *Whirlwind* simply could not help himself. He tilted his head and said, "young lady, I would deem it an honour to buy you a drink, if you would allow me."

Rose replied, "That would be nice, but I must advise you that I am very much in love with a young woman back in Stockholm, and not really interested in a men at present."

The *Whirlwind* hid his disgust, but mulled in his warped mind that had been manipulated by religion, the perceived evil of people having sexual relations with those of the same sex. He found it absolutely abhorrent and firmly believed that the Bible was the adjudicator of all things in life, and his Bible said homosexuality was an abomination. He was particularly disenchanted by the Scandinavian countries openness about homosexuality, and the growing acceptance it was receiving in America under that Arkansas free-love advocating Presidential fornicator, Bill Clinton. What America needed was a Jesus-loving Republican in office who would get things back to normal. Yet, he decided, for the sake of appearance and the distraction of observers, to engage Rose in idle conversation as they shared a drink. Despite his cold, calculating nature, the *Whirlwind* knew how to turn on the charm when it was called for in tenuous situations.

Rose was a bit naïve for a 24 year old, and her tongue was loosened by the numerous drinks she shared with a man, whom she found extremely interesting. She was impressed with this person who had introduced himself as Harrison Reed, an American looking for investments in Sweden. His flawless Swedish surprised her, as most Americans she had met could only speak English, as they all assumed the whole world was supposed to learn their language. After all, America was superior in every way – at least, according to most Americans. The *Whirlwind* was giving the impression that he was not the typical arrogant American, and this impressed Rose.

As they continued conversing and drinking, Rose made a fatal mistake when the *Whirlwind* asked about her partner. She replied, "Oh, she is a waitress in Stockholm. She has had a very difficult life, living in foster homes most of her youth, after her mother was killed the same night that Olaf Palme was assassinated."

The Girl Who Stirred Up The Whirlwind

A light clicked on in the *Whirlwind's* head, as he realized this was a most propitious event. He had inadvertently stumbled upon someone who could provide the final piece to the puzzle of the whereabouts of the one person who could connect him to the murder of Olaf Palme.

Rose's suspicions were slightly aroused when it became obvious that Harrison Reed seemed to always bring the conversation back to Jasmine, or as she was known by Rose, Felina Jacobssen. He kept asking the name of the café where she worked, saying he would drop by for lunch one day and say hello. When she finally told him that she worked at the CafesLetekatten, she wondered if she had made a mistake. This seemed to be a man with a sinister purpose. But what could it be?

The two conversed well into the night, but parted with cordial farewells when the train arrived at the downtown Stockholm terminal. Or, at least that was the impression given Rose. The truth was that the *Whirlwind* deftly pulled his fake beard and eyebrows off in an alcove and discreetly followed Rose to her apartment. Standing outside, he waited patiently, letting out a smirk when he saw the lights go on in a corner fourth floor apartment. It would be easy to locate. He would not know what Jasmine looked like; after all, she was only 8 the last time he saw her in 1986. She would be 20 now. But obviously, she would be the only other person in the apartment, and what difference did it make if someone else was there with them. He would just kill them all. This was his chance to put his fears to rest, but he had to do it quickly, because he was due to catch a plane back to New York City in a few hours. He had no weapons, as he could not risk getting caught at the Norwegian-Swedish border with a gun. After all, the Scandinavian countries, unlike pistol packing America, did not allow its citizens to roam the streets with concealed weapons. Hell, in America, it was everyone's dream to own an AK-47. He thought to himself, damn stupid Swedes, they didn't realize that real freedom meant that you had the right to always be "packing." He needed a weapon, something that would allow him to dispatch the both of them quickly. Strangling them would take too long. He reached in his back pocket, took out his wallet and removed one of his credit cards under the name Harrison Reed. He had used credit cards before to kill. They could be deadly weapons if wielded properly. To make sure it was extra sharp, he leaned against the brick building behind him, tilted the card slightly and rubbed it back and forth on one side. One swipe across the neck and the jugular vein would be severed. There wouldn't even be a scream as the victim choked on her own blood. Two swipes and two victims dead, and his fears put to rest once and for all. Wilton, too, could then rest assured that his brief exposure to Jasmine on the stair landing that day was sealed forever from discovery with her death.

The Girl Who Stirred Up The Whirlwind

He surveyed the street up and down, and it was deserted. He pulled up his coat collar to conceal his face and walked across the street to the old apartment building. This was Sweden, so it was rare for any building to be locked. Crime existed, but not to the extent it did in societies like America, where poverty was institutionalized as part an economic system based on greed and there was no safety net for the marginalized. He opened the glass door, turned to his right and walked up the old wooden stairs to the fourth floor. Gripping the credit card in his right hand, he could feel the adrenaline pumping through his veins as he anticipated the coming thrill. He was breathing methodically and shallowly, as he prepared for the coming rush that would overwhelm him as he once again extinguished human life. He was all powerful, now. It was better than sex for him. Hell, he even had an orgasm sometimes when killing. He thought to himself that Rose was of no real value anyway. She was a fucking tattoo artist. What possible worth was she? She was also a lesbian, which was an affront to all the *Whirlwind* held dear in his religiously corrupted mind.

He knocked on the door, and the unsuspecting Rose did not bother to ask who it was. She assumed it was Jasmine coming home early from work, having once again forgotten her keys. As the door opened, the *Whirlwind* did not even take time for recognition, he just raised the card and swiped it across the jugular, and as Rose grabbed for the pulsating vein to try and stem the flow of blood, the *Whirlwind* raised his right foot and kicked her backwards as he rushed into the room, closing the door behind him. He did not have to worry about Rose, she was still alive, but she would not be able to get off the floor. She could not scream. She was already dead, but just didn't know it.

Furiously running about the apartment in search of the one he really wanted to kill, the *Whirlwind* could not believe he had once again missed his chance to dispatch Jasmine. She was not there, and his time in Stockholm was running out. It would have to wait for another trip to the city. His C.I.A. handlers would tolerate no divergence from the plan of escape for him. Yet, he just couldn't resist picking up a tube of lipstick and writing on the bathroom vanity mirror, *you are next, bitch.*

Damn, he felt good! Walking out of the building, he enjoyed having the cold night air slap him in the face with a mist that seemed to be crying out in exaltation at the havoc he had wrecked in Trondheim, Norway and Stockholm, Sweden. The *Whirlwind* left a trail of devastation everywhere he went.

CHAPTER 6
A ROSE TATTO ON HER LEFT BREAST

Coming home from work at 1:00 AM, Jasmine felt trepidation as she ascended the stairs. When she got to the 4th floor stairwell, it was bathed in complete darkness. It was so dark that she had to grip the wooden railing to feel her way up the stairs in the pitch black that seemed to wrap itself around her in a blanket of overriding dread. She heard the sound of broken glass crackle beneath her feet, and then she knew that the light bulb was not just burned out. It had been broken by someone. That old feeling enveloped her, the same as it had that night so many years ago when she witnessed the murder of her mother and had to run into the night to avoid the same fate. She had drifted into a life of desperation, as she became a vagabond on the road travelled by so many who suffer in a world with far too little compassion. Yet, she had never let her circumstances sour her on life. She knew that her predicament was a barrier, not a prison.

Despite a life lived in virtual hiding from a force she could not understand, she always had hope that one day she could feel genuinely safe. She sensed that an unspeakable horror awaited her at the door to her apartment. However, there was a determination on her part to push open the slightly ajar door that she felt would open into another tragedy in a life of quiet desperation.

The Girl Who Stirred Up The Whirlwind

She did not scream, nor did she cry. Looking down at her beloved Rose lying dead on the floor with blood still streaming from the gapping neck wound, Jasmine tepidly walked to the kitchen alcove where she quietly opened a drawer and picked up a serrated knife. The room was bathed in a bluish light caused by the flickering outside neon apartment sign. She dared not turn on a light. If she did, she knew that the horror of what lay on the floor would be too much for her to bear. With the knife held in front of her, she moved toward the bedroom. Looking down at the bed, she fought back tears, knowing that she would never again be wrapped in the arms of her beloved Rose. She went to the bureau drawer and began to remove a handful of clothes she would need for the next few days. Tossing them onto the bed, she looked down at the trash can that was lined with a plastic bag. She emptied the trash and put her clothes in the plastic bag. That was her life, a plastic existence where everything seemed to wind up in a trash bag. It wasn't about living. It was about surviving. Yet, she knew that she was one of the majorities of the world who were not afforded an opportunity to live, only to exist. That was the modern world to which far too many were relegated to nothing more than survival.

As she exited the bedroom, holding the bag in one hand and the knife in the other, she glanced into the bathroom and saw what the *Whirlwind* had scribbled on the mirror, *you are next bitch*.

Not flinching in horror, but rather feeling a new found determination, Jasmine moved forward, and as she passed Rose's body, she forced herself to not look down. She did not want to remember Rose that way. She preferred to cling to that magnificent memory of the warmth she felt in her presence, that feeling of a vibrant connection that made them both seem whole. That, like so many other things in Jasmine's life, was taken from her. All she had now were the glorious memories of what was her only true love. She exited the building and faded into the dark, misty night like she had done so many times before.

For six years, she meandered throughout Stockholm, taking one demeaning job after another. She was a waitress, an adult products sales clerk and a masseuse in a house of ill repute. For a time, she even worked as a street prostitute until one night when a john slapped her around. It was then that she was offered jobs with several licensed houses of prostitution, but that required a government background check, and that would only lead to trouble, as her real identity would be discovered.

She was always looking over her shoulder, always wary of strangers and, yet, everywhere she went, those who got to know her, even for the briefest moment, loved her. She was a woman who garnered respect from all with whom she came in contact. Her devilish smile, her calm demeanour and the compassion she exuded for the downtrodden made her a revered figure among those who cried out for compassion where there was none.

However, in 2004, all the turmoil she had faced before would pale in comparison with what was about to occur. Jasmine Alexander was the most beautiful thing in Stockholm, a demure angel of love in despair, and two evil devils of vileness were going to destroy her.

The *Whirlwind* and Wilton slipped innocuously into Stockholm four scant hours ahead of Aaron Adams. That four hours would prove fatal to Christer Pettersson who, by 2004, had become a well-known person throughout the city, as the man who all assumed had gotten away with the murder of a Prime Minister and had even been compensated by the government for what the courts ruled was unfounded harassment and imprisonment.

Several associates of Pettersson had come forward over the years to claim that he categorically stated he had killed Olaf Palme. Yet, these sources were all compensated informers for the police or had received large sums of money from news organizations.

Some of these people substantiated a story that had been circulating for years about Pettersson mistaking Palme for a drug dealer. Palme, immaculately attired with his stylish wife by his side was mistaken for a low-life drug dealer who was on Pettersson's hit list? As often is the case, the more elaborate the tale, the more likely people are to believe it. For most truly informed investigators, this tale was the most outlandish of all and could not stand up to thorough scrutiny.

Since Palme's death, Sweden, although still a society with more compassion than the USA, had drifted from Palme's commitment to economic and social fairness. Like most of the world, it was hemmed in by powerful U.S. interests that saw each nation as ripe grounds for exploitation by corporate interests. Even though Palme had been gone for nearly 20 years, the hatred that the USA and even Swedish capitalists had for him had never truly abated. As a symbol of fairness in a world run by exploitive corporate thugs, his name was anathema to all capitalists who constantly wanted more and more.

The truth about the assassination had been unravelling for years, especially after Colonel Eric de Klerke, a former South African police officer, gave evidence to the Supreme Court in Pretoria, South Africa that Palme's murder was carried out by an infamous assassin called the *Whirlwind*. This man code-named the *Whirlwind* was actually a C.I.A. operative working with the South African Intelligence Service. He had not been seen in

The Girl Who Stirred Up The Whirlwind

South Africa for many years and was assumed to be dead. Dead indeed! He was alive, lived in New York City and was going under the name of Harrison Reed. And now, he was in Stockholm, preparing to concoct his elixir of evil once again.

The *Whirlwind* was anticipated in Stockholm. He went directly to Stortorget Square, where the C.I.A. section chief had placed a small vile of a rare, undetectable poison behind the same loose brick that had been used to convey his orders to assassinate Olaf Palme eighteen years before. Meanwhile, Wilton, who had been alerted, along with the *Whirlwind*, where to locate Pettersson, was already headed toward the alleyway where he had taken up temporary residence as derelict after being evicted from his apartment. So thorough was the C.I.A.'s penetration of the police department that the mole had even told the C.I.A. the colour of the blanket he used to keep warm.

There was little time to lose with Pettersson, as he had a meeting scheduled with Olaf Palme's son, Mårten. Wilton surveyed the scene, turned his collar up to hide his face and nondescriptly strolled through the alleyway until he sighted Pettersson with a red blanket over his legs, as he sat in a corner drinking a Heineken. Completely unnoticed by Pettersson, he walked back to the alley entranceway and waited for the *Whirlwind* to arrive with the fatal elixir that would shut Pettersson up permanently.

The Girl Who Stirred Up The Whirlwind

The drug would not kill him instantly, but simply put him into a coma, from which he would never awaken. The trick was how to administer the drug to him? The *Whirlwind* had a syringe that he had picked up on the way at a government licensed drug injection site. Sweden was one of a number of countries that realized you did not stop drug addiction by putting people in jail for what was a sickness, rather than a crime. For that reason, they dispensed needles to combat disease, and even had sites where nurses would supervise drug induction to assure an addict's safety. The *Whirlwind* had paid a street addict to get him the syringe from the dispensing house, and as he and Wilton discussed their next step, Wilton said that he was fearful that Pettersson might recognize him; consequently, the Whirlwind, after filling the syringe with the poison, walked down to the end of the alley where Pettersson was still sipping on his Heineken. Sitting next to Pettersson, he asked if the alley was a good place to spend the night.

Despite being a patsy for the Palme assassination and a drug addict, Pettersson was no fool. He noticed that the *Whirlwind* seemed to be making sure his face stayed out of the light. Looking up at him, Pettersson said, "You aren't spending the night in the alley. You a newspaper guy? I'm sick of asking for money to tell the truth, and you guys thinking I will spill my guts cheap. Just wait until tomorrow. Mårten Palme is getting it all laid out. I'm going to destroy a lot of people.

The Girl Who Stirred Up The Whirlwind

The *Whirlwind* looked right, left and straight ahead to make sure no one was watching. He reached up with his left palm and pushed the back of Pettersson's head against the concrete wall, knocking him out. He removed the syringe from his coat pocket and injected it into Pettersson right behind his left ear. The job was done. Next was Jasmine Alexander.

It would take Pettersson 15 days to die, and the cause of death would be listed as apparently an injury received when he hit his head which eventually led to a cerebral haemorrhage. Palme's son spent days by Pettersson's bedside, hoping that he would regain consciousness and reveal the truth about the death of his beloved father. It was not to be.

Thus ended the life of one more victim of the political shenanigans during the Reagan and George Herbert Walker Bush years that nearly rivalled Bush Two's disregard for human rights and fairness. All individuals standing in the way of this criminal operation were summarily done away with. Only one more person needed to be eliminated to make certain that the truth about Olaf Palme was finally buried forever. Jasmine Alexander did not know it, but the man who had killed her mother was now prowling the streets of Stockholm in search of her, so that the final link to American involvement in the assassination of Olaf Palme could be silenced forever.

The Girl Who Stirred Up The Whirlwind

When the sixty year old distinguished looking man stepped off the plane in Stockholm, Christer Pettersson was already in the hospital. The *Whirlwind* and Wilton had no idea that they were about to go up against the administrator of justice, the revealer of truth, the inflictor of righteous retribution. This was the man who was the enemy of those who preyed upon the weak, and who was a friend to those who had no friend. In a city that could swallow you whole, he was going to find what could not be found. Aaron Adams had come to do battle against the forces of evil.

As he was going through customs, Aaron almost immediately noticed the headlines in a Stockholm newspaper that a woman in front of him was holding. He couldn't read Swedish, but he saw the name Christer Pettersson and immediately knew there was already a fly in the ointment. Fortunately, the woman spoke English and gave him the details of Pettersson's apparent impending death.

Aaron's job had already been diminished by half. Yet, he knew from experience that one of the most difficult persons to find was the drifting, solitary, wary woman. Jasmine Alexander might not even know she was connected to Christer Pettersson, but they shared a mutual knowledge that made them both expendable. She was assuredly not helpless and was probably migratory. Like all women, she possessed that one thing that made it possible to manipulate men almost at will. Men rarely thought with their heads. Rather, they thought with what was between their legs. Yet, he sensed that Jasmine was a stray chicken in a world of foxes. It was his job to protect her from the foxes, but first, he had to find her.

Fortunately, unlike the USA, Sweden was a country where everyone was expected to learn three or four languages to be effective communicators in a world that cried out for understanding. That made it easy for a New York private eye to communicate with everyone from the lowly trash collector to the bank president. Ironically, in Sweden, because of unions, the trash collector was one of the more highly compensated professions, as it was an equalitarian country where one's job title was not used as a detriment to financial well-being.

Making his way to a library, he began to sense that someone was following him. He had been tailed so many times in his career that he almost had a sixth sense about it. Stopping at the entrance, he turned and scanned the sidewalk in front of the library. Looking across the street, he noticed a tall, thin, slightly balding man who seemed to be lingering about the front of a building. Aaron thought to himself that he could lose any tail, but why bother. There was no reason to lose him yet.

In the library, he was greeted cordially by a librarian in Swedish. Aaron, responding confusingly in English, said, "I am afraid I don't speak Swedish."

Smiling, she replied, "Ah, I can tell by your accent that you are American. Are you in Sweden to escape from the wrath of that warmonger George Bush? A lot of Americans have had enough of him and his henchmen."

Aaron grinned and said, "Well, it would be a nice thing to escape from, as he is going to bring the country to the brink of complete collapse, but I am here on business. I am trying to locate someone, and I would like to find an address for her."

The woman, apparently eager to help, enthusiastically replied, "I can help you with that. We have a name index base that lists everyone in the country." As she was speaking, she was guiding Aaron toward a computer in the reference section.

Motioning for him to sit down, she continued, "You just type the name in here, and it will give you all the known addresses. If you know the person's age, it will help refine the search. I will be glad to assist you if you want."

"Yes, please help. I would appreciate it."

The Girl Who Stirred Up The Whirlwind

Leaning over Aaron, he could feel her breasts against his shoulder. Aaron had long ago given up on ever being virile again, but he had to admit the feel of the 40ish woman did bring back pleasant memories of a time when he was a bed-hopping scamp who really knew how to woe the ladies. He thought to himself that was long ago and was forever relegated to a past that was, as Scarlett O'Hara would have said, "gone with the wind."

She asked him to type in the name. As he typed Jasmine Alexander, the woman stood up straight and got a look of concern on her face. "That is a name from the past that few people would even remember, but I knew her mother. I assume you mean the Jasmine Alexander who disappeared the same night as Olaf Palme's assassination."

As the computer ran a name and address check, scrolling rapidly through a government data base, Aaron looked up and said, "You remember where she lived?"

"Of course, I knew where she lived. My name is Heidi Helmut, and I kind of worked with Jasmine's mother. You see, Sweden is a country where everyone can get a free university education, but sometimes the stipend for living expenses is not quite enough, so I worked as a prostitute a day or two a week for the extra money. You Americans would frown on that, but in Sweden, we have a different attitude about sex."

The Girl Who Stirred Up The Whirlwind

Aaron, ignoring the search results, turned and said, "America frowns on far too many things that make sense. I am not like most Americans. I know sex is nothing more than a recreational activity. What America needs is a little more common sense and a lot less religious hypocrisy. My name is Aaron Adams. I am a private investigator from New York City, and I am here to locate Jasmine Alexander and save her from a terrible fate."

Heidi replied, as she pointed at the search results which showed one known address for Jasmine Alexander. "You see, that is the address where her mother lived 18 years ago. No one has heard or seen Jasmine Alexander since that night she disappeared. My guess is that she is dead, and the body was disposed of where it will never be found. I saw her a couple of times. She was a cute, but incredibly precocious, little girl. She had an infectious smile that slowly crept across her face, almost as if she were telegraphing her next mischievous act. Her mother loved her dearly, and you could tell that Jasmine felt the same way about her mother, but Phyleece Alexander had some serious drug problems that kept her from being the mother she should have been. Yet, you could always see the intensity of her love for Jasmine."

"You want to tell me how to get to this address?" Aaron said as he pointed down at the computer.

"Sure, I can tell you. It's not far from here at all. Come up to the reference desk and I will draw you a map. You can take the bus or walk. It's easy to find."

As she drew the map, Aaron noticed that her blouse opened slightly to expose just enough of her breasts to make him wonder what her nipples looked like. She knew what he was up to, looked up and said, "aren't you too old to be a lecher, Mr. Adams?"

Aaron, smiling replied, "when I am that old, I will be dead."

Heidi, realizing that Aaron was, no doubt, a man in his sixties, still felt an attraction to him and blurted out, "well, if you are still alive at 6:00PM, I get off work, and would love to have dinner with you and hear how your search went."

Aaron, somewhat shocked, not only by her obvious boldness, but by her interest in an old worn-out man, replied, "I'll be here at six. But don't expect much more out of me than company. I am afraid that my days of being a Lothario are far behind me."

"Good company is much more important than the superficial elements that mask themselves as affection. I look forward to seeing you," Heidi said with a mischievous grin.

The Girl Who Stirred Up The Whirlwind

As Aaron was leaving, he noticed the tall, thin, slightly balding man meandering through the stacks near Heidi's desk. At the same time, out of the corner of his right eye, he observed another man waiting at the top of the steps just outside the library door. He was being tailed by professionals, no doubt about it. The word was obviously out that he was looking for someone who was of interest to the C.I.A. These guys were just another example of how no one could escape the long reach of the American government that would go to any lengths to control those who dared stand-up to authority. Just like using terrorism to fight terrorism, these people thought they were defending freedom by denying the very freedom they so vehemently defended. With the appointment of George Bush as President by the Supreme Court in 2000, America's fate was forever sealed in a tomb of coming despair. The end of economic fairness and the abrogation of freedom would go unopposed by those who simply lined up for their invisible chains, unaware that they had just made the final surrender in the long battle against despotism and the nepotistic aggrandizement of the culture of greed. Evil had triumphed.

Deciding not to worry at present about his tail, Aaron simply ignored the man from outside the library, who apparently had been a replacement for the tall, thin, balding guy. This one was a little less discreet, but he was still pretty good. Most people would have never picked him up, but Aaron was not most people. He had simply been at the game too long to be fooled.

The building would have housed middle class renters in America, but this was Sweden, so the relatively modern structure was where the so-called poor lived, because shelter, food and medical care were considered the basic rights of all citizens. Poverty in Sweden was not a crime the way it was in the USA. Rather, it was considered a crime of society to allow people to slip through the cracks. Compassion wasn't something that was preached about in pulpits on Sundays and forgotten the rest of the week. Compassion was the government's responsibility. This was the face of that dreaded socialism that Americans were propagandized into believing represented inherent evil. Yeah, it was evil alright – evil for the moneyed class.

Aaron found the buzzer for the super, and was buzzed up without any questions. A rather statuesque elderly figure, a beautiful woman for her age, still seemingly fresh and vibrant, greeted Aaron in Swedish and asked him in as if she had known him for years.

Aaron, explaining that he did not speak Swedish, was surprised that someone her age was so fluent in English. The intelligence of the Swedes just overwhelmed Aaron. He thought to himself, "This is what a country can do that spends more money on education than bombs and bullets. Unlike Americans, Swedes did not think the whole world was out to get them."

Offering him tea as she pointed at a nearby overstuffed white chair, Aaron politely declined and said, "I am Aaron Adams, a private detective from New York City. I am trying to locate a Jasmine Alexander, and I understand this was the last place she lived before she disappeared the same night her mother was killed. Any chance you would be able to maybe give me some information on her?"

Her interested piqued, the lady replied, "I was super here 18 years ago when it happened. Her mother had a drug problem, but she was a good tenant. What a night. It was the same night our Prime Minister was killed. The little girl, Jasmine, oh, what a nice little thing. She was an absolute delight. She was eight as well as I remember, but had the maturity of a young woman. I suppose she had to, dealing with her mother's problems and all. Can't figure out what could have happened to her. She just disappeared into the night."

"You never noticed anything strange until that night?

"No, nothing at all. This is a pretty quiet building with good tenants. Her mother was a prostitute. We all knew that, but she never brought customers home."

"What about afterward, did anything happen that was out of the ordinary? Something that might seem suspicious to you. Anything you can share might be helpful, no matter how trivial it might appear."

She seemed to be in deep thought, mulling over what had occurred 18 years before. "Well, the police went through all the apartments. The apartment next door, the tenant was a Mr. Heed Hildegard, he seems to have also disappeared. He had rented the apartment for years, but was rarely seen. He paid his rent yearly, so the apartment stayed empty for a long time, as it was assumed he would be back. He just never came back after the murder. The police went all over the apartment, but found nothing out of the ordinary as far as I know. There were not even any clothes or cooking utensils. It was almost as if the person living there was nonexistent."

Just as Aaron was about to ask another question, she blurted out, "wait a minute! They did find something else unusual. Yeah, I remember it now. At least, I suppose it would be considered pretty unusual. Mind you, they did not share the information with me in any way, but I am a nosy old lady, so I was listening to their discussions and I heard one of them say something about how strange it was to find absolutely no fingerprints whatsoever in the apartment. Don't you think that was unusual?"

"Yes, yes, that would be very unusual, unheard of I would say. Even an empty apartment would have some fingerprints from past tenants or cleaning people."

Seemingly satisfied with herself, the old lady said, "so, I was helpful then?"

Aaron, smiling, replied, "very helpful."

"Good, good," she replied.

Aaron leaned forward in his seat, rubbed his chin with his right hand and asked, "what about this Heed Hildegard? Can you tell me something about him?"

"That is the strange thing. I took over as super after he had moved in, but even when you saw him, you didn't see him. Know what I mean? He was like a phantom – there one minute and gone the next. He seemed to only go out at night, but you could never hear anything in the apartment. Hey, I put my ears up to the door, nosy old woman that I am, and simply never heard anything. I once tried my pass key, and he had changed the lock. When the police tried to get in, they had to get a locksmith to open the door. The rent check was always slipped under my door, and it was paid yearly, like I said, by a company in Switzerland. Something called the Kimkassee Corporation. The cops ran a check on it, and no such company existed, only a bank account that had been closed."

Aaron realized he was on to something. "You say he was like a phantom. You never once saw his face?"

"Never, but once when he had his scarf on around his face one really cold day, I did get a look at his eyes. Can't remember what it was now, but there was something strange about them. I spoke to him, but he never acknowledged me, just moved on up the stairs like I wasn't even there. Wish I could remember what it was about his eyes."

Aaron thanked her and as he was leaving said, "you have any idea if Phyleece Alexander had a pimp?"

Smiling, the lady said, "sure, I know him. He tried to recruit me when I was younger and thinner."

Aaron replied, "you still look fine, ma'am."

Obviously pleased by what Aaron said, she chortled, "Adrian Patay. They call him Pretty Boy.

Been in the business since he was 16 and still out there hustling girls who are down on their luck. He's actually an O.K. guy. You can usually find him hanging out somewhere on Tenstaganen Gata.

Aaron left the building with a good feeling. He was making progress. It was too late for Christer Pettersson, but he still had a shot at saving Jasmine Alexander. Ironically, Frank Penderent popped into his mind at the same time that Frank was boarding a bus in Cincinnati, Ohio for St. Joseph's, Missouri on his circuitous route to Lonoke, Arkansas. Both men were being followed. Aaron knew it, but Frank did not.

As he followed a map drawn by the landlady, looking back over his right shoulder, Aaron picked up a blurry image about 100 metres behind him. The guy was a trained pro, but he was not as good as he thought he was. Aaron smiled and continued toward Tenstaganen Gata.

Finding a few obvious drug addicts leaning against a building as they passed around a joint, Aaron asked if they knew where he could find Pretty Boy Patay. One guy blurted out in perfect English, "just go down to the end of the block. You'll find him hanging out in front of the Café Chokladkoppen. He uses that place as his office. If he ain't outside, just go in and you will see him holding court in one of the booths. You can't miss him. He'll be the fanciest dresser in the place."

The Girl Who Stirred Up The Whirlwind

Pretty Boy wasn't outside, so Aaron stepped into the café. Pretty Boy was certainly an appropriate name. Although obviously nearing his 50's, he still had that youthful vigour and swagger about him. He was standing by a booth conversing with four women, occasionally placing his hands on his hips like a preening peacock spreading its feathers. Tall, muscular, with broad shoulders, long and immaculately coiffured salt and pepper hair and a thin grey moustache, his face was as smooth as silk, and as he waved his hands back and forth, it was obvious that they were probably manicured daily so meticulous was there appearance. This guy was a real dandy.

The immaculately tailored suit with wide lapels fit him perfectly, seemingly not a single wrinkle anywhere on the material. Yet, on him, it was more an exaggerated costume than an article of clothing. It was more than a sartorial statement; it was the bearer of a complex and contradictory exploitative attitude toward women, whom, because of his bearing and manner, obviously fell under his captivating spell. This was a man who exuded fascination, not fear. He was a steward of the whimsical and a purveyor of the farcical.

This man's clothes were his identity. They gave him an exalted place in the social order of his world. The clothes were more than a colourful stage-prop hanging from a lithe and toned body. They defined the man.

Aaron could not help but smile, as his eyes met Pretty Boy's and for a brief second they looked at each other, contemplating their next move, as it was obvious to Pretty Boy that Aaron was there to see him. Neither man knew what it was to concede to the manners of subservience. Striding toward Aaron, Pretty Boy became more erect, arching his back upward to make his height more pronounced. He accentuated his swagger as his thickly padded, killer-diller coat that had shoulders padded like a lunatic's cell seemed to move melodiously with each step.

In Swedish, Pretty Boy said, "you here to see me, man?"

Not understanding him, Aaron replied, "You speak English?"

Immediately realizing from the accent that Aaron was American, Pretty Boy replied, "of course, that is the only way you can communicate with Americans. They are too arrogant to learn any other language."

In perfect Spanish, Aaron replied, "some of us know other languages, but we don't have much use for Swedish."

Pretty Boy replied in perfect Spanish. "So, you want to speak English, Spanish, German or maybe French?"

Impressed, Aaron said, "English is fine. You have proved your point. We Americans are language illiterates."

Laughing, Pretty Boy pointed with his meticulously manicured hands toward an empty booth and they sat down across from on another. Pretty Boy, now a bit more respectful of Aaron said, "so, what can I do for you American?"

"Well, I am trying to locate a woman who is the daughter of one of your former ladies of delight. Her name is Jasmine Alexander. I believe her mother, Phyleece Alexander was a member of your stable of women."

Smiling and shaking his head, Pretty Boy seemed to get a serious, contemplative look. "Yeah, I handled her. Phyleece was a real hand full. I never hit my women, but I admit that I did hit her one night; the night she was killed. She was a drug addict, and I threatened to turn her in to child welfare to get that little girl of hers out of the misery. She came at me flailing and wailing, went crazy, so I slapped her across the face and she fell to the pavement. I tried to help her up, but she just kept fighting me. Said that she was going to go out on her own, and that I could go fuck myself. She went running down the street, and I never saw her again. She was killed that night and her little girl just disappeared. I read about it in the papers, and I have always wondered what happened to the little girl, but something funny happened a couple of years ago that made me think that perhaps the little girl wasn't dead."

His interest piqued, Aaron leaned forward. "And what was that?"

"First, why are you looking for her?"

"I am a private investigator, Aaron Adams from New York City. A friend of mine has information indicating that she is in danger. I am here to help her if I can."

"You seem like a righteous dude. So, I'm going to share something with you. You see, I have a stable of girls who are the cream of the crop. Well, cream for the freelancers that is. The government licences whorehouses, but they are too expensive for a lot of people, so I take care of girls for 20% of their take. They work the streets serving the small change guys who deserve a good fuck just as much as the affluent guys. Anyway, a couple of years ago, I hear about this chick who is a real looker. I mean prime stuff. Great body, terrific smile, demure personality, all the attributes that make for a first class street hooker. She was a waitress up at Café Tössebageriet on Tenstaganen Gata. I know the owner, so I figure I will go up and check this chick out and see if she wants to make ten times what she's pulling down as a waitress."

The Girl Who Stirred Up The Whirlwind

Aaron was actually beginning to like the guy. Hell, he was better than the corporate executives who took advantage of the hard-working employees while padding their own wallets. At least Pretty Boy was letting the girls keep the biggest part of the take. Aaron thought to himself that the Walton's certainly wouldn't let the employees of Wal-Mart keep the biggest end of the take. Hell most Wal-Mart employees had to get social assistance to survive on the pittance they were paid by the billionaire inheritors of a fortune build on the backs of working people. Pretty Boy was an executive with a heart, something extremely rare in world where those at the top looked with disdain at those who had to really work for a living.

Pretty Boy continued, "So, I go up there and find this gorgeous chick who reminds me of Phyleece Alexander. Her name was Felina Jacobssen. I offered her a real opportunity, and she says that she had already tried hooking, but it just wasn't something she wanted to do for money. She was more interested in sex for pleasure than as a business. O.K., I respect that, so I say to her, think it over, and I'll be back in a few days. Then she gives me this smile. I swear, I thought I was looking into the face of Phyleece Alexander. Same damn smile exactly. I am really unnerved. I leave, but go back a week later, because I can't get this chick off my mind. Find out her girlfriend – her lover was killed and she's disappeared."

Aaron, fascinated now, said, "so, you never saw her again?"

"Right man, absolutely right. I still can't get that look out of my mind. This chick is the spitting image of Phyleece Alexander before Phyleece went overboard with drugs. But her body, wow, this chick's body is what you say, not perfect, even a little big maybe, but so perfectly proportioned in all the right places and that smile. What a killer smile. It starts in the right corner of her mouth and just mischievously creeps across her lips showing gleaming white teeth. I'm telling you, she gives you an erection with just that smile. Oh, what that mouth could do to a man's member; damn, makes me horny just thinking about it."

Getting up, Aaron said as he prepared to leave, "so, I tell this fellow at the café that you sent me, think he might put me onto this woman? You think she could actually be Jasmine Alexander?"

"I'm not saying definite, man. All I know is it has haunted me every since I saw the chick. The resemblance is uncanny. Don't know what the owner could do for you. Name's Eric Hender. He never saw her again, but you can tell him Adrian sent you. Maybe he can give you something that could help. If you ever find her, regardless of whom she might be, hey man, tell her that Pretty Boy has a job waiting for her anytime she wants it, and, for her, I'll only take10%."

The Girl Who Stirred Up The Whirlwind

Aaron shook Pretty Boy's hand and asked for directions to Café Tössebageriet. He strolled out into the late afternoon sun, and immediately picked up his tail. He was beginning to get irritated, but decided to wait before confronting the guy. After all, he didn't want to create any waves, at least not yet. He was short of time and Jasmine, herself, might not know it, but she was running out of time also.

Again, Aaron thought about Frank Penderent and wondered if he was in Lonoke, Arkansas yet. He had told him to contact Carrie and Allen Pink who had a cabin in the backcountry where they went for love trysts some weekends. They were just two lovers who minded their own business and lived a quiet existence in a little town where they were anomalies. Unlike most of the others there, they had no religion and were liberal minded. Aaron had met them years ago when he was in town working with a friend on a case. They would all be fine. Jasmine Alexander was his primary concern now. He had promised Frank to save her from certain death, and he was not going to let him down.

Café Tössebageriet was a small place with a huge red neon sign in front. Eric Hender, a fat man with a huge smile, stood behind the counter in an old-fashioned white apron. Hearing that Pretty Boy had sent Aaron, he ushered him back into the closet sized office and asked him to take a seat.

The Girl Who Stirred Up The Whirlwind

"So, what can I do for you Mr. Adams," he said, smiling broadly as he eased into an old, well-worn leather chair.

"I understand you had a young lady who went by the name Felina Jacobbson working for you a couple years ago, and she mysteriously disappeared."

"Oh, I wouldn't say there was anything that mysterious about it. Her roommate was killed. She came by and said she couldn't afford to get mixed up with the police. She was pretty distraught. I mean the two girls were in love, and you know how love is when you are young. You think it is forever, but men our age know that is not usually the case. Anyway, I gave her cash for what I owed her, even a little extra, and told her to take care of herself. She smiled that cute little smile of hers, kissed me on the cheek, turned around and left without saying a word. Damn fine young girl. The best I ever had working for me. She was a real honey. She was always helping out people on the street and her fellow workers who needed a lift. The girl was carrying some heavy baggage herself. You could just tell it, but she always had time to help others. I never asked her what her troubles were, but told her that I was there for her if she needed me. I've had a lot of people work for me over the years who were avoiding the police for one reason or another. Hey, I've had my own troubles with the police. Spent a couple years in stir before I got myself straightened out. Being in trouble with the police doesn't mean you're a bad person. Most of the time it just means you got caught for doing something that other people got away with. Hell, half the Stockholm Police Department should be in jail themselves. Yet, they are riding around all arrogant telling the rest of us to stay in-line."

"That sounds a lot like the New York City Police Department," Aaron sarcastically replied.

"Yeah, it's the same all over the world. The big money boys get away with all kinds of stealing that is just called doing business, but the rest of us have to pay the piper. The police don't give a damn about the average Joe, but they fall all over themselves trying to cater to the rich and powerful. Welcome to the new world order of that asshole who is running America now. George Bush is a prescription for disaster. My guess is you Americans will elect him to a second term, and by the end of it, you won't even recognize the country. You Americans aren't really that smart you know. Present company excepted."

Aaron, taking an instant liking to Eric Hender, would have loved to continue their philosophical exploration of the problems encountered by the small guys ground up in the machinery of capitalism, but he was pressed for time. He had to find Jasmine Alexander, and he needed to know if

Hender had an inkling of who the girl calling herself Felina Jacobbson really was. He said in a pleading manner, "so, do you think her real name was Felina Jacobbson? You see, I need to find a woman named Jasmine Alexander, and Pretty Boy seems to think this girl might have been she, as she resembled the way he remembered her mother, especially her smile."

Sighing and looking contemplative, Hender quizzically replied, "Yeah, you're right about the smile. You can never forget it. There was something magical about it. She could have been this Jasmine Alexander. My guess is that her real name was not Felina Jacobbson. You see, she had no papers. I paid her under the table, like a lot of people I hire. I know the name Jasmine Alexander. That was the little girl who disappeared near here the night that her mother was killed. That wasn't big news, because it was the same night that Olaf Palme was assassinated. Hey, the high and mighty are a lot more important than a little poor girl and a drug-addicted prostitute. Although, I must say that Olaf Palme would have cared about both of them. He was a man who tried to do the right thing for us ordinary people. That's why he was killed. The rich and powerful can't tolerate someone offering a hand up to working men and women."

"Well, at least Sweden is a little better than the USA when it comes to helping out the marginalized of society."

The Girl Who Stirred Up The Whirlwind

Shaking his head up and down, Hender said, "Yeah, you got that right. I am thankful to be a Swede, but every day, the same moneyed interests are trying to take over Sweden the way they have the USA. If you don't mind my asking, why is this Jasmine Alexander so important to you? I mean I wouldn't want to get the girl in any trouble."

"It's a long story, but basically, if I don't find her soon, she is going to wind up just like her mother. There is a contract out on her."

Sitting up straighter and obviously concerned, Hender said, "she was such a sweet thing, and she was really in love with her roommate, Rose. One day I even got a glimpse of one of Felina's magnificent breasts. With her, it would be disrespectful to call them titties. Anyway, one night she showed several of us her left breast, right near the nipple, where she had gotten a tattoo of a rose, done by her girlfriend, the one who was killed, named Rose. Now those breasts were a sight to behold, never seen any more perfectly formed and they were real, not plastic. Damn, if I had been a younger man, I'd been all over that. That girl Jacobbson or whatever her name was, she was something special. I mean you don't run across her kind everyday. I wish I could help more." He raised his right index finger and continued, "Hey, wait a minute. I know where there might be a photo of her. She avoided having her picture taken, but right after she met her girlfriend Rose, a guy took a picture of the two of them together. Rose wanted it to carry on her trips. Said that it would make her feel close to Felina when she was away. He was a street busker, sometimes hangs outside here playing his guitar and harmonica. They asked him to take the picture right outside in front of the café. He had one of those new fangled digital cameras that the girls were too poor to afford. It is a long shot, but he might have a copy. I wish I could draw. I would give you a rendering of her, but I have no artistic talent whatsoever."

Then, a worried looked seemed to slowly grow on Hender's face. "Oh no, I may have really screwed up. Earlier today there was a guy, a real weird acting gent with a South African accent, asking about the busker. Yeah, he said he wanted to use him for a party he was planning. I gave him the address. It is Hagagatan 12. Just go outside the restaurant, turn left and go three blocks to Gyllenkrooksgatan, turn left there and go two blocks, then right on Hagagatan. He lives in a basement flat, Hagagatan 12, number 1-A. The busker's name is Christian Eriksson."

Aaron, his interest piqued, leaned forward and said, "you able to describe the fellow who asked about him?"

"Not really, he had a turned up collar. Went all the way to his chin but I did notice his eyes were a little unusual. He had no eyebrows. He was sinister looking, really made me uncomfortable being in the same room with him. You think he may be the person looking for Jasmine Alexander?"

"Definitely one of them, and if he shows up again, don't do anything to anger him. This is not a man you want to mess with, believe me."

"Gotcha Mr. Adams, and you going to see this Eriksson fellow then, I suppose. Hope I didn't screw things up."

"You didn't know about the situation when he was here. Don't blame yourself for anything. If Felina Jacobssen or Jasmine Alexander can be found, I'm the man who can do it, but I am up against some pretty good adversaries and they have the might of one of the most sinister organizations in the world behind them. This is not going to be easy. Thanks for your help," Aaron said as he got up, shook hands with Hender, turned and headed for Hagagatan 12.

Aaron sensed that Felina Jacobssen and Jasmine Alexander definitely was the same person, but time was rapidly running out. He was up against Wilton and the *Whirlwind*, and there were two others involved, the guy he left back at the library and his tail. Hell, this was what Aaron lived for. He loved bringing down the arrogant bastards who thought they had nothing to fear. As he strolled outside, he turned and headed down the street, noticing that his tail was creeping along about 100 metres behind him. He instinctively slapped his coast pocket over the left breast to feel that big bastard of a 45 that always gave him a feeling of security. Damn, he suddenly realized he was in Sweden. It was a country that didn't allow its citizens go around packing. Smiling at his mental mistake, he whispered out loud, "this is a country with some sense; I will have to devise another means of killing here. This is a country where everyone does not dream of owning an AK-47."

Knocking on 1-A, Aaron could not help but notice that the door was slightly ajar. When there was no answer, he nudged the door open a little more with his right foot and peered into the darkness. Darkness was Aaron's friend. He relished it. It gave him strength. He eased into it unafraid, but cautious. He could feel the evil in the air. It was a tangible element that he could almost touch. The blackness was overwhelming. He could only feel the furniture, not see it, as he moved forward like he was in a tunnel so black that one cannot get out of it, for there is no light, only an endless pit at the end that would take your hand and pull you into eternity in the dark bowels of the earth.

He could hear faint breathing in the distance, but saw nothing. Damn, how he wanted to pull out the

45 and break the silence with a thundering volley of lead to light up whatever awaited him at the end of the dark pit of hell. A cuckoo clock suddenly went off to Aaron's left, signally that it was 4:00 o'clock, so he turned to look outside, almost pleading for some light, but this was Sweden in the fall, and the daylight hours had already diminished as darkness crept up early in the day. There would be no light, no light to shine in the blackness that was overwhelming him. He felt a lamp on a nearby table and fidgeted for the switch so that he could bathe the room with even a small ray of light that would allow him to see where the breathing was coming from in the darkness.

As he switched on the lights, a dark cloaked spectre hurtled toward him, knocking him over onto a chair that collapsed under him. He had no time to grasp at the figure, as all he could do was reach out to brace his fall. He tried to scramble up from floor and pursue the spectre, but it was as if it was a ghost that simply disappeared into the ether. Finally, struggling to the door, he looked out into the street and about 100 metres away, on the opposite side of the street, he saw the cloaked figure meet up with his tail and the two of them scurried down the street like long distance runners sprinting for the finish line. He could not catch them. He turned back, walked into the room, closing the door behind him and there it was. On the floor, right under that obnoxious sounding cuckoo clock that was sitting on a mantel above a walled up fireplace was a body. No doubt, it was the busker, Christian Eriksson. Aaron was too late. Whatever information Eriksson had was now in the hands of the infamous *Whirlwind*. Aaron knew that time was of the essence. Flipping on light after light, he bathed the place in brightness and looked all about, trying to see what might be a clue, any clue to what happened and whether or not the so-called *Whirlwind* had gotten a picture of Jasmine Alexander. Then, he noticed something in Eriksson's hand. It was a small torn piece of paper. Bending down, he pried it from the dead man's hand. It was only a sliver of paper, but it was photographic paper. The Whirlwind had Jasmine's photograph, and all Aaron had to identify her by was a rose tattoo on her left breast.

CHAPTER 7
THE WRATH OF AARON ADAMS

Feeling morose about losing the opportunity to actually get a picture of Jasmine, Aaron decided to head back to the library and see what additional information he might glean from Heidi Helmut. As he was strolling toward the library, Frank Penderent's bus was pulling into Lonoke, Arkansas. He immediately went to a pay phone and called the number given him by Aaron, who gave him strict instructions not to use a cell phone. It was answered by Allen Pink, who had been told by Aaron, in a brief phone conversation, to take his friend Frank to the cabin deep in the Arkansas back country and to be sure no one followed them. Allen gave Frank instructions to walk down Main Street and to look for a blue 1985 Ford pickup that would have him and his girlfriend Carrie in it. Allen would only stop if it appeared that there was no one following Frank. If he did not stop, Frank was to simply go back to the terminal and take a bus back to Little Rock. Then, he should call Allen again and there would be further instructions.

As Frank walked down Main Street, with its boarded up buildings that were a reflection of the economic malaise caused when Wal-Mart arrived in a small town to destroy free-enterprise, he kept glancing behind him. There was no one following him. He was certain of it.

The Girl Who Stirred Up The Whirlwind

Frank was right, there was no one following him on foot, but at the bus terminal, two men sat in a Hertz rental car with the engine idling, closely watching Frank walk down the street. They had been following the bus since it left Cincinnati, waiting for the opportune moment, to not only take out Frank, but whomever he was meeting. There absolutely could be no loose ends when it came to protecting the agency from being exposed for nefarious deeds conducted in the name of democracy. Allen and Carrie were now about to come into the sights of these C.I.A. killers who had been given the green light to eliminate anyone who might be privy to what Frank Penderent had found out.

Allen Pink was a gregarious young man of about 29 who, although a bit overweight, was still a handsome young man in his soul and carried himself with an air of self-confidence that seemed to elicit respect, even from those who saw him as an anomaly in a place that demanded conformity. He saw through the artificiality of those who clung to religion and out-dated values as an escape from the drudgery of life in a small town where everyone was expected to follow a certain regimen of respectability. To him, respectability was not important. Caring about people and questioning authority were at the centre of his belief system. It was these attributes that had made him a friend of Aaron Adams, who had often come to visit an old army buddy who lived near Lonoke. When Aaron had tried to pick-up his girlfriend, Carrie, at a local bar, Allen, rather than being offended, actually complimented Aaron on his taste in women and told him that, anyway, he was too old to handle a woman with Carrie's spirit.

Carrie, a short, demure, retiring, but voluptuous 28 year old with those proverbial come-hither bedroom eyes had moved from California to Lonoke after meeting Allen on a chat-line six years before. Like Allen, she refused to follow the prescription of respectability that seemed to define most Americans who always bowed to patriotic servitude as a result of propaganda, conditioning and fear. She was a free spirit who had no religion, no interest in material things and felt no compunction to yield to the authority of those who demanded conformity. She and Allen were both throw-backs to the rebellious, anti-materialistic youths of the 1960's. Perhaps that was why Aaron had gotten along so well with them both, because he was nothing more than a fugitive from the 60's himself, still trapped in that era when it seemed possible that things could really change and that the culture of greed could be defeated. Everyone else had given up, but Aaron still clung to the hope that someday, somehow, that spark of rebellion would be reignited, and once again people would take to the streets to demand justice and fairness in a world that had been completely turned over to the evil barons of greed who ruled with the iron fist of repression.

As Frank neared the end of downtown, he saw lights being flashed from low beam to high beam behind him. A blue pickup pulled up, the passenger door flung open and a soft female voice said "get in, quickly."

Climbing in, Frank was delighted to finally be in the presence of people with whom he might let down lct his guard. He sighed and eased back in his seat, the old truck bouncing him up and down as they cruised down the dark, deserted road. Carrie demurely smiled at Frank as her eyes twinkled and said, "Welcome to Arkansas, the place where Bill Clinton got blown before he met Monica."

All three burst out in laughter and after introducing themselves, Frank actually felt safe, but it didn't last long. Allen kept looking in the rear view mirror and said, "we are being followed. I guarantee it. We have no idea why you are here. Aaron said we were better off not knowing, but he asked us to hide you out, and we will do anything for him. He is a righteous dude if there ever was one."

"He is right about you being better off not knowing, and I appreciate what you are doing. But I don't want you two to risk your lives for me. You can just drop me off anywhere you want. The guys after me are no amateurs. They mean business."

The Girl Who Stirred Up The Whirlwind

Allen, slightly grinning, motioned with his head toward the back of the truck cab, where there was a gun rack with a 12 gauge pump action shotgun in it. "Man, you're in Arkansas, we're all packing here. I'm not afraid of nobody when I got that baby with me."

Carrie, her body bouncing up and down with the motion of the truck that had long-ago worn-out its shocks, noticed that Frank was glancing out of the corner of his eyes at her large, globular breasts that jutted out defiantly in her form fitting blouse that hugged her generous curves. Thinking how ridiculous men were, she almost laughed out loud at a person who was facing death, but still couldn't put aside his sexual desires. She intentionally let her right leg brush his, just so he could continue to keep his mind off the trouble they were all facing. She enjoyed being an attractive woman immensely, and she had no qualms about using her charms. Allen, seeing what she was doing, looked to his right and gave her a little wink, knowing that she was always ultimately his, because they had a simpatico that transcended mere sexual attraction.

Realizing that once they got onto the dirt road that led to the cabin, the two men would probably make their move, Allen, without saying a word, communicated with his eyes for Carrie to get the shotgun. She reached behind her and placed it in her lap.

The Girl Who Stirred Up The Whirlwind

Turning onto the dirt road, Allen motioned for Carrie to take the wheel as he gently nudged the driver's door slightly open. Slowing down to a snail's pace, he picked up the shotgun from Carrie's lap and stepped outside, keeping pace with the truck, then running across the road into a gulley where he ducked behind some trees as Carrie slid over behind the wheel and sped up the hill, pulled to the right and parked once they were over the crest. She turned off the engine and said, "don't worry, Allen knows how to use that shotgun better than anybody in Arkansas.

What happened next is not for the faint of heart, because Allen was a man who felt no qualms about destroying those who used a dark cloak of supposed righteousness to conceal their evil intentions. He had no idea who the two men were, but he had been told by Aaron, an individual for whom he had tremendous respect, that Frank Penderent had been targeted for elimination by the American government. Allen understood that repression and dastardly deeds that were a violation of human rights sanctioned by the dope in the White House had turned America over to a pack of right-wing, religious and corporate ideologues. He, Carrie and Aaron all knew that there would be an eventual calamity as a result of this idiot's malfeasant disregard for the average citizen, but most Americans were too wrapped up in religion and patriotic propaganda to see that they were all being played for suckers.

The Girl Who Stirred Up The Whirlwind

The car with the two agents in it was heading toward Allen, its lights turned off in the darkness to avoid detection. Allen, with the shotgun poised and ready, suddenly stepped from behind a tree and fired into the hood of the car where the drive belt would be disabled. Steam billowed into the humid night air, seeming to form a ghost like figure above the car. The headlights weren't on, so the darkness provided Allen with cover. He had no intention of killing the agents, only stopping them. From behind the tree, he shouted, "Outta the car with your hands up, assholes."

The two men exited the car, but rather than having their hands up, they opened fire in the direction of the voice, while diving to the ground to make themselves harder to see. Scanning the darkness, they slowly crawled under the car for cover. One said, "Should we call for backup?" The other replied, "can't take the chance, this is a clandestine operation. Keep cool, it is only one person. I am sure, and he is an amateur. The shot came from that wooded area over by that gulley. I'm going to turn the lights on while you fire in that direction."

Allen sensed what they were about to do. So, he slowly crawled to his left, making sure that he did not rustle any bushes that might attract their attention. He did not want to do it, but they were forcing him into an untenable situation, where killing them would be his only way out.

Allen, his options now limited, watched as one agent leaped into the car and turned on the lights while the other one emptied his gun firing where Allen had been. Now on their feet, and behind the opened car doors for cover, one agent shouted, "we represent the U.S. government. You're in a heap of trouble friend."

Allen couldn't resist replying. "I am no friend of anybody representing a government that tortures people and ignores the plight of the poor."

Then, the two men pivoted in the direction where Allen's voice was coming from, pulling the car doors against their bodies like shields, as they aimed their guns into the darkness. Allen, now crawling back to where he could get in front of the car again, couldn't resist continuing the banter. "All I want to do is walk up the road to my truck and haul ass outta here. Throw your guns into the brush to your right, or turn around and walk back to the highway. There's no need for anybody to die tonight."

The agent on the passenger side said, "listen asshole, you are into something really big here. You don't want to mess with the people we represent. We're not going anywhere. You better toss that goddamn shotgun onto the road, and we'll let you live, maybe even let you avoid jail, but your options are running out fast. You better make your decision quick."

The Girl Who Stirred Up The Whirlwind

Allen, never one to mince words, replied sarcastically, "you men are already dead. You just don't know it. As far as me not wanting to mess with the people you represent, we are out of the cell-phone coverage area here. Go ahead, try it. Nobody knows where you are, and as for me being in trouble, if there are no witnesses, I got no trouble."

After each discussion, Allen crawled to another position. Meanwhile, Frank was getting anxious as he sat in the truck over the knoll with Carrie. Seeing he was nervous, Carrie, cool and collected, said, "don't worry. Allen is cool under pressure. He thrives on things like this. He lives to stand-up to authority." Then, that sheepish little smile crept across her lips as she continued, "the only authority he is afraid of is me."

While Carrie and Frank were laughing at her statement, Allen decided that there was no way out of the situation that wouldn't end in disaster either for him or the agents. When you dealt with authority, you either caved in or stood your ground, and those who stood their ground in America had always paid a dear price for doing so. For some reason, Leonard Peltier, who had dared to stand up to FBI intimidation at Wounded Knee in 1973 popped into his mind. Peltier would pay for his boldness by spending the rest of his life in prison. Yet, Allen was not willing to submit to intimidation. He would stand his ground.

Allen took a deep breath, rolled over on his back and pleaded one last time with the agents. "I don't want to do this, but you're leaving me no choice."

Allen's answer was a fusillade of hot lead aimed in his direction, but he kept rolling to his right until he eventually came up to the side of the agent on the passenger side of the car. He stood up in the now chilling night air, and knowing they would have on bullet proof vests, he fired two quick rounds at the agent's head. Brains and bone fragments scattered all across the roof of the car and the other agent started running for the gulley and cover. Popping up again, Allen aimed for the back of his head. His head exploded like a ripe watermelon being dropped on concrete.

Walking over to them to make sure they were dead, Allen shook his head in disgust. They could have walked, but typical of government arrogance, they could not see their own malfeasant devotion to a cause that was an abomination to decency in a country that had simply lost its moral compass. They would not be the last to die for a man in the White House who had conned them into believing they were standing against tyranny, when in effect, it was the man in the White House who represented tyranny of the vilest form – the tyranny of the 1% who reaped all the good things while those at the bottom were bound forever into subservience to an ideal that did not exist anymore and willingly volunteered to fight so-called evil-doers in other countries while the real evil was at 1600 Pennsylvania Avenue, in the board rooms of corporations and on Wall Street.

Saddened by what he had done, but with unbowed head because they gave him no choice, Allen walked briskly up the road in anticipation of wrapping himself in the sweet arms of his Carrie. He couldn't help but wonder what his friend Aaron was up to in Stockholm.

Aaron, approaching the library, noticed a mass of police cars out front and a large crowd mulling around. Finding a younger person to address, because he assumed they would speak English, he asked, "what's going on?"

The young man replied, "A librarian was murdered back in the stacks. Someone cut her jugular. Real messy, they just brought her out. I knew her, not personally, but from going into the library over the years. Real nice lady, she was."

Aaron instinctively spurted out, "Heidi Helmut?"

The young man said, "You know her, too?"

Aaron, despondently replied, "Yeah, I knew her." He turned to walk away and continued, "you're right, a real nice lady."

Aaron's indignation was beginning to build. Yet, he knew he had to keep it in abeyance until he found Jasmine. When he did, then the *Whirlwind* would pay. This was now about more than just finding Jasmine Alexander. It was about a killer who had no restraints placed on him by the U.S. government. Well, Aaron Adams had no restraints placed on him either, because he could mercilessly kill those who stood against justice. The *Whirlwind* would suffer the wrath of Aaron Adams.

CHAPTER 8
I AM A HURRICANE

Aaron seemed lost. What could he do next? Yeah, maybe stand on the street corner and ask every woman in Stockholm who seemed to be between 18 and 30 if they had a rose tattoo on their left breast. Hey, Sweden was a liberal country, but it also had laws against harassment. Not a good idea thought Aaron, as he instinctively strolled toward Café Tössebageriet, and his new friend, Eric Hender.

Aaron retired to the closet size office with Eric Hender, and over a cup of coffee, he shared what had happened to two people that day. One, Christian Eriksson, who obviously had a photograph of Jasmine or, as Eric knew her Felina, and the other, Heidi Helmut, who probably didn't know enough about what Aaron was up to. Not being able to answer questions that were put to her had cost her dearly. Aaron warned Eric, that he, too, should be careful, because these killers had a green light to erase any evidence of what had occurred nearly twenty years ago. There would be no mercy shown to anyone who might have knowledge of what happened. Anyone connected to Jasmine Alexander now or in the past might be in danger.

When Eric asked if they should go to the police, Aaron looked him directly in the eyes and said, "I always go to the police as a last resort. I have always found them to often be more crooked than the crooks they go after. My guess is that the U.S. government has the whole Stockholm Police Department infiltrated with moles that go right to the very top. Just be careful, and keep yourself a kitchen knife close at hand, just in case."

Eric leaned forward, and said, "I know how to take care of myself. I have been doing it since of I was twelve and my pop skipped out on my mom and his four kids. I just wish I could help you more with finding Jasmine. I'm an old man, and I've lived a pretty good life. That girl deserves better than she got. She had no real chance, like so many who are just victims of circumstance."

"Eric, was she a lady of precise habits? I mean could you always expect her to do the same thing day in and day out?"

Eric, contemplating for a second, seemed in deep thought. "Yeah, I'd say that. She was supposed to be at work for the noon shift most days. Told her 11:00 o'clock was fine, but like clockwork, she always came in at 10:30. And she always had a certain way of placing the silverware on the tables. Did it the same way all the time – made sure the knife handle was exactly even with the handle of the fork. Would even go behind the other waitresses and fix theirs that way. She also loved going to the cinema, but always went to the

Grand whenever possible. It was the first place she and Rose went to the movies together. She and Rose would go there for the 10:00 o'clock show on Friday or Saturday nights."

A light went on in Aaron's head. That was it, he could find her. "So, tonight is Friday night Eric. How'd you like to go to the movies with me?"

A bit bewildered Eric replied, "sure, but what's the catch."

"Years of experience tell me that people rarely change their habits, and when someone has fond memories of a place, they don't just forget it. They go back for nostalgia reasons. My guess is that Jasmine, or as you know her, Felina, will be at the movies tonight or tomorrow night."

"You mean the Grand?"

Aaron nodded his head in the affirmative and the two men were set for a course of action that would inexorably alter their lives.

Hanging outside the Grand Friday until midnight produced no one who even came close to resembling Jasmine Alexander, so all day Saturday, Aaron spent time trying to catch up on sleep at his hotel, while Eric, as usual, was at his restaurant. Late Saturday afternoon, Eric went out back to deposit some trash in the bin. He was met by the man with no eyebrows (Wilton), who grabbed him by the shirt and shoved him behind the bin. Another man, seemingly more sinister, stood in the alley entrance, apparently as a lookout for anyone who might venture down the alley. Beside him was a tall, thin, bald headed man with a scowl on his face. Wilton leaned in close to Eric. "You're going to be given one chance to answer my questions truthfully. One chance is all you get. What have you told Aaron Adams about Jasmine Alexander?"

Eric was not afraid of death. He had long ago decided to never live his life in fear. He took a deep breath and actually smiled. "I told him nothing, because I know nothing. I don't know no Jasmine Alexander."

"O.K., then! Felina Jacobssen. Whatever name you prefer."

"I already told you all I know. I gave you the name of the man who took her picture. Wasn't that enough?"

Wilton smiled and motioned for the *Whirlwind*, who strode toward them like some ancient Greek God coming down from Olympus. Each stride accentuated his evil intentions. Here was a man supremely confident in the righteousness of his cause, no matter how sinister or evil the intentions. He was the slayer of hope.

The Girl Who Stirred Up The Whirlwind

The *Whirlwind* was not a man. He was a shadow of evil moving methodically and with malevolent intent toward poor Eric. He was a barbaric calamity waiting to rein terror on all who dared stand against what he saw as the only true, righteous country on the face of the earth. This was an individual who saw nothing evil about what he did, because he was in service to his country, and he firmly believed that extremism in defence of one's country was no vice. This was the doctrine of total depravity that engulfed so many who had illegally manipulated an election and stolen the reins of power in a so-called democracy. Now, in power, these minions of mayhem were hell-bent on the destruction of everything in their path as they marched toward the economic enslavement of humanity to a creed of greed. As the Bible, that these purveyors of evil so boldly proclaimed to revere, intonated, these men were so fallen, so darkened in their hearts, minds, and completely ruled by the sins of arrogance, pride and entitlement, that they were unable to turn from the sins of self-righteousness and embrace the truth of redemption offered through genuine love of your fellow man. They did not know how to reach out with compassion. They only knew how to destroy all who dared stand in defiance to economic slavery and ideological servitude to a cause which was an abomination to justice. And these men's ideals were defended at all costs by men like the *Whirlwind*, who was, himself, without realizing it, a brainwashed patriot who was fighting for an ideal that was nothing but an illusion – an illusion that captivated those too weak minded to think for themselves. Eric almost laughed out loud as a quote from George Carlin flashed through his mind. *I do a real moronic thing. It's called thinking, and I am not a very good American, because I like to form my own opinions. Thinking for yourself is un-American.*

Eric, as the *Whirlwind* leaned in close to him, noticed something strange about his eyes, just as had Jasmine when she was a little girl. He had two brown eyes, but there was a tinge of green in his left eye. How strange thought Eric – I am about to die and I am noticing my killer's eye colour. He thought to himself that the eye was not satisfied with seeing, nor the ear satisfied with hearing. Very few people consistently saw or heard what was around them. People's lives were too superficial for them to genuinely see and hear what was being done to them by those who were in control.

As he waited to die, Eric thought that his realization was both comforting and horrifying at the same time. Things were simple, easy to understand. The constant wars between countries, between religions, between ideology, literally and figuratively, was a result of individuals not seeing the evil in men like those who now faced him. People like the *Whirlwind* were servants to those who lived in shadows and wandered through the periphery of people's lives. These demons were darker than even the *Whirlwind* and his henchmen, because they had a façade of respectability that masked their true intentions. They were human shaped entities that simply trekked through the world, lurking, watching and controlling all who toiled day-to-day in supplication to the rich and powerful who ruled with complete impunity.

A grey sheet of clouds stretched across the sky, casting a pall of darkness in the alley as Eric prepared to die. There was no need to scream out. There was no need to plead. The decision had been made. He was just more collateral damage in the battle between evil and evil. No matter who won, in the end, the result would be just more evil.

The *Whirlwind*, almost in a whisper, said, "This is it for you Hender. I can make it quick and easy or so painful that you will beg me for death. One more time, what have you revealed to Adams that you have not told us?"

Defiantly, Eric shouted, "fuck you!"

The *Whirlwind* motioned with a nod of his head toward Wilton. Wilton removed a large handkerchief and stuffed it in Eric's mouth to stifle the coming screams, as he grabbed him from behind the shoulders, and pulled backwards, jutting out his mid section toward the *Whirlwind*.

The Girl Who Stirred Up The Whirlwind

Sinisterly smiling, the *Whirlwind* reached into his pocket and removed a large pocket knife the size of a ruler. Slowly opening it for maximum scare affect, he waved the serrated blade in front of Eric eyes, all the time smiling. Looking down at Eric's crotch, he reached down and unbuckled his belt, unzipped his pants and as his pants dropped to his ankles; the *Whirlwind* began to cut away Eric's boxers, exposing his dangling member to the brisk air. Reaching down and taking one testicle in his hand, the smile became even more sinister as he said, "going to remove the gag for a second. Tell me what you have told Adams and I'll end this painlessly; otherwise, you're going to know some real pain. Pain like you never imagined."

When Wilton removed the gag, Eric shouted, "haven't used it in years, asshole. The damn thing is useless. Go ahead!"

As Wilton jammed the handkerchief back in Eric's mouth, the *Whirlwind* carved off Eric's right testicle. Eric's screams were muffled by the gag, but the pain was etched in his eyes. The *Whirlwind* whispered, "Gonna try again. Let's see if you have something to say now."

Again Wilton pulled out the gag, but Eric spat in the *Whirlwind's* face and said, "motherfucker, carve the hell out of me. I know nothing, but if I did, I wouldn't tell you, anyway!"

The Girl Who Stirred Up The Whirlwind

Wilton immediately put the gag back in Eric's mouth. The *Whirlwind* threw up his hands, turned and started out of the alley toward where the thin, tall bald guy was standing. Wilton put his knee in Eric's back, pulled hard and snapped his spine. Eric fell to the ground and Wilton bent over, picked him up and placed his head in the trash bin. He brought the lid down hard on his neck and joined the two others as they walked out of the alley into the street. They wouldn't kill Aaron Adams yet, because he might be a help in locating Jasmine Alexander. They had a picture of her, but Aaron had the know-how to locate her. Why not use him just in case they needed help. Then, after they eliminated Jasmine Alexander, the *Whirlwind* would personally dispatch Aaron. He loved taking out guys who thought they were tough. Eighteen years of worry were close to being put to rest. The end was in sight.

As Aaron walked toward Café Tössebageriet, he picked up a tail. This was a different guy. It was the one who had followed him into the library. Yeah, he figured there were four field agents probably involved with finding Jasmine Alexander. There was the *Whirlwind*, Wilton and the two guys who had been tailing him. He would wait to deal with his tail. What he needed now was a bite to eat. Then, he would wait for 10:00 PM and he and Eric would head to the Grand. He would have to shake his tail then to protect Jasmine from exposure.

The Girl Who Stirred Up The Whirlwind

Seeing the mass of people and the police cars in front of the alleyway beside Eric's restaurant gave Aaron a sinking feeling in the pit of his stomach. Things were falling apart and time was running out. Not wanting to be detained by the police, he simply found a reasonably young person, whom he assumed would speak English, and asked, "so, what happened."

A young man of about 20 replied, "Somebody killed the owner of Café Tössebageriet, cut his goddamn balls off."

Aaron turned and looked for his tail, but saw no one. He thought to himself, "enough of this cat-and-mouse game. I am going to start taking these bastards out before they kill anybody else. I might not find Jasmine, but I'll leave a string of dead bodies as a warning to anyone who dares get in my way."

They had just killed a good man, and Aaron Adams was not one to let something like that go down without some form of retribution. These killers weren't messing around with the typical person. Aaron Adams did not roll over for anybody. He had no concern about dying. Hell, he had been a walking dead man for years, ever since the case of the mysterious box that had cost him the love of his life. His blood was beginning to boil, and he didn't care who got in his way. Even the U.S. government was not immune to his wrath.

The Girl Who Stirred Up The Whirlwind

As he strolled down the street, his hunger no more a matter of concern, he once again instinctively felt for his forty-five that wasn't there. Damn, he missed the great equalizer, the demon that spit death, the ejector of the hot lead of retribution.

He was burdened with sorrow, but he was about to shine the light on years of darkness. Rivers of blood would flow, as he unleashed the fury and rage of a man who simply knew no fear in a world where people lined up for their invisible chains that bound them forever in subservience to the elite who ruled with the iron fist of repression. He refused to bow before evil that was cloaked in a veneer of respectability and self-righteousness. No man, no government, not even God, himself, could stand against this man who refused to accept the unacceptable. There would be hell to pay, and this was the man who would deliver the bill.

The goddess of wrath begat him.
The god of retribution taught him.
The mother of redress and reprisal nourished him.
Vengeance was the food that strengthened him.
Anger, retaliation and rancour motivated him.
The great monster of reciprocal vendettas led him.
He was the dispenser of justice to the unjust;
Defender of those who can't defend themselves.
Be aware when his ire is aflame.
If you be his enemy, prepare to die.
Be wary - the wrath of Aaron Adams.

The Girl Who Stirred Up The Whirlwind

Striding with purpose down the street, Aaron knew his tail was there, but he made sure that he did nothing to indicate he was aware of him. He would play a cat and mouse game until nearly 10:00 o'clock. Then, he would eliminate his tail once and for all. He did not relish killing, but he had no compunction about doing it when it eliminated the vermin in service to those who thought they were born to rule by virtue of birth or wealth. He thought to himself how wise the revolutionaries in Russia were when they eliminated the entire Romanoff family, thus ending for all time the right of those born with that name to rule over others. Those who ruled or gained their fortune by virtue of birth were the true parasites in world filled with idiots who bowed before royalty, the powerful and the wealthy. People who exalted those with birthrights were simply solidifying the right for the few to rule over the many. Aaron Adams would never bow before any man or woman. He saw true royalty in those who toiled for pocket change in the fields of despair in service to the exalted in their palaces, Rolls Royce's and yachts. Yet, those who were made slaves still worshipped at the feet of those who kept them in bondage. Aaron hated the complacency of the oppressed, and he realized that there was no help for those who refused to demand the fairness to which they were entitled. However, Aaron was still their champion, still the defender of those who seemed unwilling to defend themselves.

J. Wayne Frye

The Girl Who Stirred Up The Whirlwind

By 9:15 PM, Aaron had nearly worn out his tail, as he led him on circuitous route to an area he had noticed the previous day. Near the library was a boarded up abandoned house that sat on a dimly lit cul-de-sac. No doubt, his tail was the very man who had probably either killed or been in on the killing of Heidi Helmut and Eric Hender. Aaron would show him no mercy.

Leading the man down the cul-de-sac, as he got in front of the once obviously opulent building, Aaron noticed an amber glare dancing and flickering about the sidewalk. The building seemed to call seductively to Aaron to enter so that he could annihilate some of the sorrow and rage he felt for the loss of his friend, Eric.

Aaron made sure the tail saw him remove the boards and enter the abandoned house. He walked inside and waited. The interior of the place was papered in torn and dilapidated wall paper stained with water marks. A large circular bar extended down one side of the room. Behind it a huge walnut bookshelf almost reached the high ceiling. Upon its shelves, rested pyramids of shimmering glasses that appeared to have been sitting there for years, as they were coated with heavy dust. The elementary senses of it all seemed to emanate a former grand opulence that must have certainly prevailed in the now abandoned testament to another family of privilege that had moved on to more majestic and ostentatious accommodations.

The Girl Who Stirred Up The Whirlwind

Aaron realized that his tail was too smart to enter into a dilapidated, abandoned old building where darkness and surprise would give Aaron the advantage. Did he sense that Aaron was setting him up for the kill?

Aaron looked out through the boards into the dimly lit street and saw nothing. The guy was good, damn good. Unlike Aaron, chances were this fellow had a heater. Getting guns for C.I.A. operatives was no problem, even in Sweden, but Aaron would have a much tougher time locating someone who would sell him a gun, and if he got caught with one, this wasn't America, illegal handguns were simply not allowed. A long stretch in prison was guaranteed. He was at a disadvantage without his forty-five. If the guy was aware that Aaron was on to him, he might just pop Aaron when he stepped onto the street.

Peeping through the opening between the boards, then Aaron saw it: three men strolling down the street. One was the tall, thin bald headed guy, and it was no doubt that the other two were Wilton and the *Whirlwind*. The one in the centre, obviously the *Whirlwind*, had a cell phone clued to his ear, and the others flanked him on each side and had their hands under their jackets, seemingly in anticipation of a nefarious act on the behalf of Aaron. The three of them walked to a building about 50 feet down the street and disappeared into a basement stairwell.

The Girl Who Stirred Up The Whirlwind

O.K., Aaron knew where the other guy was, but what good did it do him? There were four of them now. If he had heard the conversation between the four men, he would have probably gotten a swelled head.

The *Whirlwind* said to the three others, "out of the whole bunch of men for us to go up against, this guy is the best. He stands head and shoulders above most agents we have in the field. This guy killed more people one-on-one in Vietnam than any other soldier. He was a trained assassin of the highest order. He once took down two men with a hand gun so fast that they couldn't even raise their weapons. He is faster with a gun than death itself, but my guess is that he probably hasn't been able to get a gun in Sweden yet. That gives us an advantage. But remember, this guy is just as dangerous without a gun. He doesn't just kill, he is a slaughter machine who has survived when most would have perished. He lost the love of his life a few years ago, and since then he hasn't cared whether he lived or died. I believe he may think he is a God, impervious to death. In fact, I have heard that he has often laughed in the face of death. Keep that in mind, and keep him in that building. We have a good idea now where we can find Jasmine Alexander. She is already dead, but just doesn't know it. Wilton and I will be back after we take care of her. Then, we'll tackle this guy, end this fucking thing and get the hell back home."

The Girl Who Stirred Up The Whirlwind

Aaron watched Wilton and the *Whirlwind* defiantly walk up the street like two gunfighters in the old west getting ready to step onto the dusty streets and have a shootout. These two guys were actually having fun. Now, he had two agents to contend with, and he only had 45 minutes to make it to the Grand. Was that where Wilton and the *Whirlwind* were headed also? Had they come to the same conclusion as he about Jasmine returning to the theatre where she had spent so many enjoyable hours with Rose? Jasmine had no chance of surviving the murderous intentions of the *Whirlwind*, but with Aaron by her side, her odds were much better. He had to make it to the Grand, but first he had to get by the two agents who were waiting for him outside. They were obviously left there to contain him by a man who knew the dangers they faced if Aaron were allowed to roam about freely.

Surveying the room, looking for anything that he could use as a weapon, Aaron noticed leaning against a far wall was an old metal bicycle rim. He walked over, picked it up and looked for a back way out. Getting in the front was easy, but getting out the back presented insurmountable problems for an ill prepared Aaron. The nails in the boards covering the exits were driven so far in that there was no way he could pry them loose without a hammer claw. He had to find a way to distract the guys outside. Then, he could make a dash for the main street and the crowd that would be milling

J. Wayne Frye

around on a Saturday night in downtown Stockholm. His problem was just how to get to that area.

The only way out was through the front, but he would be an easy target if they had guns, and he was sure they did. He peered through the boards and knew that they were still ensconced in the basement stairwell, waiting for him to make a move. Looking at his watch, he realized time was critical as he was ten minutes from the Grand, and it was already 9:23.

Aaron had killed many times before, sometimes with remorse and often without it. In Vietnam, he had great empathy for the poor bastards he killed, because they were just fighting to free their country from colonial exploitation by the greatest military power in the world. He had more in common with the so-called "gooks" than he did with the politicians and generals who were ordering him into battle. You didn't see the generals going into battle, and the politicians and their children were all kept safe from conscription, which was the norm for the day. Toward the end of his tour of duty, when he had a North Vietnamese regular under his knife, ready to slit his throat, he told him in broken Vietnamese, "hey, we shouldn't be trying to kill each other, we should be allies against the rich American bastards who are trying to rape this country. I am through killing for a pack of sanctimonious hypocrites who have brainwashed the American public into supporting an immoral war."

The soldier ran away up the hillside and Aaron walked back to headquarters where he told the major, "fuck you and fuck this war. You want somebody to do some killing for a bankrupt idea that is going to make slaves out of people in this country the way Americans are slaves to corporations, get somebody else. Put me in jail or shoot me. I'm fucking through!"

His war record was so stellar, including many decorations for bravery, that they figured just letting him go would avoid any bad publicity for the army and a war that was already causing riots in the streets. As a trained assassin, he had recorded over 100 kills, what more should they ask of him? They even gave him an honourable discharge, because they feared the commotion he would raise if they didn't. He was always a man who defied authority, anyway.

In civilian life, he had also been put into situations where he had to kill. It was just part of his profession sometimes. When he eliminated those who made a career out of working for the 1% who ruled the world with complete disregard for those enslaved by the culture of greed, he never felt any remorse, because they had become cogs in the well-oiled machinery of repression. The two men he was about to kill probably had families, but so did those they helped oppress. It would be unfortunate, but the two men had made a choice to serve the interests of the few at the expense of the many, so Aaron would feel no emotional remorse whatsoever in dispatching them into the darkness that awaits us all. Aaron let a faint smile purse his lips, as he thought that the two of them were probably secure in the knowledge that they had the upper hand, but they did not know who they were up against. Oh, they might have heard of him, but they had no idea of just how skilled Aaron was at killing. They were about to find out.

As Aaron was preparing to go into battle, Carrie, Allen and Frank were still heading toward the cabin. Allen turned off the road, drove the truck into a grove of trees and they got out. He said to Frank, "we are about an hour from the cabin by foot. There are no roads in or out." Then, he switched on a flash light and shined it straight ahead. "In the dark, it may take us two hours, but when we get you there, you'll be safe. No one even knows it is there but me, Carrie, Aaron and his two friends from Little Rock."

Allen motioned to Carrie with a nod of the head, and she instinctively and dutifully went into the truck and removed the shotgun from the gun rack. He took it from her, and he and Frank began the long trek to the cabin, while Carrie waited by the truck.

The Girl Who Stirred Up The Whirlwind

After dropping off Frank at the cabin, which was fully stocked with food, Allen returned to the truck and he and Carrie went back to the scene of the shooting. Burying the agents deep in the woods, he managed to get the car started and drove it as far down the road as he could before it got severely overheated. Then he furiously drove it into a thicket, until he finally came to a small pond that was deep enough for him to drive the car into. It disappeared beneath the surface and he headed back to the truck. He and Carrie drove to Lonoke and continued their lives as if nothing unusual had happened. They took a bath together and, as a result of an adrenalin high, had some of the most passionate sex they had experienced in a long time. They would patiently await word from Aaron, who, himself, was about to rise up in battle against the minions of despair who were out to silence the last person who might connect the murder of Olaf Palme to the *Whirlwind*.

The two agents waited patiently for Aaron to emerge, as they knew it was only a matter of minutes until the *Whirlwind* would dispatch, with extreme prejudice, Jasmine Alexander, then return for the elimination of Aaron Adams, unless, of course, Adams tried to make a break before then.

The agents' breathing was coarse and shallow, as they held their weapons in their hands, silencers on, to muffle the noise. Their eyes were glued to the opening they had seen Aaron enter.

The Girl Who Stirred Up The Whirlwind

Aaron knew they would have silencers on their weapons, and that would make them less accurate. Looking up at the street lamps, they were all burned out except for one almost in front of him, and it was even blinking a bit. He reached down and managed to completely loosen a spoke from the rim. He had a deadly weapon now that he was holding in his left hand. Looking up at the lamp, he slid the board covering the opening a little to the left, and knew that the two agents would realize he was about to make a move. Holding the board open by placing his left foot against it, he moved to his left behind the opening, looked up at the lamp again and began to sway the rim back and forth in preparation to throw it up at the light. A solid fling sent it skyward and the hissing sound of bullets being fired through a silencer could be heard as he scored a direct hit on the light and the street was bathed in darkness. He dropped to his stomach and started to crawl out the opening to an old abandoned car that was parked about twenty feet away. They had not seen him, because there were no shots fired.

Transferring the sharp ended spoke to his right hand, he crawled under the car and waited. They would come out now, because they knew he was not packing; otherwise, he would have shot the light out. They thought they had him, but they would not live to realize how wrong they were. Being careful not to move, even breath loudly, he waited in the dark for his prey.

The two men moved across the street cautiously at a snail's pace, their weapons in front of them. As they neared the opening in the building, Aaron quietly rolled out from under the far side of the car, and with the spoke in his hand suddenly sprang on them from behind, stabbing the partially bald guy in the jugular. As baldy was falling to the ground, dropping his gun into the storm drain opening, much to the dismay of Aaron, the other one turned and by then, Aaron already had the spoke out of baldy's neck. As he tried to fire the gun, Aaron used his left hand to deflect the weapon and it also flittered into the same storm drain opening.. Aaron rammed the spoke deep into the agent's side, penetrating his liver, and he collapsed onto the pavement. Baldy was dead, but the other agent looked up, pleading with his eyes.

Aaron bent over and tried to retrieve the guns. He couldn't. He said to the pleader in a very calm manner, "you're already dead, but chances are you'll live a good hour, maybe until the *Whirlwind* gets back to berate you for fucking up big time. Whether he gets Jasmine Alexander or not tonight, tell him that he does not have to come looking for me. I am coming after him, and I'm even more relentless than he is. There are not enough C.I.A. agents to keep me from killing him for what was done to Eric Hender. I don't know if the *Whirlwind* did the killing or not, but I know he ordered it. He may be the *Whirlwind*, but I am more fierce and unpredictable. I am a hurricane.

CHAPTER 9
THEY DRIFTED INTO DEEP SLUMBER

She was more than a woman; she was a vision of all that was possible in a world where compassion had long ago been sacrificed at the altar of greed. She saw the fallacies of a world where there was an eternal pursuit of all the superficial toys that corporations manipulated people into believing were required for the good life. Yet, the opulent homes, the expensive trips, the luxury cars, the fancy restaurants, the finely tailored clothes made in sweat shops, the utter mass of disposable goods and the mountain of pills to make you high and then pills to bring you back down were nothing but grotesque masks to hide the extreme emptiness of most people's existence in a world where they had made themselves willing slaves to a dark void of nothingness. There was no substance to most people's lives as they pursued that which, but for the few who were privileged, was unattainable. The showroom seemed bright and shiny, filled with the wonders that made for a good life, but the stockroom was empty.

Jasmine Alexander had lived a life that often consisted of quiet desperation, but she still saw the glorious possibilities of a world where the few did not rule with arrogant indifference to those who had to beg for their daily bread. She saw the inherent glory and beauty of those who did the real work and were compensated with a pittance for their efforts. She glorified in embracing those who knew only want in a world where power and privilege were revered, even by those who suffered the misery caused by the privileged who gorged at the trough of plenty while disdainfully ignoring those who suffered the indignities caused by the evil they perpetrated. She understood that it was the working class who fought the battles, the working class who made all the sacrifices, the working class who freely shed their blood and furnished the corpses, while never having a voice in either declaring war or making peace. It was the ruling class that made all the decisions, but the working class who bore all the burdens.

So, this extraordinary young woman's real beauty was inside, but the outside was also a reflection of perfection that firmly matched what constituted the inner self. Yet, this physical perfection was not what would be considered the classic beauty of the precisely symmetrical face, the hour-glass figure with a punctilious bust to waist ratio, the meticulously trimmed hair, or the overall thin frame that was the concept promulgated by those who sold the idea that beauty and sophistication could be purchased at a price. No, this was a woman whose physical perfection was an extension of the inner self that was a glorification of the possibilities of a world where the least were just as exalted as those born into privilege and those who savoured success in a world where success was defined by how much material wealth you had, rather than by how many people you had reached out to with the hand of compassion.

Jasmine Alexander's beauty far transcended all that would be considered classic attractiveness, grace, charm, form and comeliness. Her shoulder length, thick, coal-black, partially curly hair had an unkempt appearance and flopped about seductively as if she had just finished a wild unfettered, vigorous fornicating session with a virile man who had pounded her into blissful oblivion. It cascaded down the back of her neck and enticingly bounced about her shoulders. It was as if by warm breezes it was lovingly kissed and then touched delicately by a golden mist to make it have a wild and wanton grace as it flopped all about.

Ah, but what beauty shone in her dark brown, come hither eyes that were like blinking beacons lighting the way for ships heading for the rocks in a brazen, tumultuous sea. They seemed to beckon and lure, to offer untold delights to those fortunate enough to be tendered the joys of unbridled passion from a woman who knew no erotic restraint.

Her lips were thick, full and ripe, seemingly longing to wrap themselves around a man's member and suck out the life force that was the essence of each man's desire. There was nothing subdued about their provocative nature. It was if they were seeking another mouth to caress in wanton craving that blended two souls into one as tongues duelled in shameless desire.

Her huge, globular shaped, perfectly formed breasts jutted out like two mountain peaks soaring into the heavens and bounced like jelly fresh out of a mould. Her waist had a slight bulge to it, right around the navel, but on her, it was an invitation to the delights that lay just below the bump on the erotic road of carnal pleasure. Her calves were sufficiently thick that no one could ever take her for a ballerina, but they were muscular and rock hard to the point that they seemed to plead for a gentle stroking from the hand of a lover who would bow in supplication to the desire to simply touch that which seemed to cry out for attention. Oh, and her muscular thighs were so taunt that men's minds could only stare in disbelief as they fantasized about what it would be like for her to wrap them provocatively around a lunging lover and pull him into her mound of desire, never letting go as she pleaded for the pumping of seminal fluid into her body, as if that fluid gave her life a purpose. Jasmine was a woman whose inner thoughts matched that which was on the surface, because she knew no restraint when it came to her sexuality. And this was visually apparent to all, men and women alike, who were privileged and honoured to gaze longingly upon the loveliness of her body and soul.

J. Wayne Frye

The Girl Who Stirred Up The Whirlwind

She wore bargain store clothing but gave them a provocative charm with each stride she took down the street toward her beloved Grand Cinema as they seemed to hug and accentuate every sensuous curve of her provocative body. She was a woman who did not need to adorn her body with the brand name threads of opulence like others whose beauty was based on how much they spent to look good, rather than looking good naturally and with no pretensions. This was a woman who boldly walked in beauty like bright twinkling stars lighting up a dark night. And all that was best in her seemed to mesh in her dancing brown eyes that glowed tender and soft in the shimmering light of the Stockholm night. Every dark tress of her raven hair floated like waves on a peaceful shore as her face seemed to glow with nameless grace. Her cheeks were rosy in the brisk night air, but her calm elegance in each determined stride cried out that here was a woman of no shame, blessed with a gold encrusted heart.

Aaron was sixty years old, and had parked his virility in a garage that had been locked for years. Yet, he had never lost his appreciation for the female form. Although his libido had gone limp, his mind was still an erection of desire. As he concentrated on the sway of the woman's ass from side to side, he fantasized about what it would be like to caress it and enjoy the softness the way he used to with so many women. The sway of the woman's ass was not just provocative. It was overpowering, as if she emitted power from its shapeliness that was almost crying out for the touch of a lover. Obviously, from the way men, and even some women, were staring at her as they passed her on the street, he assumed the front must be every bit as alluring as the back.

Damn, he thought to himself. I have to get my mind on Jasmine Alexander. I only have a few minutes to save her from the *Whirlwind*. He decided to speed up and pass the woman, leaving her and her magnificent ass behind as he headed for the Grand Cinema, which was now, only a few blocks away. As he went passed her, he could not resist looking back over his left shoulder for one last glimpse of what he assumed would be a vision of loveliness.

When first she gleamed upon his sight as a lovely apparition, his heart began to flutter and he noticed her eyes that seemed to twinkle with the twilight of life unencumbered by the restraints of convention. She was like a twinkling ornament that stands out among those that have no substance. Like the cheerful morning dawn, she seemed to exude hope for a better day. Her coal-like hair shimmered under the street lights and the world about her seemed to disappear for Aaron. There was only her in the misty night air, and all about him, the rest was just peripheral and meaningless. There was little sound, only the cloaked whispers of those who meandered up and down the street. He knew that she would forever own his soul as a waylay on a road that would now offer no end. She was not just a woman. She was a spirit that had risen up to haunt his very existence for all days to come. She had a profound countenance and offered promises so sweet with her succulent lips that seemed to beg for kisses. There was an angelic light about her that shined like the brightest star in the heavens. She was the perfect woman for warmth, comfort, strength and skill, as if she was nobly planned. All about her there seemed to be an angelic light.

Aaron was mesmerized and could do nothing but stop and stare as she moved toward him. Seeing his absolute transfixion on her, the young woman, who by now was flabbergasted by the apparent lack of restraint from Aaron, came to an abrupt halt in front of him, tilted her head to her left side, and through succulent, lush, pouty lips said, "a man of your age, should be careful when staring at women. You could have a heart attack."

Aaron, for one of the few times in his life, was at a loss for words. All he could do was stutter, "I,I,I,….."

Then it happened. A smile lit up the woman's face as she said, "cat got your tongue?"

The mischievous smile seemed to go on forever and was accompanied by a bright twinkling of her eyes that seemed to radiate a prankish nature. And then it dawned on Aaron. His heart raced rapidly and Aaron knew. Yes, the smile – the smile. That was the clue. This was Jasmine Alexander! He was sure of it.

Boldly Aaron blurted out, "do you have a rose tattoo on your left breast?"

Shocked, Jasmine turned and as she started to run, Aaron shouted, "Eric Hender is dead. You are in trouble, big trouble. Please, please talk to me."

Stopping, she methodically turned and said, "Eric is dead?"

"Yes, he died because he wanted to help you. I want to help you. You are a target for assassination by a force that will go to any lengths to get you. I am Aaron Adams, and I have been sent here by a former member of the C.I.A. who connected you to the man who assassinated Olaf Palme and probably killed your mother the same night. You are the only living person who can identify him."

Glancing across the street at a coffee shop, Jasmine, pointing at it and said, "Let's go over there and talk."

Nodding his head in agreement, Aaron was still in a daze of bewilderment. She was a vision of all that was possible in a world that was unceremoniously marred in misery. She was a radiant rainbow of serenity in the dark skies of hopelessness and despair. It was as if a shining halo of hope and love glowed all about her. Aaron did not believe in God, so he could obviously not believe in angels. Yet, her was an angel in the flesh, walking beside him, allowing him to bask in her radiance. This was the moment Aaron had waited for all his life.

Jasmine's hips swayed provocatively as she and Aaron crossed the street. Her huge breasts, gyrating up and down, were the focal point of all the men who crossed in the opposite direction. They also caught Aaron's wandering eyes that could not divert from the magnificent creature that was rekindling that which he thought was long ago depleted.

Her beauty was not of a mere physical nature. There was no perfection in her physical appearance, although it was certainly one of grandeur in the way she bore herself confidently, unabashedly with an air of magnanimous bountifulness and grace. Aaron walked beside her, gazing out the side of his eyes at a woman who had mesmerized him like no other. He was 60 and she was 26. Why was he making such a fool of himself? Yet, he could not help himself. He had never encountered a woman who took his breath away as Jasmine did. Alas, was that an erection he was sensing in his pants? Oh my, it was. Yes, it was.

The charm, thought he looking at the moon!
Oh she was a wild and harmonized tune.
His spirit struck from all the beautiful!
On some bright essence could he lean, and lull
himself to immortality: He pressed
nature's soft pillow in a wakeful rest.
But gentle heart! There came a heavenly bliss.
His unfettered love came into Jasmine's abyss!
She came and did not fade, did not fade away .
Upon him, she held a starry sway.
He was trapped in passion to the hour.
Now Aaron began to feel her strange power
coming fresh upon him: Oh be kind!
Keep back thy influence, and do not blind
the sovereign vision. Dearest love, forgive
for he can never leave thee and live!
Pardon him, airy planet, that he prizes
one thought beyond all argent luxuries!
There is but love. Love divine for Jasmine.

As they sat down at a table, Aaron still mesmerized into a hypnotic-like captivation, seemed almost totally incapable of speech. He could but gaze upon that which now infatuated him.

Jasmine, tilting her head, forlornly said, "you say that Eric is dead?" Then, she snapped her fingers as if to awaken Aaron from a slumber.

Shaking his head, to clear the cobwebs of desire and awe, Aaron replied, "yes, a fine man, who had great respect and admiration for you, is dead. A victim of the scourge of a society that thinks all is permissible in defence of its bankrupt idea of economic servitude."

"You sir, have an unusual attitude for an American. You live in a country where all the tools of society are used to protect property. So, it has laws against stealing food but none against starving. It has laws to protect homes from burglary but none against homelessness. The police, the government, the military in America exist to enforce these laws. They are the modern Gestapo for the 1%, and their tentacles reach into this country, too. I have lived in fear, because I know those tentacles are deadly and will be used to silence anyone who stands for justice against that behemoth of evil in service to the barons of greed who rule with complete impunity. Eric was a fine man, but his admiration for me was probably misplaced. If I was stronger, I would have stood up for justice, rather than scurrying in fear of that which has plagued me for 18 years now."

Aaron reached out and placed his right hand on her velvety soft left hand that lay on the table. With steely determination, he said, "do not be afraid any longer Jasmine. I am about to exact some long over-due justice."

Smiling, Jasmine replied, "and just how, Mr. Adams, are you going to do that?"

"My dear Jasmine, I have devoted my life to comforting the afflicted in a world of despair and to afflicting the comfortable and smug who have no heart and no compassion for those of us who are expected to bow in supplication to the privileged. I am about to unleash my wrath and wreck carnage of the most vile kind on the C.I.A.'s best trained assassin. The *Whirlwind* is his name, and the jack-booted foot of repression is his game. I have already dispatched two of his brethren tonight, and if the C.I.A. continues to mess with me, they will be extremely short of employees. I am here at the behest of a friend, who could no longer tolerate the evil carried out in the name of liberty. He asked me to help you and Christer Pettersson. It is too late for Pettersson, but I am here to see that you are kept safe from the machinations of evil perpetrated by those who believe in no restraint when it comes to defending the interests of their country, right or wrong. I hope you will permit me to help you. You can put your faith in me, and I shall never waver in my devotion to your welfare."

Smiling that mischievous smile, Jasmine replied, "I have a feeling, with a man of your character Mr. Adams; I have absolutely no choice whatsoever but to humbly accept you as my knight in shining armour."

The Girl Who Stirred Up The Whirlwind

They smiled at one another, and there was an instant simpatico between two people who saw the evils of a world where the few ruled at the expense of the many. They were about to become a formidable duo in the fight against those who destroyed others in service to depravity.

Warning Jasmine that the *Whirlwind* and Wilton were determined to eliminate her, the two of them contemplated, for a brief moment, going to the Rikspolisstyrelsen (Swedish National Police), but they both knew that there was simply too great a likelihood that the C.I.A. had moles throughout the department who would work against keeping her safe. They could not take the chance. Then, Aaron said, "Please do not take this wrong. I know I have been less than stellar when it comes to probity in looking at you. I apologize for my rudeness. It is just that, well, frankly, I have never seen a person with more charismatic beauty than you have. I was just taken aback by what I saw. I think it would be best for you to stay with me tonight at my hotel. You are completely safe. After all, I am almost old enough to be your grandfather. And believe me, although I am not immune to sexual fantasy, my days of being able to fulfill them have been long gone. I will sleep on the sofa. I sincerely believe that if you had made it to the Grand Cinema, the two assassins would have been waiting for you. I am committed to eliminating them as a threat to you, but I need some time to do so."

There it was – that mischievous smile that slowly crept across her lips as her eyes twinkled with pixie-like glee. "Well, I have rarely fended off a potential lover, because I am somewhat of a brazen hussy. Consequently, I will not deride you for your fantasies, grandpa. However, I will insist that you sleep on the sofa, and I may even put a restraint on one part of your body to make sure it doesn't wander about too frivolously in pursuit of that which you say you are incapable of performing."

Aaron smiled back and said, "Hey, you better not try restraining it, or it might have a reaction that you didn't anticipate."

As they walked down the street toward Lilla Rådmannen, the old, stately hotel where Aaron was staying, they spoke in muffled whispers, like two people trying to hide something from the world. Aaron felt a sense of pride, old man that he was, with this fine, alluring young woman by his side. She made him feel alive, really alive.

The hotel was old, but freshly painted and scrubbed. The large, ornate door swung open easily as Aaron stood to his left, holding the door open with his right hand for Jasmine, who looked up at him with that slow, mischievous smile that slowly crept across her lips.. As she eased by him, slightly brushing against his elbow with her hip, he felt a slight tingle between his legs.

The Girl Who Stirred Up The Whirlwind

The lobby was a bit musky smelling, but it exuded an air of formality from years long past when the place catered to elite Stockholm society. It was a favourite of American tourists who wanted to savour a bit of the old time Stockholm atmosphere. Like archaic things in the modern, throw-away plastic world, it seemed a bit out of place, but it was exactly what Aaron looked for in temporary quarters. Being ostentatious was not his style. He liked the simple and non-complex. The hotel had the right feeling for Aaron, both rhythmically and physically. The old way of life was not necessarily better, as there had still been that socio-economic gulf, but, at least people were less tied to the technological slavery that was so apparent in the present. This was a place that made a man who still refused to have a television or cell phone feel comfortable. Aaron often thought that technological progress in the modern world was like putting an axe in the hand of a pathological killer. It was used to destroy more than it was used to build. It was obvious to him that technology, as Einstein had said, had exceeded man's humanity. That was why Aaron felt comfortable in a place like Lilla Rådmannen, as did the other Americans who were now staring at the two of them.

As he and Jasmine made their way to the lift, the hotel clerk and several people in the lobby seemed to look at them curiously as they obviously assumed that a man of Aaron's age had just bought the company of a young lady for the rest of the night. Jasmine looked at him and said, "they think you are about to defile a young, innocent thing with debauchery of the vilest kind."

She winked at him, grabbed his arm and led him into the elevator, getting pleasure from putting on a show of defiance to those who gawked in disbelief. As the elevator door stood open, she whispered, "You'd think we were in America, not Sweden. Of course, you know that this hotel is full of Americans. We Swedes have a much more lax attitude about sexuality than you uptight Americans." As she finished her last sentence, right before the door closed, she made sure the on-lookers saw her drop to her knees in front of Aaron's crotch. As the door snapped shut she looked up and smiled, saying, "Don't get your hopes up, Aaron. I just like to put prudes in their place. I detest those who judge others. They need to read the Bible where it says, judge not, least you be judged."

Laughing out loud, Aaron took her by the arm as the door opened and he led her down the hall to room 407. As he put the old-time metal key in the keyhole she playfully said, "That's the only hole you'll get in tonight, Mr. Adams. You would be wise to remember that."

Aaron, pushing the door open, replied, "Jasmine, I know where I stand with you, and believe me, you have nothing to fear from an old man."

J. Wayne Frye

The Girl Who Stirred Up The Whirlwind

Aaron offered Jasmine an oversized pair of his pyjamas, and she sheepishly went into the bathroom to change. As Aaron sat on the sofa, listening to the shower run, he contemplated what it would be like if he was a virile young man. He was acting like an adolescent, but he simply could not help it. He was overwhelmed with fascination, and what was worse, Jasmine knew it. She could see it in everything Aaron did and said, and she was actually making things worse by teasing him. She was brazen, but was she, as she said, a hussy? One thing for sure, she certainly wasn't shy about her sexuality.

Coming out of the bathroom, she smiled and looked back at the bathroom door as she said, "it's all yours. I only sleep with clean men."

Placing his clothes on the commode lid, he stepped into the shower and noticed that he had a partial erection, something of which he was actually proud. He found himself reaching down and grasping his member, even pulling back and forth on it a couple of times in hopes that it would actually get completely erect. It didn't. Looking through the obscured shower door, he sensed another person was in the room, and he saw the shapely shadow of Jasmine, who was apparently removing his clothes from the commode lid and placing something else down on it. He was too timid to swing open the door to see what she was doing. He just waited for her to leave.

Stepping out and drying off, he looked on the commode lid and there were his pyjamas neatly folded. Obviously, she had taken them off and walked out with his clothes.

Putting on his pyjamas, Aaron walked into the bedroom and saw his clothes neatly placed on the sofa. Jasmine was lying under the covers, obviously naked. Smiling up at him, she chortled, "I have never slept any other way than in the nude since I was about 14. Hope you don't mind. There's no need for you to sleep on the sofa. This is a queen size bed with plenty of room, and you have already said that you are an old man who has lost his sexual prowess, so I am sure I have nothing to fear. Come to bed where you can get a good night's rest. From what you said tonight, we will have a full day tomorrow. Besides, I want my protector as close to me as possible."

Aaron could only work with silence as his frame of reference. He knew not what to say. She lay there, inviting him in bed beside her. Then, there it was, that sheepish grin that pierced across her lips, slowly, deliberately, mischievously soliciting him into a true chamber of delights that he knew he had never experienced in the absolute grandeur they would be with her, but he no longer had the virility to tackle the task. He felt both exhilaration and disconsolation. He was dejected and forlorn that age had robbed him of a pleasure that he enjoyed so much in his youth.

The Girl Who Stirred Up The Whirlwind

Jasmine, sensing his consternation, pursed her lips and muttered softly, "do not fret my dear Aaron, there is much more to affection than a throbbing, pulsating hard erection or a moist opening that craves pounding. Come to bed, and I shall show you that I am not a woman who demands much more than the soft caresses of someone who cares. I have not had that since my dear Rose was killed. It was with her that I last felt the true warmth of someone who cared. Tonight, I think that warmth is within you. I have sensed it in everything you have done and said. I have teased you mercilessly, and I am sorry, because I should not have been so flippant and disregarded your heartfelt affection for me. I, too, genuinely feel a connection to you, and age is not a detriment to two people who long for the closeness of one another."

She flipped the covers back and lay there, totally unashamed, almost glorifying in her nakedness. Oh, the magnificence of her was overpowering. Aaron still could not utter a word. All he could do was stare in amazement at the grandeur that lay before his aging eyes. Her soft, silken, coal-black hair that had been pulled from beneath her neck and tossed back against the headboard shimmered in the dim light that filtered through the partially closed curtains. Her soft, smooth face glowed with the radiance of the morning sun coming up on a distant horizon. There was warmth in her partially parted lips that seemed to plead to be wrapped around a man's stiff member, so that she could literally suck the life out of it. Her lips were pleading for the warmth of another's mouth so they could slowly part and welcome a darting tongue to bring her passionate longing to fruition. Her neck was slender and had two small creases in it, predating a time when she would age and be wrinkled, but even in old age, that magnificence would still be there. Hers was a beauty that did not cease with age. It lived forever in the hearts of those whom she touched with her loveliness of spirit.

Looking down at her globular breasts that jutted out like two mountain peaks, he gazed longingly at the large, somewhat flattened nipples that appeared almost lost in a huge background of the dark brown areola that seemed to go on endlessly in a circle of desire. Her slightly pouched alluringly sensual stomach had a huge naval opening that made Aaron think what a delight it would be to deposit his seed in it, watching the gooey white substance flow out of it onto her smooth stomach.

Seeing how much Aaron was enjoying looking at her, Jasmine slowly parted her legs. What a magnificent specimen of womanhood thought Aaron. Continuing his survey of the most erotic body upon which he had ever gazed, the sight of her massive plume of pubic hair sent a resounding sensation through his body that titillated him to the very depths of his soul. There was a thin bead of hair that led down from her navel and slowly spread out in a thicket of coarse blackness that spread onto her thick thighs. It seemed to longingly call out to be nestled and gently blown on by a searching mouth with a tongue that wanted to dispense a eulogy of undying worship to the glory before it.

Jasmine, with wanton desire showing across her reddened face, slowly spread her legs wider, and deep within the darkness was the place from whence all men came. And most spent their lives trying to get back in it. It was a place of warmth that lured, tempted, enticed and coaxed. Yet, on Jasmine, it was more than a pit of desire. It was a home that offered shelter from the stormy seas of life that had, for so long, overwhelmed Aaron. The vulva was now clearly visible, seemingly pulsating with temptation. There was a clear excellence to it, tender and fat, a bright and fervent unbroken circle of wantonness filled with the strength of a woman who knew no sexual restraint. It had a boundless strength to its faultless court of plumage. It parted like a huge valley in a canyon of heavenly delights. Had religion any soul or heart, it would sing the praises of a woman like Jasmine, rather than pouring out the venomous poison of sexual restraint.

Finally, Aaron found words. "Jasmine, I want to possess you."

The Girl Who Stirred Up The Whirlwind

Then, the dear girl raised her arms and locked her hands under her head, exposing hairy armpits. This was the most natural woman Aaron had ever encountered. Aaron swept upon her, his mouth finding hers as they floated into the sweet oblivion of more than desire. This was the blending of two souls in perfect harmony. Time, place and age were irrelevant as Aaron's tongue darted about in her mouth. He instinctively reached up with both hands to gently fondle the soft hair beneath her arms. She moaned with delight as he caressed it lightly. The tingle went all the way down between her legs. She pushed Aaron downward, wanting to feel his mouth on the pit of her yearning.

Aaron was finally in the forest grove that covered the object of his desire. He was greeted with fine flaps full of sweet tasting juice that he savoured deliciously on his tongue. He nestled in harmonious pleasure, blowing, kissing, rubbing his face in the delicacy that lay before him. Had he believed in God, he would have pleaded with him for a swelling erection so that he could pound the nymph of delight into sweet oblivion beneath his thrusts. Still, she moaned in pleasure from what he could offer, and before long, she again pulled him up to taste her own essence as their mouths met with unbridled passion.

Although his member was only partially erect, she spread her legs as wide as possible, so that it could rest in her gapping opening to the root of her passion. Aaron rubbed back and forth with his partially erect member and her moans became louder as she whispered, "give me your essence my love. Let me feel the warm gooey substance that gushes up from deep within your soul. I need your warmth. Seed me with your desire."

An explosion like an erupting volcano raged forth from Aaron, and he groaned with delight as his member pulsated uncontrollably, dumping stream after stream of the warmth from within into the parted opening. Jasmine, miraculously working her muscles in the gapping valley of pleasure, milked Aaron dry as he lay on top of her, exhausted. She wanted every last drop.

As Aaron rolled off her and lay breathing heavily beside her, she reached down with her fingers and gathered up what Aaron had deposited in the gapping opening. Bringing it to her lips, she closed her eyes and placed her fingers, that were moist with Aaron's essence, into her mouth, savouring his taste as she sucked every drop and swallowed with a sigh of contentment. She cuddled up next to Aaron, resting comfortably in the safety of his strong arms. Without a word between them, they drifted off into a deep slumber.

CHAPTER 10
THE SPIRIT WAS BROKEN & DESTROYED

The morning light filtered in through the partially opened curtains, flickering in Jasmine's face and woke her with its warm rays. She was still wrapped in Aaron's arms, and she looked with curiosity as he lay there breathing peacefully. This was the oldest man to whom she had ever made love. Even the brief time when she was a prostitute, she had always avoided men over 50, figuring that she would just have to work too hard to get them off. Why, she always rather pensively thought, should you just make a lot of extra work for yourself. She preferred them young, dumb and full of cum. Pop them off quickly, take your money and move on. Although she had many lovers for whom there was no charge, just a strong desire for sex, she had never found someone to whom she had the emotional sexual attachment she had with her beloved Rose. Yet, with Aaron, she felt that same attachment. They had sex, and it was adequate, although not physically as exhilarating as many of her other partners. Still, there was something much deeper in what she felt when making love to Aaron. There was a profound emotional attachment that took it far beyond mere sex. Was Aaron her new Rose? Was he the life-line of hope that she desperately needed in a world where she was continually on the run from the forces of darkness that were always threatening to overwhelm her?

J. Wayne Frye

The Girl Who Stirred Up The Whirlwind

She was fascinated by this older man. She lay there in his warm embrace and surveyed the person to whom she now felt such a strong bond. It was not a physical attraction, because Aaron had long passed the age when he cut a swarthy, handsome figure of confidence as he strode about with a somewhat arrogant swagger. Yet, thought Jasmine as she gazed upon him, here was a man of consummate strength of character. It was written in every line of his moderately wrinkled brow. There was a serenity to him like no one she had ever seen before. Yet, looking at his square jaw and tightly clenched lips made it apparent that this was a man with whom you did not trifle. Even at 60, in appearance, he was striking and ruggedly good-looking in a way that Jasmine could appreciate. His magnificent confidence was manifested as a physical attribute that brought comfort to Jasmine's troubled soul. He was obviously so physically strong that he could withstand violence with a constitution of storied determination. His large, calloused, rugged hands were like granite, and could, no doubt, fell almost any enemy with one blow. Still, there was a peacefulness to them, as if they could protect and defend against a malevolent force with a mere soft touch of reassurance, rather than the force of wrath. There was an innate quality of strength that seemed to emanate from his core. You could almost feel the strength that lay in his worn and scarred body that had obviously been involved in far too many altercations.

The Girl Who Stirred Up The Whirlwind

Jasmine felt a tingling sensation between her legs and the moisture began to build. The sheet was up to Aaron's waist, so she gently and carefully, so as not to wake him, pulled it down to his feet. There it was – old, wrinkled, worn-out and scarred from years of overuse she thought, as a smile crept across her face. He must have been something in his youth. She thought that he probably was actually proud of it in "the day," as it was still a nice specimen of manhood, even at 60. It was half erect, and looking longingly at it, she licked her lips. She wanted it in the warmth of her mouth. She needed to feel its considerable girth between her teeth. She wanted to suck on it – to make it gush forth with the essence of the man she now loved.

Removing herself from his arms, she reversed position, putting her feet by Aaron's head, and moved her face down between his thighs. At first, she only blew on it and gently kissed it. It was on the rise, not fully erect, but rising. She nestled her face in his black pubic hair, rubbing it with her nose and licking his sack that contained the fluid she so vehemently desired. The now awake Aaron moaned and reached out with two fingers to manipulate her gently between her legs. She crawled on top of him, putting her mound of desire squarely in his face, where she could feel the warmth of his darting tongue. She began to work furiously, desperately wanting him to burst forth the fluid of passion into her waiting mouth.

The Girl Who Stirred Up The Whirlwind

Aaron had to stop his furiously frantic licking, as he was so overwhelmed at the shameless way she was pursuing her carnal instincts. She wanted an old man. There was genuine passion in her desire for Aaron. She cared about this broken down wreck.

He began to breath rapidly and moan. Then came the explosion. Oh, it was like a volcano going off. The pulsating was frantic, as Jasmine gobbled up his essence and collapsed on his member, it going flaccid in her mouth. Yet, she continued to blow, kiss and worship it like it was her God. She wiggled her hips a bit and Aaron, taking the cue, began his rhythmic but furious licking again. Within a few seconds, she was overwhelmed with the ecstasy of blissful release. Exhausted, they lay that way for several minutes before Jasmine crawled off him and returned to the warmth of his strong arms. She seemed to melt into them. She cuddled up tightly, almost trying to crawl into his skin. They were one!

They took a shower together, and fondled each other as the water cascaded over them. Aaron had no life left in his member, and they both laughed at its refusal to partially rise one more time. It did not matter, because their relationship was now beyond sex. Jasmine said nonchalantly, "I better lay off you for awhile. I wouldn't want to give you a heart attack. I might be convicted of murder by pussy and mouth."

The Girl Who Stirred Up The Whirlwind

They had a laugh and Aaron went into the bedroom, as she told him to go down to the hotel clothing store and buy her something to wear, anything in size 12 and to be sure and get her a toothbrush out of the vending machine. She needed no underwear, because she wanted Aaron to be able to feel her moisture whenever he wanted, as it now belonged to him and was always available for his pleasure.

Waiting for Jasmine to dress, Aaron sat on the sofa, contemplating all that had led him to this moment. A series of circumstances had brought love into his life again. He wondered what was going on with Frank Penderent, Allen and Carrie. Were they safe? Was the C.I.A. on their trail? Was there a way they could avoid what was an almost guaranteed coming calamity from an out of control organization dedicated to the preservation of the status-quo. In a country that refused to allow any divergence from the accepted norms of what was considered patriotic behaviour, those who dared speak out against tyranny were silenced one way or another. George Bush and Dick Cheney were war criminals who would never be tried in a world where all other countries cowered in fear before the American military machine. The two of them had lied the country into un-winnable wars in Iraq and Afghanistan, while economic ruin awaited in the wings, as the government had been handed over to the corporate barons of greed to use as they pleased.

　　　　　J. Wayne Frye

The Girl Who Stirred Up The Whirlwind

Aaron made a call to Little Rock, Arkansas private eye friends, Brian and Dixon Long, with whom he had shared many a day in the backwoods cabin near Lonoke. He asked for Dixon, but Brian said he was in Los Angeles on business for about two weeks. Weary that somehow there might be a tap on either line, all he said to Brian was, "C and A. The place. They will tell you what is going on. They may need your help. Thanks, and I will be in touch."

Hanging up the phone, he waited for Jasmine and the coming pursuit of the *Whirlwind*, so they could get him before he got them. He had his head down, but heard her quietly open the bathroom door. Raising his head, he saw her standing there in the doorway, wearing the blue dress that Aaron had bought for her. She had long unerring lines, the sweep and amplitude of the great artist's stroke seemed to have brushed her with stardust as she sparkled before his eyes. Itched on her face was a passion that lurked beneath the surface for the man before her. He could see it in her demeanour. Each smile and twinkle of the eye was a letter in the record of what happened between them the previous night. Her rag-tag, gnarly, unkempt hair flopped all about as she stood there, the light coming through the slightly parted curtains casting a spotlight on all her glorious beauty of body and soul. The light shimmered on her crotch and Aaron recalled the dark beauty that lay there. It was warm in the room and she lifted her arms, putting her hands behind her head to fluff her hair, exposing the dark underarm hair, much to Aaron's delight. She was chic-looking, with a freshness borne like a butterfly soaring about on a summer day. Shaking her head and continuing to fluff her hair, Aaron looked into her eyes. She glared back at him. Her lips were slightly parted, exposing a hint of white from her upper teeth. She moved gracefully toward Aaron, her full hips swaying provocatively as she exhaled and inhaled, her magnificent breasts rising up and down and jiggling like two swollen water balloons. She was built with curves like the hull of a racing yacht headed for the finish line, cutting through waves of blue mist. If you work diligently with every erotic fibre you have, a person is capable of a denotative surplus. Oh, and was she making a statement of surplus. She had an abundant surplus of everything Aaron desired, and she knew it. Her gravitas was driving him crazy. He stood up and swept her into his arms, their mouths seeking out one another. So wild and unrestrained, their kiss was almost violent in intensity.

Jasmine thought to herself, as she faded into oblivious bliss in his arms, of a time and place where they could forever dwell in rapturous ecstasy.

To her, Aaron was more than a man; she had slept with a shadow of intensity. His kisses were bullets that flew ravenously into her open mouth.

The Girl Who Stirred Up The Whirlwind

It was as if there was cardiac arrest as he raised her dress and fondled her most intimate part.

She hungered for his body. She unbuttoned his pants, dropped to her knees and removed the object of her desire. She did not just take it in her mouth, she devoured it like a homeless person who had not eaten in weeks and suddenly had a banquet laid out on a table. She tasted that first drop and savoured it like fine wine. Soon, Aaron let lose with a torrent of joy juice that hit the back of her mouth with such ferocity he was afraid she might be injured from the blow. The intensity overwhelmed him, and he collapsed on the sofa, Jasmine crawling to him, still worshipping his stick of pleasure. She looked up and gave him that mischievous, devilish smile. She was so proud of herself.

Jasmine stuck out her tongue, and there was still a small drop of the gooey white stuff on it. She flipped it back into her mouth and Aaron thought that life, his life, fit in that little drop. She had devoured him. She had satiated him. She had captivated him. She had captured his heart and soul, and he surrendered willingly.

How long would Aaron's heart remain in jeopardy with blank amazements that went to his very core? He had tasted her sweet soul and meandered into the shallow depths of desire accompanied by love. She was like fertilizer for his earthly root, making it grow gradually. Would it one day grow tall like it once did, reaching toward the sky to finally thoroughly satisfy her?

He had tasted of the golden fruit and found heavens eternal light. Before him lay past, present and future. This fair maiden was his to protect. Duty bound to be her knight, he would slay the dragons sent to destroy her.

Aaron was not a man who practiced discretion as valour when it came to the U.S. government, or for that matter, when it came to any government that tried to manipulate and control, rather than to reach out with the hand of compassion. This was now war, and he was prepared to wage it with a ferocity that the U.S. government was not used to in a world where all cowered before the behemoth of subterfuge and inherent evil purpose that was manifested in the form of the C.I.A. Aaron was different from those who feared government, because he knew that was the way you lost freedom. He understood that in a real democracy, it was the government that feared the people, rather than people fearing the government. In America, the people had no will-power, no backbone, no courage to stand against the tyranny of the 1% who ruled with impunity in a system set up to benefit the few at the expense of the many. Even in Sweden, the long tentacles of this commitment to protecting the interests of the wealthy and powerful in America was reaching out to snare all who even hinted at a system of parity and equality of opportunity. The C.I.A. was at the forefront of protecting the privileged by whatever means available.

Finding the *Whirlwind* would not be easy, but Aaron had a plan to flush him out - a plan that would instil fear in a man who was used to being the pursuer rather than the pursued. He was about to turn the tables on the *Whirlwind*, and prove to him and the C.I.A. that messing with Jasmine Alexander was a mistake of monumental proportions that could well incur the wrath of the one man who could bring their house of cards tumbling down like a tornado cutting a swath across the Midwestern plains. Anything in his path would suffer the havoc of total destruction.

As they were leaving the hotel, Aaron, knowing that Jasmine dealt with the seedy underbelly of Stockholm daily, asked her if she knew anyone in the city who might be able to get him a gun. She replied, "this is Sweden, not the United Sates. You just can't go into a Wal-Mart and buy an AK-47 here."

Aaron, smiling, replied, "But you can buy a gun for hunting if you are Swedish?"

"There's a waiting period and a background check even for that kind of gun. I do know someone who might have a connection. You may have already met him while searching for me. His name is Pretty Boy Patay."

Aaron, grinning, replied, "Yes, I have had the esteemed pleasure of meeting your old friend, Pretty Boy. Shall we go to his office?"

Jasmine, somewhat sheepish that he had talked to the man who encouraged her to be a prostitute, said, "well, I just can't hide anything from you can I, Aaron?"

Aaron, street corner philosopher that he was, replied, "a prostitute is much better than a C.E.O., she is only adequately compensated, not rewarded with excess pay and parsimonious benefits, and she does give people value for their money. She has a product that does not wear out, no matter how much it is used. I'd say she is giving customers long-term value and a life-time warranty."

Arm-in-arm, they headed toward Pretty Boy's café office, laughing as they strolled down the street toward a destiny that would probably end badly for them both. However, they were together and in love.

The day was dreary and overcast, but these two people sailed though the black of day or night in a forest that had no discernable, comprehendible end; millions of people thread it in millions of ways. They both had many trysts in the past to brighten the darkness, but where or with whom? Of that they no longer cared, for they now had faith that a lifetime's bliss had appeared in a flash, with a smile upon its lips. Scents, touches, sounds, snatches of songs brushed them with a rapturous stroke. Now, their lives were blessed. All those others who came close to them and moved off in the darkness – they did not know if they existed or not. Were they but figments of imagination on a journey to find each other? Together, these two lovers had shed yesterday's skin with an obsessive breath that brought them to life.

Back in the Langley, Virginia C.I.A. headquarters, the Deputy Director was holding a meeting in his office with the Head of Field Operations. There was deep concern that Frank Penderent was a loose cannon that might just blow the lid off a deep cover operation from 18 years ago that had eliminated a man who was about to lay bare before the United Nations the lengths to which a country would go to enslave the entire world to corporate theocracy. Then there was this guy named Aaron Adams, who had come into the picture. Talk about a loose cannon. This guy was known to have gone up against authority before, and the results were usually disastrous – for authority. And the young woman named Jasmine Alexander needed to be dispatched as soon as possible to prevent the whole affair from unravelling in a torrent of recriminations. Oh, and the *Whirlwind*, he might not be a loose cannon, but he was, after years of success, beginning to get sloppy. Damn, the whole affair was what the D.D. referred to as a cluster-fuck of monumental proportions. Turning to the Head of Field Operations, the D.D. said, "goddamn, this is a catastrophe waiting to happen. We have to get a handle on this, and damn quick. This thing could bring a lot of people down, past and present."

Bill Donnelly, the Head of Field Operations, was dour, stern, and silent in expression and manner. His taciturn approach to things often gave the illusion of disinterest, but he was a man who deeply believed in the cause of his country, and that there was no act too severe to commit in its defence. Right or wrong, it was his country, and he would go to any lengths to protect its interests. Apparently, he had never read Mark Twain's quote "loyalty to country always, loyalty to government, when it deserves it" because he was now faithfully serving the Bush Administration war criminals who, had they been Germans in World War II, would have been in the docks at Nuremburg. He dourly offered his assessment to the D.D. "I don't think so sir. You see, the two agents who were killed in Arkansas were obviously on Frank Penderent's trail. We have spirited the bodies out of Arkansas and their families will be told they died in a car accident that will be staged in Manassas, Virginia tomorrow. So, no problem with that."

The Girl Who Stirred Up The Whirlwind

Nodding his head, the D.D. was in agreement. Bill continued. "We know that Penderent was picked up by Allen and Carrie Pink. Our guess us that it was Pink who probably killed the agents, or maybe him and his girl friend, both. Probably not Penderent, as he was nothing more than a reader. He never had any field experience in his career, a real nerd, according to reports. O.K., we have the Pinks under surveillance now. We aren't going to sweat them yet, because we think they will lead us to Penderent soon. We'll give them a couple of days. Then, if all fails, we'll fly them to Guantanamo and a little water-boarding will get the information we need to find Penderent."

The D.D. seemed a bit relieved and said, "This is top priority. These people have to fall, and fall soon. You know that!"

"I do, sir. I do. Of course, there may be another slight problem."

Concerned, the D.D. replied, "slight problem? Slight fucking problem? There is no such thing when dealing with an assassination that might be uncovered by a bunch of idiots who don't know their scumbag asses from a hole in the ground. Those kind of fucks are incredibly dangerous. They are just ordinary fucking people. They have no clue to what goes on in the real world when it comes to running this country. We have an administration that is running all over the world committing all kinds of illegal acts to defend our homeland. They can't afford for something like this to come out when they have already snowed the United Nations into supporting an illegal and immoral war. We know everything is permissible in defence of the American way, but there are some dumb fucks who actually believe in openness and fair play. Those people are dangerous, and that is the kind of people we are dealing with here – dumb mother-fuckers who are too stupid to realize that they need us to look after them. We know what is good for them. They don't have a clue. So, slight problem? Bill, there are no slight problems. Give it to me. What is this slight fucking problem?

Calmly and unemotionally, Bill replied, "it appears another private detective has been brought into the melee by this Adams character. His name is Brian Long. He and his brother are Little Rock P.I.'s. We are monitoring all calls from Sweden right now, and we picked up a call from this Aaron Adams to him. It was very cryptic, but we were, well – well kind of able to figure it out. Apparently, he is going to contact this Allen and Carrie and see just what the next step is with Penderent. My guess is that they will lead us to him within a day or two."

The D.D. shook his head and threw his hands up in disgust as he rocked back in his high priced leather executive chair. "This is looking pretty fucking precarious. Stay on this. You're relieved of all other assignments. This is fucking top priority. Everything else is off the table. I'll be away the rest of the morning, as I have an appointment with the Director and the Vice-President. The V.P. is going to be pretty fucking upset that we haven't wrapped this up yet. He may order us water-boarded if we don't get a handle on this. He is a fucking sadist when it comes to protecting this country. Hell, I am beginning to think we may need some protection from him, ourselves." Realizing what he just said, he interjected, "forget I said that Bill – fucking forget it."

In his taciturn, matter-of-fact way, Bill nodded his head up and down in agreement, got up and walked out. The D.D. leaned back and sighed.

Meanwhile, in Lonoke, Allen and Carrie Pink were telling Brian Long about what Aaron had asked them to do for Frank Penderent, as they headed for the cabin. Parking the truck on the main highway, they hiked up the dirt road before entering the brush and heading toward the cabin. Brian, even when he was younger, had never been much of a outdoorsman. He and his brother had just bought the cabin with Aaron as a place where they could bring a couple of women, some booze and get away from the hustle and bustle of city life with no phones, no television and no internet. There was another way in by boat that was much easier, but this way was safer, as the dock near the river back in Lonoke would simply attract too much attention. Brian knew that the C.I.A. and the F.B.I. were probably covering it anyway, along with every other boat landing and dock on every river in the area. They left nothing to chance. Hell, what did they care how much overtime was involved. They were on the taxpayers' dollar. If the taxpayers only knew how much of their money was wasted on keeping things secret and committing acts of terrorism, they might rebel. Hell no they wouldn't. They were too busy trying to keep their heads above water while buying cell-phones, flat screen televisions, new cars and brand name clothes to be concerned with the loss of the freedom that was only illusionary anyway. Most people lived in a haze of misconception about freedom. They were too ignorant to realize freedom had long ago been sacrificed for expediency and service to the privileged class. Dixon, Brian, Allen, Carrie, Frank, Jasmine and Aaron were different, though. They knew the truth about the enslavement of all humanity to corporate greed and the needs of the privileged in a world where most people had been brainwashed into worshiping at the altar of avaricious greed.

Huffing and puffing, Brian pleaded with Allen and Carrie to please slow down. Allen, ever the clown, said, "I never slow down. Just ask Carrie. We do it once, and I am ready to do it again. You simply can't put any restraints on this old country boy. I am a piston in an engine that goes 24 hours a day."

Carrie, smiling at his boldness, interjected, "yeah, and I am the engine the piston is always in. I am afraid the engine may need a major overhaul soon."

Having a good laugh gave Brain his second wind. He motioned forward with his head, urging them to continue on to the cabin. Little did they know that behind them was a crack team of C.I.A. counter-insurgency operatives, four men who had been given the job of eliminating anyone who posed a threat of exposure.

Through briar, bramble and dense foliage, they finally made it to a small clearing, and there it was, the cabin. Old, dilapidated and giving the appearance if being unlived in, it was the perfect hide-out. Allen, with his trusty shotgun in his hand, surveyed the scene. Brian, pulling his revolver from under his coat, motioned for them to approach the cabin cautiously. You could never underestimate American law enforcement or government agencies. They would stoop to any trick to protect their interests. They would bear any burden in making sure that the truth never got out. The truth was dangerous to these people. They feared it, because the truth might make those who had been propagandized into believing they were free, realize their own enslavement.

Allen moved toward the door cautiously as he surveyed the scene. Knocking quietly three times as he said he would when he left Frank, he called out, "it's me, Allen."

Frank Penderent slowly opened the door, and looked relieved to see Allen. "Come on in."

"O.K., but I have Carrie and another guy that Aaron sent with me. Don't be nervous. Everything is fine. This man knows a place where you can avoid detection, completely."

Swinging the door open, Frank exposed himself just enough for one of the sharpshooters to take careful aim and blow the top of his head off. Allen, wiping brains and blood off his eyes, grabbed Carrie by the hand as a bullet whizzed overhead, threw her to the ground and they scurried behind an old rain barrel. They began to crawl toward the back of the cabin. Allen carefully cradled the shotgun and motioned with his eyes for Carrie to follow him into the woods. Their only chance was to make it to the river, where an old boat with an outboard motor was always tied up. Just maybe they could make it down the Fourche La Fave River to Hollis, where he could get a car from a buddy. Then, he and Carrie could head to Mexico. They were finished in America, and they both knew it. They were now targets of a government that showed no mercy in pursuit of those who dared oppose it. They fretted about

Brian, but knew that he would have to fend for himself, as this was now simply about survival, and it was every man for himself. Still tepid about how to make it to the river without exposing themselves, Allen motioned for Carrie to stay where she was. He was going to flush the guys out. He had no idea how many of them there were, but he and Carrie needed to make their move quickly. Chances were this was a deep cover operation, so there would only be a few people privy to what was going on. He figured probably no more than three or four men in the woods at the most.

Allen was a man of cold, calculating, thorough thought before acting, but now, he was facing a situation that required immediate action. He had no idea what Brian was up to, as he had completely disappeared from view, and he had no inkling where the sharpshooters were. Exposing himself to these guys was tantamount to committing suicide. A fire might just give him and Carrie, maybe even Brian, the cover they needed to get to the river. Not being a smoker, he had no matches in his pocket, but he did have a shotgun. Glancing at the propane tank beside the cabin, he knew what his next move was. He crawled back toward her, and without saying a word, he simply looked at the tank and indicated she should put her head down. Then, he saw Brian crawling behind the cabin with his gun in his hand. He gave a low whistle to get his attention, and pointed toward the propane tank. Brain gave his approval and rolled toward the thicket behind the cabin, putting his hands over the back of his head to shield himself from the coming blast.

Allen aimed carefully, and fired both barrels at the propane tank. The explosion was instantaneous as there was a massive shower of earth and wood from the disintegrated cabin raining down from the sky. Up and running, the three headed toward the thicket behind the cabin, never looking back, even as bullets whizzed by them. Deep into the thicket, they hurried toward what they assumed would be the safety of the river. Just before arriving at the shore, Brian stopped.

Allen, standing in front of Carrie to shield her from any potential bullets, shouted at Brian. "what the hell's wrong, lets go. There's a boat over by that cypress tree."

Brian opened his coat. There was a massive amount of blood around his abdomen. He said, "go, go you two. I'm done for. Give me the shotgun."

Carrie pleaded with him. "You can make it. We can get you to a doctor."

Brian, stoically accepting his fate, said, "it's over, even if I get to a doctor. These assholes will not let me live. Get the hell out of here."

The Girl Who Stirred Up The Whirlwind

Allen tossed him the shotgun and extra shells. Not saying a word, he nodded his head in respect, grabbed Carrie by the hand and headed for the small boat tied to the cypress tree. The motor started up on the first pull and they looked sorrowfully back at Brian, knowing that he was a dead man.

Brian had been in Vietnam many years before, so he was not totally foreign to battle. He sequestered himself behind the largest tree he could find and waited for the men. The guys were pros. They did not expose themselves, but old instincts die hard. He listened intently for any sign that they were near. He heard a faint sound to his left. He noticed a bush moving slightly and fired in that direction. Hearing a loud cry, he knew there was one man down, but how many more were there? A single bullet tore into the tree a few feet above his head. He had exposed his position.

Rolling to his right, another bullet tore into the ground under him, skimming along his back. As Brian still lay on his back, a man coming from the right was firing rapidly, the bullets tearing into Brian's flesh. Brian cut loose with a mighty blast that felled the guy, nearly cutting him in half.

In intense pain, Brian struggled to his knees and took a bullet to the left side of his face. Seeing where the bullet came from, he fired in that direction, and knew that there were now three men down. Were there any more? He fell forward on his face and could faintly hear the whir of the boat motor in the distance. Allen and Carrie were going to make it. He managed a faint smile, but it disappeared quickly, as he saw a large black shoe in front of him. The man placed his other foot on the shotgun, as Brian struggled to lift it. A kick to Brian's face turned him over. He spat out a couple of broken teeth and said, "do it asshole. Do it."

The man placed the tip of his rifle on Brian's head and pulled the trigger. Brian went limp as brain matter spilled onto the ground. It was over for him, but in the distance, Allen and Carrie looked longingly behind them, as they realized all the shots being fired were signalling an end to Brian. The lone gunman left ran to the cypress tree by the shore and took careful aim at Allen. He was too far away. The bullet fell short into the water. He kept firing, but the distance was just too great. Disgusted, he began to make his way back to the road, secure in the knowledge that there would be others who could take care of Allen and Carrie. He was wrong. The resourceful Allen would make his way to Mexico with Carrie, where they would eventually board a ship for Cuba. In that socialist anachronism to the possibilities of a world where greed was kept in check, the ravishingly beautiful Carrie would become an eloquent spokesperson for socialism and its possibilities to lift people from the yoke of an oppressive economic system that enslaved so many.

J. Wayne Frye

The Girl Who Stirred Up The Whirlwind

As for her dear Allen, that is a subject for another book. He became the heart and soul of the "new Cuba" that once again stood in proud defiance and promulgated the equalitarian ideals of Fidel and Che for the poor and disenfranchised who were waiting for a message of hope in a world overwhelmed by predatory corporate exploitation. He, along with his dear Carrie, would be the vanguards in the battle for serene sanity in a world gone insane with greed. So, what had seemed a certain catastrophe for them actually freed them in a way they never dreamed possible. Many years later, when they were visiting the United Nations with a Cuban Delegation, unafraid to be in America because of their diplomatic immunity, they contacted Aaron who profusely apologized for getting them involved in the disastrous attempt to help his friend Frank Penderent. They would simply smile and say, "do not apologize, it gave us a life we never dreamed possible. We are truly free, truly part of a nation that reaches out with the hand of compassion to the afflicted. We are grateful."

While the catastrophe in the back country of Arkansas was unfolding, Aaron and Jasmine were embarking on a vendetta against the *Whirlwind*. Finding Pretty Boy Patay was easy. The café that served as his office was always open for business. In Pretty Boy's corporation, there was always demand for the product he provided 24 hours a day.

The Girl Who Stirred Up The Whirlwind

When he saw Jasmine come in with Aaron, he was all smiles. His dandy manner gave way to pure delight at seeing her. He went over to them before they were hardly in the door, threw his arms around Jasmine, and with a note of pure joy in his voice, said, as he looked at Aaron while wrapping his arms around her, "damn, you found her, man. This is the most desirable woman in all Stockholm. If she agrees to work for me, I'll give you a major finder's fee."

Jasmine, extricating herself from Pretty Boy's grasp, with a note of disdain, softly said, "I am not interested in working for you." Then, she glanced joyously over at Aaron, as she continued, "I am employed full-time taking care of Mr. Adams here, and believe me, it is a lot of work, but I enjoy my work immensely."

Aaron, his chest puffing out with pride that she was letting Pretty Boy, and the rest of those gawking at them, know that she was his, all his, could not understand why an old man could be so lucky.

Aaron quietly said, "We need to have a word with you in private."

Pointing at a back booth, Pretty Boy escorted them to his private office, and Jasmine very politely said, "Aaron needs something, and I told him you could get it."

The Girl Who Stirred Up The Whirlwind

Looking over at Aaron, Pretty Boy said, "and what do you need Mr. Adams?"

Aaron very quietly whispered, "A revolver."

"And what would you need that for? This is Sweden; we don't have cowboys running around with AK-47's to kill indiscriminately like they do in America. Packing a rod is a pretty serious offence here. You could get in a lot of trouble, and, by association, I could also get in a lot of trouble. What is my guarantee that, if caught, you wouldn't lead the authorities to me?"

Jasmine interjected: "you have my guarantee Adrian. You know I have always been on the level with you, even if you didn't like what I told you. Aaron is not the kind of man to roll over under pressure. He does not forget those who do him a favour."

Pretty Boy, sensing a chance to toy with Jasmine, said, "So, what would I get in return? Maybe a week's work out of you, or maybe an hour to share some fun with you?"

Aaron would have ordinarily taken offence to that remark, but Jasmine put her hand on his arm, as if to say, "let me handle this." She replied to Pretty Boy sarcastically, "look, if that is what it takes, Aaron knows that sex is nothing but an entertainment exercise between two consenting adults, but do you really want to have sex with someone who is completely indifferent toward you?"

"Well, I do it all the time Jasmine. I am a scumbag."

Aaron interjected, "you got that right, Patay."

Smiling, Pretty Boy said, "I'm putting you two on. I would do anything for Jasmine. She finds me pretty disgusting, but she tells me to my face. Her, I respect more than any woman I have ever met. If I was down on my luck, she'd still give me a hand up, because she knows I am not all that bad. That's the kind of person she is. I'll get you what you want, and I'll do it at my cost, probably 5000 Swedish Krona. Get back to me in about two hours, and I'll tell you where to pick it up."

Sliding out of the booth with Jasmine by his side, Aaron said, "thanks. We'll be back in two hours. I assume you want to meet here."

Smiling, Pretty Boy winked at him and said, "this is my office and my home, baby. I'll be here."

While they were waiting, Aaron strolled through Stortorget Square with Jasmine. He felt like a teenager again, with her hanging on his arm like she would never let go.

The Girl Who Stirred Up The Whirlwind

Looking up at him longingly, Jasmine, with that sheepish and mischievous grin, said, "so, just why are you so intent on bringing down this guy called the *Whirlwind*? I know how you feel about me and that you want to protect me, but why agitate the authorities? Do you really think you can take on the U.S. government and win?"

"It's not about winning or losing, my dear Jasmine. I know, in the end, the little guy always loses. Ultimately, that is the way it is absolutely every single time. For me, it is about standing up to authority. I simply bow before no man, as no one ever should. Money, privilege of birth and power should not make a person exalted. The *Whirlwind* is a tool of a system that tries to keep all humanity in bondage. I am a man who loves agitation. If you love freedom, you love to agitate. Not agitating is like planting crops without plowing the ground. It is like wanting rain without thunder and lightning or wanting an ocean without the roar of the crashing waves. As long as I have breath, I will struggle against the moral and physical enslavement of humanity by those who wield the sword of oppression. Power concedes nothing without violence. It never has and it never will."

Fascinated that such a plain spoken, simple man could have such deep philosophical thoughts, Jasmine said, "And you do not think that peaceful solutions can be found to the world's problems?"

Calmly, Aaron replied, "do you think Hitler would have been stopped with anything other than violence? Do you think that Cuba would be free of American domination today had Castro not used violence to overthrow the dictatorship? Do you think the Sandinistas would have overthrown the oppressive regime in Nicaragua without violence? Why does the whole world cower in fear of America? It certainly isn't its moral superiority? It is because the world fears America and its penchant for using violence to get the results it wants. I refuse to bow to American power or any other power that wants to rule with force. I have seen what happens to those who meekly ask for their freedom. If you are not willing to use violence to get your freedom, you will never get it. I long for the day when the people march with drawn weapons on the headquarters of Exxon-Mobile, Wal-Mart and all the other towers of evil that take more and more from the working man, and it is never enough. Che Guevara said it wasn't the President of the USA who was the problem. Assassinating him would not change things. You destroy capitalistic oppression by killing the CEO's of General Motors and GE, the bank presidents, the stock manipulators, the directors of the defence industries and scions of privilege who inherit wealth rather than earning it. I long for a world where the playing field is levelled, so all can reach the heights to which each human being is destined. This is a world filled with abundance. The only problem is all that abundance is in the hands of the few, who see no moral obligation to share with the less fortunate among us. The *Whirlwind* is a tool of this insidious evil. And furthermore, he is threatening the thing I love more than anything else in the world. I will flush him out, and I will see that he is never again a menace."

Squeezing Aaron's arm tighter and tilting her head ever so slightly to rest it on his shoulder while they walked, Jasmine genuinely felt safe like she had never felt safe before in her life, as she looked up at him and said, "you're the mother-fucker who is going to light the fires of liberty one heart at a time aren't you? You know that truth is only available for those who seek it, because most people are too easily manipulated to seek out the truth."

Aaron, realizing the depth of Jasmine's compassion for those living a marginalized existence could not help but share one last philosophical thought with her. "A nation can survive fools. Ronald Reagan proved that, and America will probably survive the biggest buffoon in my lifetime, George Bush, but it always pays a dear price for the narcissistic ranting of those who believe the USA is ordained by God to lead the world. With God on your side, all things are possible, and all manner of evil is permissible. The American people are too blinded by patriot babble and religious mumbo-jumbo to realize that the real enemy is in their midst. It's not some foreign country. It is their own countrymen, the very ones who are manipulating them for personal gain. The real enemy is not at the gates. It is inside the gates. These malevolent anti-bodies are sly and rustle silently through the corridors of power. These are the real terrorists, not the people who are crashing planes into some building. Those crashing planes into buildings kill a few. These traitors inside the gates kill millions through their nefarious shenanigans that keep fairness and common decency from being within the grasp of those they see as sheep that can be led to the slaughter. They appeal to the base instincts that lie deep within the hearts of all men. These people are nothing more than a plague."

Almost laughing at the soliloquy of discontent delivered by her beloved, Jasmine could only mutter, "you are something else Aaron Adams. You amaze me. I think you really are my knight in shining armour aren't you?"

Aaron proudly replied, "as long as I have breath."

They strolled back to the café, entered and looked around for Pretty Boy, and there he was in all his sartorial splendour leaning against the bar to Aaron and Jasmine's left, seemingly holding court like an aristocratic baron in finery that was sewed with golden threads. This guy was a dandy!

The Girl Who Stirred Up The Whirlwind

Pretty Boy, leaving his admirers, headed over and greeted the two with a nod of the head, indicating they should follow him to the back booth. On the way, he grabbed a wiping cloth from one of the bus boys. He sat down across from Aaron and said, "slide your hands under the table."

Pretty Boy used the cloth to take something out of his coat pocket and passed it under the table to Aaron, who could feel that it was a gun. It felt like a 38, which wasn't as powerful as his trusty 45, but would still get the job done. Pretty Boy, looking to his right at Jasmine, who was sitting beside Aaron, smiled and whispered softly, "consider it a present in honour of the most exciting woman in all of Stockholm. Then, he picked up a napkin and, with it, reached in his pants' pocket as Aaron was sliding the gun into his coat pocket. Pretty Boy motioned for Aaron to put his hands under the table again. He placed a napkin full of bullets into Aaron's hand and said, "of course, the extra 36 bullets are 5000 Krona. They aren't a present."

Smiling, Jasmine interjected, "that's our Pretty Boy, always doing somebody a favour, but figuring out how to make a few Krona in the process."

"You got that right baby girl," replied a giggling Adrian.

Aaron, now feeling like he could genuinely go up against the *Whirlwind* with hope of surviving, said as he was counting out 5,000 Krona and handing it to Pretty Boy under the table, "you're alright for a low-life pimp, Patay. I think I might learn to like you."

"I grow on people, baby."

Jasmine, getting up, looked down at Aaron and said, "Let's go before you actually make me start liking this fashion plate of splendorous nonsense."

Patay looked up at her and winked. "Hey baby girl, you know you like me. When you get tired of hanging with this old man, you know where to find Pretty Boy." Then, he pointed at Aaron with his index finger and continued as Aaron got up. "As for you, you got a fine woman. Make sure you treat her right."

Aaron nodded his head in agreement. He and Jasmine headed for the door, walked out into the misty air and started on a journey into terror – the terror perpetrated by those determined that all hope be sacrificed at the altar of patriotic servitude to a cause that had long ago been hijacked by those who knew no mercy in a world of pain. However, they were both unafraid, because, regardless of what happened, they had each other. They would fight for justice together, and if necessary, they would die arm-in-arm in a battle to expose the truth about Olaf Palme's assassination. Now, they were going after the *Whirlwind*.

Aaron, with Jasmine clinging tightly to his right arm, looked at her and wondered why he had been so lucky to find this young woman who saw the good in him. He was a man who had been in a violent profession for so long that he had few qualms about using violence himself, and he had no moral misgivings about a world where only those who were willing to use violence accomplished their ends. It was a sad commentary on humanity that over the years nothing had really changed from the times men lived in caves. In those days, the physically superior ruled with complete impunity. Today the physical superiority was replaced with superior monetary power, but the concept was the same. In many cases, the violence used by the capitalist class was worse than the physical violence that had been used before, as it was even more callous. In the predatory marketplace, all semblance of compassion was sacrificed at the altar of greed. The bankers had no compassion for those they put on the streets. The insurance companies had no concern for those they fleeced. The corporations had no sympathy for the employees who toiled for meagre wages so the owners could have lives of splendorous excess. The violence was more subtle, but it was just as harsh. In the past, the bodies were broken and destroyed. In the modern world, the spirit was broken and destroyed.

CHAPTER 11
YOU HAVE ALL I WILL EVER NEED
MY DEAR AARON

Aaron and Jasmine knew that the *Whirlwind* was on the prowl in search of her, and that with Aaron by her side, he was now a target as well. Two agents had already been dispensed of by Aaron, and now the two most deadly were in pursuit of him and Jasmine. However, Aaron knew that they were now aware that he had turned the tables, and it was they who were also targets – targets of a man who was just as relentless as they were. The only difference was that Aaron had an allegiance to a woman he loved and refused to be brainwashed into service for a cause that was nothing more than a facade for the enslavement of people to the capitalist class that saw them as moochers who deserved to be looked upon with disdain.

Ironically, those being exploited lined up to accept their fate. They had even willingly given up what little liberty they had in a country run by thieves for the temporary security offered by the idiot in the White House. They were all too wrapped up in propagandized patriotism to realize that it was George Bush who was in charge when the worst terrorist attack in history took place. They had turned their security over to a man who had blatantly ignored warnings of an impending attack. His only goal was to enslave Americans to

J. Wayne Frye

the privileged class of which he was a part. What hope did a country have as long as the people were too blind to see they had sanctioned their own enslavement? What hope did a nation have that acquiesced to allowing their leaders to use terrorism to fight terrorism? What hope did a nation have that thought greed was an enviable trait? What hope did a country have that ignored the plight of the people trapped in poverty. What hope did a nation have that made health care a privilege rather than a right?

Aaron had lost hope for the country he loved long ago, and he had dedicated himself to simply surviving the best way he could in a nation that was like a ship in stormy seas heading for the rocks without a competent captain at the helm. The day of reckoning was coming. It might be tomorrow. It might be next week or next month, even next year or in four years, but George Bush was going to destroy the few positives that were left of America's image in the world, and he was going to allow the barons of greed to crash an economic system that was too heavily tilted toward those at the top. In the end, he would walk off with his golden parachute pension, book and speech deals for millions and leave his successor a mess to clean up like no other President since Herbert Hoover.

Added to this disdain for the malfeasance of the play-cowboy from Texas who thought a Bible in one hand and bevy of missiles in the other made him a defender of democracy, Aaron saw the American bandied commitment to democracy as nothing but a manipulated excuse for all kinds of malevolent acts conducted in the name of righteousness.

This was the same kind of evil that had been used to eliminate that champion of the common man, Olaf Palme. There was no act too dastardly for these two evil men who genuinely believed that the world must be made to bow before the superiority of a country where the only interest was securing as many nations as possible for exploitation by the corporate entities that were the true masters of America.

Aaron knew that the one way to flush out the two killers was by letting their handlers know that he and Jasmine were about to expose the whole nefarious plot that had led to the death of Olaf Palme. Their handlers would even encourage the two of them to go to the police, because they had ultimate control of the police, but by threatening to go to the American press, that would be the blow they feared most, especially the *New York Times* and the *Washington Post*, two newspapers that had been kept out of the corporate hands of the right-wing, flag-waving media empires that now controlled the news disseminated to Americans. Television, newspapers and radio had been handed to those who supported oppression and propagandized enslavement of people to patriotic servitude.

Yet, there were at least two outlets that were still relatively free to report real news rather than sanitized and filtered versions that supported the status-quo that forever bound the common man into subservience to the privileged classes of America. Aaron was about to blow the lid completely off a deep cover operation from 18 years ago that would perhaps finally end the obscene reverence in which Americans held that buffoonish, anti-communist, flag-waving, trickle-down economics prognosticator and sleep-walking so-called great communicator who couldn't put two intelligible sentences together, Ronald Reagan. And just maybe it would also bring down the real manipulative power behind Reagan's throne, that blue-blood former C.I.A. Director, President and now venerated elder statesman, George Herbert Walker Bush.

Aaron looked up the address for the Import-Export Bank of the United States, as he knew that was a front organization for the C.I.A. Aaron, knowing that he would have to go through a metal detector, left his gun at the bottom of a trash can in his hotel room. He and Jasmine took the bus to the Import-Export Bank of America. Going into the lobby he sauntered up to a clerk and said, "I need to see the C.I.A. section chief, and tell him it is urgent."

The clerk, trying to look surprised, replied, "sir, this is the Import-Export Bank Building. Obviously, you have your wires crossed."

Aaron leaned slightly forward, placing his hands on the immaculate, gold-inlayed counter and said, "get me in to see the section chief. This is important."

The clerk stood up and motioned to two guards standing by the elevator who came over immediately and took Aaron by the arms, as Jasmine stood in fear. "Sir, we will escort you out. Please don't give us any trouble."

Aaron very calmly replied, "listen assholes, I am only going to say this once, so listen carefully. I need to see the section chief. Tell whoever it is that Aaron Adams from New York City is here, and that Frank Penderent sent me. Now, I am going to give you five seconds to take your hands off me, and then, if you don't, the two of you are going to be picking your teeth up off the floor, so do as I requested, now."

The two burly men motioned for the clerk to call someone, and they let go of Aaron's arms as they pointed to a seat over in the corner. Aaron and Jasmine sat down and there was a flurry of activity around the counter until one of the men came over and said "come with me, and I will take you upstairs."

The Girl Who Stirred Up The Whirlwind

As Aaron got up, so did Jasmine, but one of the men said, "only you, sir."

Aaron with a scowl on his face replied, "she goes wherever I go. Let's go up, now."

The man, without hesitation, nodded his head in the affirmative and walked with them over to the elevator and escorted them up to the fourth floor without saying a word. As they walked down the hall toward a large bronze door where a muscular man sat at a small kidney shaped desk, Aaron was told to remove his jacket. They frisked him and then frisked Jasmine, seemingly enjoying the part where they ran their hands slowly and deliberately over her crotch and breasts areas while they seemed to be daring Aaron to make a move against them. As the door was opened by the guy who had been sitting at the desk, Aaron looked back at them and said, "you boys ought to find yourselves a decent job."

Although Susan Altman had long ago retired, her young replacement, Tom Talman, had been trained by her. He was just as taciturn as she had been and just as arrogant in his belief that he was serving the cause of freedom. Sitting behind an expensive desk trimmed with gold inlays bought by the taxpayers whose money was wasted on frivolous baubles for bureaucrats, he motioned for Aaron and Jasmine to have a seat. He leaned back in his chair and said, "Mr. Adams, your boorish attitude has gotten you in here, but you may not get out. What is it that I can do for you? I have no interest in this man you call Frank Penderent. He was apparently an employee of a publishing company in New York City. I understand that he was killed in an automobile accident. I believe his obituary was in the *New York Times* just this morning.

Aaron was shocked at the news and immediately wondered what had happened to Allen and Carrie. He said, "and I suppose he had some people with him in the accident?"

"Yeah, seems he was down in Arkansas visiting some friends. Some guy – hey, a P.I., just like you, named Brian Long was killed with him in the accident. Some coincidence, uh, both of you being P.I.'s? Bodies were burned beyond recognition almost."

"I don't recall telling you that I am a P.I.," Aaron said in a curt manner.

A sinister smile crept across Talman's lips. "Let's stop playing cat and mouse Adams. You know who I am, and I sure as hell know who you are, and I have a good idea who the woman with you is. You want to know what happened to your friends, Allen and Carrie Pink. They are still breathing now, but they won't be for long. Neither will the two of you. Coming here wasn't smart."

The Girl Who Stirred Up The Whirlwind

Aaron slowly eased forward in his chair. "You aren't taking us out here – too messy, too risky. You have the *Whirlwind* and Wilton trying to find us. O.K., I'm making it easy for you and them. I am at the Lilla Rådmannen. They better come after us with their hands full, and that goes for anybody else you send. I am packing big time, regardless of the laws in the country. Get word to them and anyone else. Aaron Adams is ready to do battle."

Taken aback by Aaron's boldness, with a stern look on his face, Talman replied, "Look here asshole, you are messing with the U.S. government. Don't come in here and threaten us." Then he looked down at a bronze button by his telephone and continued. "One push of that button and you are both dead. One push, just one, that is all it takes to make you history."

Aaron stood up and placed his hands on the corner of the desk as he leaned over. "Yeah, we might be, but you will still be dead before they get through the door. I am not some Third World country you can scare with your threats, bombs and bullets. I am Aaron Adams, and I live to take-out assholes like you who think the poor you kill to spread your military and economic terrorism are nothing but disposable commodities in a world that must be made to bow to the evil of greed. Fuck you and your whole damn organization. Go ahead, hit that buzzer. I fucking dare you."

The Girl Who Stirred Up The Whirlwind

Talman arched his back and stuck out his chest, as he pulled his hand back to make sure Aaron saw he wasn't going to hit the buzzer. He was scared.

Aaron turned to Jasmine and signalled for her to get up. The two of them started for the door, and Aaron, with a defiant countenance, looked over his right shoulder at Talman and said, "Tell the *Whirlwind* I am looking forward to meeting him. I have a friend who wants to say hello, too. My friend spits lead."

Talman sighed and gave serious thought to hitting the buzzer, but knew that it was neither the place nor time to eliminate two people who were gumming up the smooth oiled machinery of chicanery and subterfuge. There would be the right place and time, and it would be in the hands of the man who had proven time and time again that he was a master at eliminating anyone who posed a threat to the spread of the country's stultified, inefficacious idea of freedom. If only he could contact the *Whirlwind*, but he was now in deep cover, and Talman could not contact him. Only the *Whirlwind* could make the contact. When would he do it? Time was crucial, because Aaron and Jasmine might be on their way to contact the press. Talman frantically hit the buzzer. The two men rushed in and he said, "Put a tail on those two. Have them watched 24 hours a day. And get me Simpson and Black right away."

The Girl Who Stirred Up The Whirlwind

Simpson and Black were two young agents as cold and calculating as the *Whirlwind* and Wilton, only they had not been at it as long, and they lacked the field experience. Yet, like all younger recruits, they had been brainwashed into believing all was justified when used in defence of the American way and to protect the world from the scourges of economic systems that were not based on the greed syndrome. They were as dedicated to the cause as anyone who toiled for the agency that was the dedicated, loyal and disciplined vanguard against those who dared stand against the new world order.

On the way back to the hotel, Aaron immediately picked up the tail. He ducked into an alley, and he and Jasmine found a recessed area behind a dumpster. He herded her into the corner and waited. One man stayed at the entrance to the alley, while the other one cautiously walked forward. Just before he got to the recessed area, Aaron stepped out in front of him. "You got business with me, asshole?"

As the guy went for his gun, Aaron gave him a karate chop across his wind-pipe and he crumbled to the ground. Aaron reached down and removed the gun from its holster just as the guy at the entryway was running madly toward them. He stood with the gun in his hand and said, as the guy was reaching inside his coat for a gun, "fucking freeze."

The Girl Who Stirred Up The Whirlwind

The guy did as exactly as instructed, while his poor partner was writhing in pain, rolling on the ground with his hands grasping his throat as he struggled for breath. Aaron, staring daggers at the man, said, "I told Talman I was at the Lilla Rådmannen. I will be easy to find for whoever wants me. But tell him that anybody he sends better come with their hands full, because I am taking no prisoners. This is war between me and the *Whirlwind*, one of us is going to die. I am looking forward to the battle. If he wants, we'll play Wild West and meet in the middle of Stortorget Square at high noon. Get him the word that there is a new marshal in town, and he is calling him out!"

The guy replied, "You're a dead man, Adams!"

Aaron let a sinister grin creep across his lips. "We're all dead the minute we are born, son. That's the trouble with most people. They fear it. I embrace it like a long lost friend. Me and the grim reaper are pals. We love riding that dark horse and swinging the scythe to destroy everything in our paths. Get the word out, I am ready to fill the graveyard with you assholes. My finger is itching and my gun is quick. And now, I have two. In fact, I think I'll have three. Hand me yours very slowly."

He handed it over to Aaron and snarled at him. "This ain't over. You know that."

"I hope not. This is what I live for," replied Aaron, who motioned for Jasmine to walk down the alley in front of him, as he walked sideways, keeping a weary eye on the guy.

At the alley entry, he and Jasmine turned and walked back toward the Lilla Rådmannen, as she once again grabbed his arm and leaned her head on his shoulder, safe in the knowledge that her protector would always be by her side to guard her against any harm.

After a leisurely dinner, Aaron and Jasmine retired for the evening, and as they bathed together in a lavish bubble bath, the two of them fondled and kissed like teenagers.

After the bath, he went into the bedroom and he placed one of his three guns on the nightstand by the bed, slid the other two into the drawer, turned the light off, but was still able to visually enjoy the magnificence of Jasmine's body as it glistened in the amber glow from the bathroom light that was left on. It filtered through the slightly ajar door and danced in twinkling beads of light about her thick, black bush that seemed to be crying out for attention.

As Jasmine reclined teasingly on the bed, her legs spread as wide as possible to entice Aaron, he unfolded newspapers and placed them around the doorway and by the window. It was an old trick he had employed for years to alert him while sleeping to any unsanctioned entry into a room. Looking down at her loveliness, Aaron wanted to rise to the occasion, but he knew it was impossible. He just didn't have that old virility that used to keep him erect constantly, even when he was sleeping. Yet, there was a great surge of energy between his legs as he felt a slight rise. Hey, even half-mast was better than no mast at all.

Jasmine looked up at him provocatively and began to slightly thrust her hips up and down, displaying her magnificent love mound that was in a mass of coal black hair that covered her lower abdomen like a giant shag carpet that was waiting for someone to play in it. Her dark-brown nipples were erect and her stomach quivered just a bit – and those lips. Oh, those gorgeous, full, ripe, ruby-red lips seemed to plead for something hard to wrap themselves around. They were begging. Yes, they were begging for what was between Aaron's legs.

Her body was a soft blanket of beauty.
Her longing look was a plea for relief.
Her lips quivered with desire.
The world around the lovers began to fade.

She slid her hands over her huge breasts,
Stopping to gently squeeze her nipples.
Unbearable sensations seemed to be rising
From deep within her soul.

J. Wayne Frye

The Girl Who Stirred Up The Whirlwind

She slid her fingers to her throbbing womanhood.
Deeper and deeper she penetrated.
A guttural moan broke through the steely silence.
Aaron's chest began to heave up and down.

He swept upon her with intensity,
Sealing his body to hers.
Their lips seeking with open mouth,
Their tongues duelling in delight.

Wrapping his legs around her,
pulling her so close that they felt like one,
Aaron secured them in an ambrosial embrace
Of lascivious desire, lust and love.

Jasmine reached down and wrapped her hand around Aaron's half-erect, throbbing member, pulling back and forth. She rolled him over on his back and worked her way down between his legs, as Aaron pleaded with himself to get stiff for her, but it was to no avail. Still, she took it into her mouth, seeming to savour it like someone who hadn't eaten in days would devour any food placed in front of them. Then, her ravenous feasting slowed as Aaron's eyes rolled back in his head and his breathes became longer and deeper.

She teased him by stopping and then slowly starting again. He could hold back no more. He screamed, "here it comes" and she swallowed his essence, every last drop. Then she gently blew and kissed the limpness, as if it were her God and it had brought her glory to worship it. She crawled up to Aaron, wrapped herself in his arms again and their lips met in a cadence of erotic delight.

Aaron felt for her wetness as they kissed, rubbing, and fingering until she was oozing with delight and melted in his strong arms. He increased his rhythmic manipulation with his fingers, and she could feel the juices of delight oozing out all over her hairy bush. Aaron felt the throbbing and began to work his way down between her legs. His licking and probing was so furious that Jasmine clung desperately with both hands onto the sheet beneath her as she kept thrusting her pelvis upward. He was creating havoc in there, a havoc that was driving Jasmine to the heights of ecstasies only a wantonly free woman could experience as she let herself float away into the blissfulness of erotic release.

She pleaded with him to mount her, but he said, "It won't get hard enough."

She said, "Do like you did last night. Just put it in the opening and rub back and forth. I want to feel you, feel you inside me just a little bit. I want you! I need you!"

Rocking back and forth vigorously, rubbing inside her pulsating mound furiously, Aaron took one breast into his mouth while using his hand to play with the other one. Jasmine moaned into his ears as she nibbled on them, "I love you Aaron Adams. I love you."

After a while, Jasmine felt the rush of an impending orgasm like she had not felt since she was in the arms of her beloved Rose. The pressure was building up and so was her breathing. She could also feel the ragged and intense breathing of Aaron, and then they both exploded one after the other with a torrent of splendorous release.

Spent of all his energy, Aaron laid serenely by her side, speechless, in complete ecstasy as he had never known before. All he could do was survey her loveliness, as she was, also silent, with that mischievous grin slowly creeping across her lips. Aaron's furtive mind soared with a mental ode to her loveliness.

Ode to Jasmine in Orgasmic Afterglow

Aaron gazed upon the loveliness by his side.
She was the day's sweetest, freshest flower.
Paradise had delivered a bountiful greeting:
There was no hesitation to Aaron's inward power!
He had knocked at heaven's door,
And an angel was in his arms for evermore.

So he was living with paradise by his side,
As if worthy of life's beauty there forever:
No wish, no hope, no longing still remained,
Here was the satisfaction of all his desire,

The Girl Who Stirred Up The Whirlwind

And in that vision of brazen loveliness,
His deep despair was growing less and less.

He was soaring to the heavens as if he had wings,
And he seemed driven to the light far above.
He and she were now bonded in an abiding love.
And at the next day's dawn it would remain.
Hours of each day delightfully following the other,
Like two doves lovingly signalling one another.

The kisses they shared were like aged wine,
Casting a net of deeply intertwined desires.
To their love there would be no faltering,
As if it burned in heaven's passionate fires.
There would be no path for them darkened,
With their two loving hearts forever fastened.

Aaron's heart was by Jasmine imprisoned,
As if it had never opened before her.
Beside her, it was a beacon that shone,
As bright as all the stars the heavens showed:
Remorse and reproach were no longer fair
To weight him down beneath the depressive air.

All the worldly turmoil was now still and quiet,
No longer crowned with a depressive shadow.
Peace flourished where the deepest rivers flowed.
Love was now within Aaron's grasp.
Its sweet tone of surrender his emptiness to fill,
His rampageous spirit was prodigiously still.

How light and dainty, clearly, tenderly formed

J. Wayne Frye

The Girl Who Stirred Up The Whirlwind

Was the sweet Jasmine of his dreams,
A shape of heavenly delight that cried for touch,
Made of bright mists of delight from far above!
He saw her body shimmering as in a dance,
Her heaving love-mound crying for entrance.

But for no more than a moment did Aaron dare
Hold an ethereal image fast in its place:
Return to your heart! Much more easily there
He would find her, moving in changing shapes:
Though she was but one, the many he discovered,
Thousand-fold and ever, ever dearer to him.

How she waited at the gate to welcome him,
And delighted him, from then on, step by step,
And ran wantonly toward him with desire.
To press against him with her quivering lips:
This image of his beloved, so quick and clear,
Was written on his heart, in fiery letters there.

The images of her are firm as a towering wall,
Held by Aaron deep and abiding within itself,
Joy, much thanks to her, in being there at all,
Knows itself only when she reveals herself,
Feels herself free in Aaron's strong arms,
As his heart only beats for her and her charms.

Aaron now had power to love again,
And he needed Jasmine's love in return.
He had been consumed by her completely,
And found the glad impulse to hope again,
To make decisions, and take action swiftly!

J. Wayne Frye237

The Girl Who Stirred Up The Whirlwind

If ever love inspired a lover, then one could see,
To Aaron, lovely Jasmine handed the key.

And that was all through her, who before him lay.
The weight of inner care on his mind and body:
Flickered with images of happiness that loomed
Through the heart's wasteland anxiousness.
Now hope dawned across an unfamiliar sill,
In gentle sunlight she shined, lying so still.

In her peacefulness that braved adversity,
Brought blessedness that passed understanding.
The tranquil peace of love Aaron would compare,
In the presence of the object of his loving:
Then the heart rests and nothing can disturb
The deepest sense: the sense of being hers.

An impulse rose in his heart's clear depths,
To give himself freely, and gratefully,
So entering into the eternity nameless,
To something higher, purer, unknown, entirely:
He bowed in piety before her, without fear.
High blessedness with her to share.

Before her gaze, as before the sun's glare,
Before her breath, as before the spring breeze,
Happiness for so long frozen, thaws
And melts away within its wintry depths:
No self-interest, no self-will remain,
At Jasmine's comeliness dissolves with no stain.

It's as Goethe said: 'Hour by kindly hour,

J. Wayne Frye

The Girl Who Stirred Up The Whirlwind

Life is offered to us, even though
Our yesterdays leave little trace, and our
Tomorrows – we are not allowed to know:
And if ever he shrinks from the evening, sad,
The sun still set on sights that made him glad.

Look the moment deep in the eye,
With joy and understanding! No evasion!
Meet it with goodwill, swiftly as it flies,
Whether in Love's pleasures or in action.
Be only where you are, be childlike ever,
You'll then be all things, be defeated never.

Leaving the Goethe like trance, Aaron sighed.
Knowing he had been granted a moment's grace,
In her sweet presence surely every man
At once feels he's the favourite of fate:
But for an instance, he feared the loss of her
To any end he would not let that occur.

Aaron thought, how can I live without her?
Imagining her shape a thousand ways.
At once indistinct, then radiantly clear,
Slow to form, then swiftly coming into focus.
What great comfort these thoughts could bring,
This ebb and flow, this coming and this going?

Loyal comrades, these two lovers were!
The world was theirs to own as a celestial zone.
Ah - consider! Despair brought them together,
And slowly spelled out the mysteries of love.
Tomorrow would offer Pandora's box at a cost,

J. Wayne Frye

The Girl Who Stirred Up The Whirlwind

But tonight what they had could never be lost.

Full of blessings, they entwined as one.
Although dark, the room glowed under love's sun.
Their bountiful lips pressed against one another.
No earthly calamity could put them asunder.
Drifting, floating in complete bliss,
They ended the night with a slow, lingering kiss.

Collapsing in each others arms with a sigh of contentment, the two lovers drifted off to sleep after Jasmine whispered to Aaron, "You see, it doesn't take anything that hard to satisfy me. Sex between a man and a woman is more than a hard pounding from a virile man. It is about the desire to merge as one in blissfulness and delight. You have all I will ever need my dear Aaron."

CHAPTER 12
THE WHIRLWIND'S LAST DAY

Awakening and having a brief lovemaking interlude, the two lovers prepared for a day of searching for the ever-elusive *Whirlwind*, before he found them. After bathing, Aaron placed two guns in his two outside coat pockets and the third one in the inside coat pocket. He was not going into battle unprepared.

It should be stated from the start that what follows contains no embellishment. This is an account of just how Aaron Adams turned the tables on the *Whirlwind*, and how he kept Jasmine by his side for fear that leaving her alone might be more dangerous, exposing her to the sanctioned assassins who were pursuing her and the few others who might well be in league with them. They both feared the infiltration of the police department by the C.I.A., and even though the left-leaning Swedish Social Democratic Party was in power, there was no guarantee that neo-Nazis and other conservative elements that were known to be in various ministries and departments were not beholding to the C.I.A. For that reason, going to the authorities was not an alternative in a world where the long tentacles of that agency stretched into almost every government in the world. Using copious amounts of money for bribery opened up almost every government to the subversive designs of an agency that knew no bounds in pursuit of what it defined as America's national interest. The two lovers simply could not take the risk of trusting anyone, because it was impossible to decipher the depths of depravity that the U.S.A. was willing to go to in order to firmly secure the world for the corporations that really ran America. Jasmine's fate was in Aaron's hands, and she willingly placed all her trust in him. He was more than her lover. He was her salvation.

Finding the *Whirlwind* would be facilitated by the fact that he was also looking for Aaron and Jasmine. Both aggrieved parties were depending on the element of surprise to mask their intentions to dispatch one another. The *Whirlwind* had gone up against professionals before, but never a professional with the cunning, craftiness and lack of fear exhibited by Aaron. But was that lack of fear now compromised that he had found Jasmine? Was he now concerned with staying alive to bask in the new-found love that had brought meaning back to his life?

Aaron, outwardly confident to allay any fears Jasmine might have, knew that he was about to go up against the very best. This was an accomplished assassin, and no doubt, the *Whirlwind* lived by the code of the ancient samurai that stated "he who values life will die a dog's death." The *Whirlwind's* life was devoted to a country that he sincerely thought could do no wrong. A person who thought like that was indeed a dangerous man. Furthermore, thought Aaron, the *Whirlwind* would have a deep and abiding belief in a God who had ordained American greatness. Patriotic fervour and ethnocentric religious self-righteousness were used as an excuse for all sorts of depraved acts. People like the *Whirlwind* did not understand that they had been told a false truth that was all illusion. The good lie of the righteousness of America had a long life, and it was promulgated by those who willingly made vassals of retribution out of people like the *Whirlwind* and others who blindly responded to patriotic manipulation by those whose only devotion was the protection of privilege. With God on the country's side, all things were possible, but the problem was, the Fascists in the White House had also made all things permissible. Torture, killing innocents and lying were all part and parcel of what had become the accepted norm, and the one entity, the church, that should have stood against these abominations, sat in silence while their man of God in the White House, who had stolen the election, was proclaimed a great lover of Jesus Christ, who would have been appalled at what was done in his name. Yes, Aaron postulated, this man was going to be a titan of evil who would go to any ends to finally eliminate the one person who might destroy him, and to take her protector to the grave also. There could be no mercy shown those who did not bow in supplication before the creed of insanity that was being called the new world order.

The Girl Who Stirred Up The Whirlwind

It quickly became apparent to Aaron that there were two men tailing them when they left the Lilla Rådmannen. They would be the next in Sweden to taste the wrath of Aaron Adams, but they would not be the last.

They cautiously followed the two lovers, waiting for the right moment to eliminate them as ordered. The *Whirlwind* may have wanted to do the job, but now, Sampson and Black were going to intercede to bring divine justice to two people who had actually made threats to a Section Chief.

Aaron knew that the two would not risk taking them out in public. So, as long as he stayed in a well-populated area, there would be no fear. Yet, if he was to find the *Whirlwind*, he needed to go back with Jasmine to where she had lived as a little girl and talk to the landlady again, because he knew that she had left something important out when she talked to him before. The *Whirlwind* had been there, been to the place where 18 years before, it had all started. He did not know what it was, but there had to be a clue there.

Aaron whispered to her "we are going to kill two people Jasmine. It is us or them. Believe me, I do not take this lightly, but what must be done, must be done. Can you handle this?"

Jasmine, in a determined voice replied, "I am prepared for anything by your side."

The Girl Who Stirred Up The Whirlwind

He nodded toward a nearby café, and they went inside and had a seat. Ordering two coffees, he told Jasmine to discreetly glance across the street at the two men standing near a curio shop. "Take notice of their looks. Put your right hand under the table."

She did as Aaron asked. He handed her one of the guns and told her to discreetly put it in her coat pocket, which she did. The waitress brought their coffee and after she walked away, Aaron said, "so, you know exactly what the two men look like?"

"I do."

"Then, without looking, describe them to me.'

With intense preciseness, Jasmine began. "The one on the left is, based upon non-metric measurements, because you Americans refuse to learn the system used by the rest of the world, about 6 feet tall. Appears to be in his early 30's. He has a square jaw and dark hair. In fact, I would say he would be considered rather good looking. The kind of man who might interest me, if I did not have you. Well, physically interest me anyway. I'd say he weighs about 180 U.S. pounds. He has on a dark blue overcoat. The distance is too far to make out the colour of his tie, but it is light in colour. His shoes are light brown. His eyebrows, again, a bit hard to discern because of the distance, are relatively thick and dark."

Aaron, impressed at how perceptive she was, asked, "and what of the other man?"

"Also early 30's. Only slightly taller than the other man. He has dark hair, thinner eyebrows, a dour look on his face, almost as if he is smelling an unpleasant odour. Not nearly as good looking as the other guy, based upon my subjective observation. Looks like he'd be a better sex partner, though." She smiled as if she said that to get a rise of indignation out of Aaron, and then she continued. "Sort of a crooked lower lip from what I can tell from this distance. Black shoes and a dark tie. He has one glove on and is holding the other glove in his left hand, sort of playing with it."

Aaron, smiled a bit and said, "you'd make a damn good private eye."

"Better be careful. I might put you out of business."

Smiling broader, Aaron said, "you are my business now, girl. And I intend to make you my business permanently."

Smiling back, and almost giggling, she replied, "goody!"

"Can you pull the trigger on those guys if you have to?"

The Girl Who Stirred Up The Whirlwind

"I've got no problem with killing someone who is trying to kill me. It's called self-preservation. Something all animals have an instinct for, and we are animals, Aaron. We prove it every day."

"You got that right. And we are going to prove it in about five minutes. Listen carefully, and do exactly as I say. You do this right and we will come out of this alive and kicking. Make a mistake and one or both of us will wind up dead."

Then, Aaron explained to her how they were going to lure the two men into a trap. Jasmine absorbed every word with an intensity that made Aaron confident that she would carry out the task like a pro. She had to if they were going to defeat the *Whirlwind* in an elaborate game of cat and mouse. This was the first test. This would get them ready for the ultimate showdown with the master assassin.

It was coming on toward evening. In the eastern sky were floating tinted mists; and the clouds were a deep purple. As Jasmine stepped onto the street sans Aaron, he sat at the table and watched the shorter of the two men follow her. Then, he got up and starting walking a few steps behind the man, as the other guy tailed him. The people on the street were moving slowly as they were opening umbrellas to ward off an intense snow that had started falling. The magic time was near when the fierce, implacable genius of Aaron would rise against the evil that was now closing all about them. Aaron felt that old rush that he thought he had left in the jungles of Vietnam. He was about to go into battle once again, but this time, he had more than himself to worry about.

Aaron could not help but smile, as he knew the two men, now separated from one another, had fear coursing through their veins, as they wondered what he and Jasmine were up to with this ruse. That would give he and Jasmine an advantage, because they knew what was about to happen. They were prepared for it.

Jasmine turned down a predetermined street that led off the main thoroughfare. She had told Aaron where she would lead them, and Aaron stayed within about 100 feet of the man following her until the people on the street began to thin out. Jasmine would signal when they were within 100 feet of the right spot by raising her left hand into the air.

Suddenly, up went her left arm, and Aaron immediately closed the distance with a dash. His tail began to run, closing the distance between he and Aaron. Jasmine made it to a stoop, as planned, that led into an old abandoned building, She hurried up the stairs, removing the gun from her pocket and dropped to one knee behind the concrete rail that ran up the side, taking careful aim at the guy following Aaron.

Meantime, Aaron removed his gun while he was running, and fired once into the back of the man's head who was following Jasmine. As Aaron's tail removed his gun to fire at Aaron, Jasmine took careful, cold, calculating aim at his face, because Aaron had warned her that both men would be wearing bullet proof vests for protection. She pulled the trigger just as he was about to fire at Aaron's back. His entire face seemed to disintegrate into a bloody pulp, and he fell forward onto the pavement.

Jasmine pocketed her gun, ran down the steps and she and Aaron streaked down the street without looking back, sure that they had dispatched both men. They got to the corner, turned left and walked nonchalantly into a crowd of people, losing themselves in the impending darkness and mass of humanity making its way home from work. They had delivered the first blow and the message would be clear to the *Whirlwind* and Wilton both, they were coming for them.

Finally, after a long period of silence, Aaron asked, "are you alright Jasmine?"

In a matter of fact manner, she replied, "of course I am alright."

Taking her hand and squeezing it, he said, "you did good woman. You did real good."

The Girl Who Stirred Up The Whirlwind

The two of them made their way to Jasmine's old apartment building, where she had shared her mother's last days. She stood silently, looking about the hallway in a state of nostalgic reminiscence as Aaron knocked on the landlady's door.

No one came to the door, but it was slightly ajar. Aaron nudged it open and there she was, the landlady was lying on the floor in front of the television, face up with that familiar open eyed stare that meant she had met her death violently. There was a slight twist to her neck. Aaron had seen it many times before. It was that resistant twist that was a result of strangulation. And you could tell that the person doing it drug it out, as the indentations on her neck showed intensity of purpose.

Jasmine, not bothered by the recent violent deaths of the two men whom she saw as representatives of evil, was sickened by this old woman's demise. She had done nothing to deserve this fate. Looking at Aaron, she blurted out, "the *Whirlwind*. He did this. Let's nail that son-of-a-bitch."

Aaron, looking down at the floor, noticed a sandy piece of earth by the old woman's left side. Picking up the sand, he held it up and examined it carefully. Jasmine looked down at it and said, "that black stuff in it is ashes."

"Ashes?" quizzically replied Aaron.

Jasmine, feeling rather proud that she was able to help, replied "yes, and there is one place in Sweden where you can pick up ashes in sand. The mounds on the island of Norra Ljusterö in the Upsalla region. It is an ancient burial ground, where people were burned near the sea so that their spirit could ascend to Valhalla. My guess is that the *Whirlwind* came here from Upsalla, where he had walked among those mounds. You think he might have gone back there, or is he still in Stockholm?"

Aaron, contemplating for a bit, finally said, "Yeah, that is perhaps his base of operations. He knows I am looking for him. He is like a tiger stalking its prey. He comes out of his lair, pursues the prey for a while and then retires back to the lair to contemplate his next move. He figures not having Stockholm as a base of operation gives him an advantage. But I also have an advantage."

Jasmine, perplexed, asked "and what advantage do you have?"

Aaron, smiling, replied "I have a secret weapon named Jasmine Alexander and her knowledge of Upsalla."

Jasmine, actually starting to enjoy the chase, said "we are going to Upsalla aren't we Aaron?"

The Girl Who Stirred Up The Whirlwind

The Decree of Odin

The great Swedish leader, Odin, established by law that all dead men should be burned, and their belongings laid with them upon a pile, and the ashes be buried in the earth. Thus, said he, every one will come to Valhalla with the riches he had with him upon the pile; and he would also enjoy whatever he himself had buried in the earth. For men of consequence, a mound should be raised to their memory, and for all other warriors who had been distinguished for manhood, a standing stone erected; which custom remained long after Odin's time. It was their faith that the higher the smoke arose in the air, the higher he would be raised whose pile it was; and the richer he would be, the more property that was consumed with him. Thus did the ashes pile up over the years, and the land around Upsalla, especially at Norra Ljusterö, was rich in this ash that blended with the sand by the shore.

The next chapter in Aaron and Jasmine's great adventure was about to begin. Aaron entertained, for a brief moment, the idea of leaving her behind, because now, he was preparing to face the *Whirlwind* on his own ground. Then he realized that leaving Jasmine alone was too big a risk. There were nefarious intentions directed toward her by too many elements in the intelligence community now. It had gone beyond just Wilton and the *Whirlwind*.

Aaron had a chivalrous streak that preferred a mano-a-mano ending? Yet, he seriously doubted that a man of the *Whirlwind's* pedigree would possess the honour inherent among a few men whom Aaron had faced off against over the years.

Aaron and Jasmine sit nuzzling on the short train ride to Upsalla, and Jasmine could see the sense of dread that had descended upon Aaron. She knew it was not fear for his own life, but for hers. She whispered, "I am not afraid dear, Aaron. I shall never be afraid of anything again, except losing you. You are the rock that is the foundation of my life. If I die by your side, I die basking in the glory of your love for me. I could ask no more glorious a death."

Aaron smiled and placed his hand on hers, gentling squeezing it to let her know how much he cared. Words of love were no longer necessary between them. The celestial glow that shown about them when they gazed upon one another was all that was required in their ethereal world of affection.

Getting on the bus for Norra Ljusterö at Upsalla Station, they looked out the window into the dense darkness of the night and a light mist formed on the window. Tiny beads of water wiggled about the window, making indiscernible patterns that would gradually dissipate into the air. They passed gingerbread-like cottages by the roadside, the colourful hue of every one visible in the murky atmosphere. Cinders from roaring fireplaces fluttered in the air, then fizzled out, leaving the outline of grey, gradually disappearing smoke in the misty air. The darkness and the mist blackened and obscured everything from sight as they crossed the bridge over the Baltic Sea to Norra Ljusterö. They gazed upon the fog-shrouded glare of distant lights, and could hear the ponderous autos whizzing by in the opposite direction as they rapidly approached their destiny.

The bus turned onto a narrow thoroughfare leading to the heart of the turmoil that awaited them. There was a kaleidoscopic cacophony of sights and sounds that seemed to be muffled by the intense darkness. Lights gleamed from the long casement windows of the ancient stone houses as they whirled by them. The lurid, sullen light of the moon seemed to be attempting to penetrate the intense darkness, as it cast its shimmering light on the asphalt street.

As they got closer to their destination, the fog became thicker, seemingly obliterating all light except the beams of the bus's headlamps that were penetrating the eerie, murky darkness as a harbinger of the coming calamity that awaited Aaron and Jasmine. The intense blackness seemed to harbour grotesque, shadowy caricatures that bounced about in a misty illusionary dance of evil for a few seconds and then disappeared into the blackness. This was no ordinary night. There was a feeling to it – a feeling of impending doom and despair.

They eventually arrived at the last stop on the route. They were in a quandary about their next step. Aaron asked the driver if there was a hotel nearby. He said, "no hotels this far out," then pointing to his left, he continued, "but if you walk toward the ocean that way, you'll see a huge estate surrounded by stone walls at the top of a knoll far in the distance. Below that estate is an iron gated entrance. I encourage you to not go into that estate. It is a place that the locals avoid for good reason. There is something sinister up there. However, it is safe to walk to the left of the gate about 500 metres and there is a large cottage among the dunes. They rent rooms, but you need to hurry, because they close up tight at 10:00 PM, as does everything else near that horrid estate. I would not recommend being out past 10:00 near the estate. It is not safe."

Aaron, now intrigued, had to ask about the estate. "And what is it about that estate that presents so much danger?"

The bus driver, looking to the back of the bus and seeing that there were no more passengers, said "it isn't danger as much as it is just being cautious. There have been too many strange things happen out there.

Aaron, now sensing that there was more to the story, inquisitively asked the suddenly chatty bus driver, "what strange things?"

"Well, there have often been shots fired a few times. There have been weird noises in the night, moaning sounds and even screams heard on occasion, but the police, when sent to investigate, never go beyond the big gate. It is almost as if they are afraid to go onto the grounds. You see, the place is owned by a corporation in Switzerland, and it is apparently used as a hunting retreat. Anyway, just like America, where, I can tell from your accent, you hail, in today's Sweden, the corporations are exempt from the same laws that we ordinary citizens have to follow. Just part of the new world order touted by that buffoon you have as President, now. You Americans should get some sense and elect a man with a brain instead of a clown trying to play cowboy."

The guy had America figured out. Aaron replied, "You got that right, but never underestimate the stupidity of the American voter."

They shared a laugh and Aaron and Jasmine exited the bus. They walked through the intense darkness toward the ocean as instructed. Arriving at the shore, they could hear the surf ebbing and flowing, but the blackness obscured almost everything from view. They looked to their left at a hill that was surrounded by thick forest and there, under a beam of light streaking down from the moon, penetrating the darkness just in that one area on the knoll, as they peered through the damp night air as it pressed its thick wetness upon them, was the massive estate to which the cautious bus driver had alluded.

As they approached the knoll, the high stone wall became visible. As instructed, they turned left until soon, on their right, was the huge iron gate. The two of them stood there, gazing into the estate and then a few stars twinkled through the haze, the light casting an eerie glow up the pathway that led to a huge stone house at the top of the knoll.

There seemed to be a wrath in those twinkling stars, as the light was almost sullen. They were quietly raging in the sky, lighting the evil forest behind those stone walls. Jasmine, turning to Aaron, her eyes deep with concern, sensed the forlornness of the place that seemed perched on the abyss that led to hell. Then a red glow danced about one of the windows in the house. It was the colour of blood.

A light tapping could be heard filtering through the stone walls of the house that was far in the distance up the hill. It was almost a cry, no, a pleading for respite from the evil that was up there. The flapping of birds' wings could be sensed in the dark, but they could not be seen in the dark haze that surrounded the estate.

The Girl Who Stirred Up The Whirlwind

They stood in the fog, not moving. The dark forest of the estate seemed to be calling. It wanted them. There was a pull that seemed to tug them toward the gate. Their names were written in the darkness. It was if the fog had been sent to fetch them, to lure them up the hill. They saw the unnerving stare of an owl that lit on the top of the gate, and a wolf howled in the blackness. It was as if the darkness was stealing their dreams, and carving a vision of destruction deep within their souls that festered with horrendous screams. Were these nothing more than mental haunts? Or, were they grievous taunts to lure them up the pathway to where the devil haunts? The shadows were summoning them to seek out the tormented dreams of human decay that waited at the top.

There seemed to be shades of death all about. There was the intense silence of eternal sleep. Evil permeated the estate, and there was now a biting cold creeping about them, seeming to portend the cunning stealth of that which could not be seen but sensed. Yes, it was sensed like shadows in the dead of night, malevolent with peril. Something was seeking them out, something from the purgatory of evil delight.

Aaron had felt this way many times in the jungles of Vietnam. He and Jasmine were staring at death with its scythe and hollow eye. Yes, death was calling and would not pass them by without a fight.

The Girl Who Stirred Up The Whirlwind

Aaron, calmly, with a determined scowl, said "we don't have to look any further. He's up there. The *Whirlwind* is up there."

Jasmine said not a word. She just reached out and grasped Aaron's arm. It was almost as if providence had brought them there, or was it the demon of darkness that lured them to his lair? Darkness had always wrapped itself in rapturous delight around the *Whirlwind*, protecting him from harm?

Aaron took Jasmine by the arm and led her from the evil. He would deal with it on his own terms at the right time. This was not the night to tackle the *Whirlwind*, but tomorrow would be another day, and Aaron was determined to make it the *Whirlwind's* last day.

CHAPTER 13
THE FORCES OF DARKNESS NEVER REST

There are two urns that stand at the door
into the kingdom of good and evil.
One urn contains the elixir of love.
The other is filled with the liquid of discontent.
Never can the two mingle.
For the liquid of discontent will devour
all the compassionate fluid in the other urn.
Discontent is an urn of sorrows
and exhibits the failures of mankind.
This evil in the urn is a driving force
that devours all who drink thereof.

Maybe if Jasmine and Aaron could scream loud enough they could release the intense emotions of their growing love. Sometimes they were so overwhelmed that they felt like they were going to explode. Joy, love and life were now wrapped up in every thought they had of each other. It coursed through their veins. Each heart beat made the love grow stronger. It surged through their bodies like a river of peace, excitement, refreshment, renewal and restoration. Love was flowing through the veins of their lives. Convicting, revealing, teaching, nurturing, healing was making them whole as they had never been before. It was beyond normal comprehension as they spent another evening wrapped in each other's arms. Aaron and Jasmine had now transcended pure lust and settled into the comfort of blissful peacefulness that can only be found with the merging of two souls into one. Having brought no luggage, they had procured toothbrushes from the wistful proprietress who had given them both a quizzical look, no doubt, wondering if a man Aaron's age had procured the services of a wanton young woman for the evening. Nonetheless, she had no qualms about renting them a room.

As they dressed, Aaron jokingly told Jasmine that his grandmother always taught him that when he had no clean underwear to simply turn his worn underwear inside out.

Jasmine replied, "I always knew there was a good reason that I wore no underwear. I shall never have that problem."

The proprietress, Lilli Vanderburg, was a woman of about 60, but still incredibly attractive. As she served breakfast to Aaron and Jasmine, she could not resist asking why they were in Norra Ljusterö. It was a perfect opening for Aaron to bring up the nearby estate. "We came up to see the mounds of Norra Ljusterö, but we are absolutely captivated by the estate down the lane from you. It is so huge and a bit foreboding."

Lillie, her demeanour becoming stoic, offered an interesting assessment. "Foreboding isn't the word for it. That is a place that dumb-founds us all in the Upsalla area. There is rarely anyone there. Yet, when there is, there seems to be something sinister going on. All kinds of weird noises emanate from the place, and people are coming and going at odd hours of the night. Supposedly, the place is owned by some Swiss company. Name is Kimkassee Corporation, I believe. Anyway, I looked them up on line once and there is no record of the company. No record at all."

Finishing breakfast, Aaron asked where he might find a hardware store. Lillie asked what he needed, and when he said some rope, as they were going to do some climbing, she said she had some rope in her shed.

Of course, Aaron's intent was to use the rope to scale the walls of the estate. He was certain that the *Whirlwind* was there. He had been in the P.I. business so long that his instincts were rarely wrong, and the fact that the Kimkassee Corporation, the same company that paid the *Whirlwind's* rent in Stockholm, owned the estate, just confirmed his suspicions.

Aaron and Jasmine had not been separated since the first night they met on the street, as she was making her way to the Grand Cinema. However, a misstep on Aaron's part would separate them for only a few minutes, but it was to be a few minutes that would alter the flow of events in a way that would put Aaron's plans askew and make him lose the advantage against the *Whirlwind*.

The Girl Who Stirred Up The Whirlwind

Lies hide the truth of intent as the mind runs against that which enslaves, so the soul will dwindle when the light hits it. Thus, Lilli had no idea that she was a conduit of evil intentions when she knocked on Aaron's door and told him that he had a call on the lobby phone from someone named Allen Pink. Lilli's place was old, and so was her communication system. She had no room phones and not even a wireless phone in the lobby. Aaron, for a brief moment, letting his guard down, turned to Jasmine and said, "I'll be right back. I don't know how Allen found me, but he wouldn't be calling if it wasn't important."

The truth was that Allen had not found him, nor was it Allen on the phone. The instant Aaron picked up the lobby phone and heard the receiver being hung up on the other end; he knew what a grave error he had made. Dashing up the stairs to his second floor room, he found it empty. Looking over at the window and seeing that it was closed, he rushed into the hallway and noticed the window at the end that led to the fire escape was open. Running rapidly, he arrived in time to see a dark sedan pulling away rapidly and heading in the direction of the estate. They had Jasmine. The *Whirlwind* had Jasmine!

Aaron waited and waited and waited. He knew they would not harm her, and that for the time being, she was only bait being used by the *Whirlwind* to lure Aaron into his lair.

The Girl Who Stirred Up The Whirlwind

When the next phone call came for Aaron, it was not hung up rapidly. A cold, calculating, determined voice said, "My dear Mr. Adams, it is a pleasure to finally talk with you. I am looking forward to meeting you in person. We are very much alike you and me. We are both men who know how to kill, and it does not bother us in the least bit when we do it. I am in possession of something you hold very dear, and I can destroy it at any time, but I am a man who enjoys a challenge. Oh, if my superiors knew I was doing this, they would probably have me targeted for elimination. But, as it is, we can play for a while, before anyone is the wiser."

Aaron, being very careful not to antagonize him into a rash act, was very reserved. "You are holding all the cards. Tell me what you want."

"Your assessment of your situation is admirable. What I want is for you to come up to the estate tonight at 11:00 PM. The gate will be unlocked. Just walk up the pathway, and we shall discuss how we can ameliorate the situation that is, no doubt, causing you great consternation." Again, the phone was abruptly hung up, and all Aaron could do was wait for night.

Jasmine had, since meeting Aaron, put her fear aside and decided to meet her fate head-on; therefore, she was not intimidated by being the prisoner of the *Whirlwind*. She did not cower.

The Girl Who Stirred Up The Whirlwind

The *Whirlwind* was a fastidious dresser. He prided himself on looking the part of a dashing and debonair man of means, and, at 51, he was, indeed, a handsome man with thick, wavy white hair that fluttered lightly as he walked. He wore a tweed coat and an immaculately pressed pair of khaki pants, and his boots went up to his calves, where his pants were neatly tucked into them. He looked like he was about to go on a fox hunt. Little did Jasmine know that he had another animal in mind to hunt. In his waist band, he wore a pistol. Oh, and he wore a sinister smile, and he wore it with pride – like it was the bane of his existence.

Then there was Wilton, who, like his Guantanamo torture patron, Dick Cheney, was a bit chubby and appeared to always have a scowl on his face. He was obviously in awe of the *Whirlwind*, based upon the way he always seemed so reverential of him in both manner and speech.

As Jasmine lay spread-eagled, tied to a bed, the moon cast an eerie glow into the room through the partially parted curtains. She knew that Aaron would come through the fires of hell for her. Still, she fretted over what price he would pay for his love. The two men who were staring menacingly down at her had no idea that she had often been in ropes over the years. If only they knew that she once had a sex partner who played bondage games with her.

The Girl Who Stirred Up The Whirlwind

Her lover had, on occasion, tied her up while playing, then carried it too far and left her afterward, laughing as he went into another room with playful delight. She thought back on those days and how she managed to free herself on occasion. If only Wilton and the *Whirlwind* would leave her alone, she might free herself again from her bonds, get out of the estate and fling herself into Aaron's waiting arms.

As the hour of turmoil approached, Wilton and the *Whirlwind* left the room. Jasmine twisted her hands behind her; but all the knots held tight. She wiggled her hands until her fingers were wet with salty sweat and blood. She stretched and strained to no avail. Each second her veins throbbed with a lover's refrain. Aaron, her dear Aaron would come and pay the supreme price. If only she might free herself, and reach him with pleas to simply quit this folly and go with her to some far off place where they might live in peace, hiding forever from those who refused to curry sanity in a world filled with pain. All she wanted was to put all this behind her, so that she could devote her life to loving the man who had lifted her from the depths of despair.

It was 10:50 PM and Aaron stood at the gate, looking up the hill at a house of horrors that harboured an evil man who served the interests of those who wanted to enslave all humanity to the evil of greed and indifference.

J. Wayne Frye

The Girl Who Stirred Up The Whirlwind

Aaron Adams was a man on fire,
As he gazed up at the Whirlwind's lair.
The darkness awaited his onslaught,
A mighty battle to be fought.

He was no longer a mere mortal man.
He was a brazen animal on the land.
Around him was an aura of light,
And within not an iota of fright.

Tiger, tiger, burning bright
In the forests of the dark night,
What immortal hand or eye
Could prevent your mournful sigh.

In the distance - a house on a hill.
With burning fire, his eyes did fill.
On swift wings to his love did he aspire?
Would he dare seize the fire?

And what shoulder and what art
Could twist the sinews of his heart?
And when his heart for her did beat,
He raised his death hand and prepared swift feet.

What hammering fist? What clanging chain?
Like a roaring furnace his brain?
What evil to fight? What dread grasp
Dare its deadly terrors clasp?

When the stars threw down their spears,
And watered heaven with tears,

The Girl Who Stirred Up The Whirlwind

He longed for dear Jasmine to see?
In her arms he longed to be?

Tiger, tiger, burning bright
In the forests of the night,
Aaron, with a vengeful hand and a damning eye,
Was preparing to make the slayers of hope die.

Aaron contemplated the enormity of his task. The *Whirlwind* and Wilton were men who would commit any wrong, bow to any wickedness to serve the interests of their country. They were facilitators of a gathering storm that had long ago lost any moral imperatives. The weaknesses, defects and moral diseases which led them to this estate of evil were at the heart of their damnable souls that were in service to an idea of moral superiority that made terror and torture just more tools in an arsenal of moral depravity.

A gentle breeze began to give way to a raging torrent of darkness among the gusty, leaf-bare trees. The moon was a ghostly galleon upon a raging sea of despair that was building at a fever pitch. As Aaron gently nudged the gate open, the pathway up was like a ribbon concealing a package that once opened would let loose the horrors of Pandora's Box. A light snow began to fall, and the wind blew little flakes all about, dancing in the air as if they were in search of a warm place to light, where they could melt and slowly build into a stream of despair.

J. Wayne Frye

The Girl Who Stirred Up The Whirlwind

Looking up at the house as he trudged forward, fighting the wind, which had now changed directions and was blowing down from the top of the hill, Aaron contemplated what was about to occur. The battle was waiting there, and the smoke that kept the two warriors warm filtered out of the ancient stone chimney. It seemed to swirl aloft for awhile, as if waiting for the wind to make it dissipate. Then, puff, it was gone, only to be followed by more swirling smoke. It was like the two wicked men who awaited Aaron. It was there for awhile, disappeared, but then was replaced with more smoke. Like the smoke, there would always be people like the *Whirlwind* and Wilton, swirling about and then dissipating. But, they would always be replaced. There was never a shortage of those who would wilfully serve the interests of evil. Aaron thought to himself, *let not my soul feel dread of the coming battle. I earnestly desire to began the murderous slaughter of those who serve evil. As I stride upward toward my beloved Jasmine, blossom my trepid soul with prowess and daring in the battle to come, so that I may stand victorious, even if in death, that she whom I love can come down from this hill of darkness into the light.*

Lips can speak both lies and truth, but far too many lips spoke only lies. The heart screams as the soul dwindles where light cannot reach it. The *Whirlwind* had sold his soul for misplaced patriotic fervour and was about to pay the price.

The Girl Who Stirred Up The Whirlwind

Aaron did not have to knock. Wilton opened the door as he approached. Aaron knew that he was not the *Whirlwind*, because he would make a more dramatic entrance. That would be his style.

Wilton said not a word, only stood there as he closed the door. Then, at the top of the stone, winding staircase stood the *Whirlwind*. There would be no doubt who he was. He was a strikingly handsome man for 51. He had a powerful air of invincibility in his demeanour, as he slowly descended the stairs. There was a fierce acuity to his determined countenance. This determination signalled an individual who subscribed to a moral code that he thought made him better than the average man. But you just knew that he sanctioned the violation of accepted moral principles in order to accomplish the goals of the higher order that he served. This was a man who could violate every principle of human decency but justify his actions by saying that they are "for the greater good." Fulfilling his vision of the ideal social order was so important that, in his mind, it necessitated doing terrible things. This was a man who believed so strongly in the righteousness of the cause he served that the normal standards of moral conduct no longer applied for him. This man was an island unto himself. The physical bearing conveyed the depravity of soul that fostered unspeakable acts in the name of defending the glory of the nation he served. This man was evil personified!

The Girl Who Stirred Up The Whirlwind

It was quiet all about. The only sound inside the house was the ticking of the old grandfather clock in the hallway, tick-tock, tick-tock. Through the vast window above the staircase, Aaron could see the stars seem to almost tremble in anticipation of the coming battle. There was no glimmer to them, no shine and no light.

Over in a far corner, a rocking chair slowly rocked as if a ghost was sitting in it. Yet, it made no sound, not even a squeak. But still there was the one sound in the deathly quiet house, tick-tock, tick-tock. The wind outside howled as it whisked about the windows in muffled, indiscernible sounds as the clock continued tick-tock, tick-tock.

Still, not a word had been spoken by anyone. The *Whirlwind* pointed at the rocking chair, indicating that Aaron should take a seat. As Aaron eased into the chair, he could sense, but could not hear the mournful moan of the howling wind and saw an old tree's gnarled branches banging against the pane of a nearby window. Still, he could not hear it in the deathly quiet of the house, but he could hear tick-tock, tick-tock.

Suddenly the silence was broken by the *Whirlwind*. "I have heard and read a great deal about you Mr. Adams. You and I should not be adversaries. We should be comrades in the fight against those who want to destroy the American way of life."

Aaron replied, "Be careful with the use of the word comrade. The people you work for are still living in the 1950's and think there are commies hiding under every bed. They might question your loyalty if you use a word like that."

Motioning for Wilton to pour Aaron a glass of wine, the Whirlwind, responded, "today is no different than the 1950's. When you have a superior way of life, there is always someone out to destroy it. America is envied by the whole world."

"You are delusional. Most of the world looks with disdain on the USA, and wants to be nothing like it. They don't envy America. They only fear it."

Stiffening his back and puffing out his chest as Wilton handed Aaron a glass of wine, the *Whirlwind* said, "You and people like you are traitors to capitalism, which is a way of life that promises every man an opportunity to succeed."

Aaron shook his head with disgust. "Yeah, opportunities abound if you have the right parents, the right education and the right privileges. People like you are supporting a system of servitude by the many to the few. You and everything you stand for disgusts me. I'm not here to argue political philosophy. You cannot reach people like you and your compatriot over there who have been brainwashed with patriotic babble since you were babies in diapers. I am here to get Jasmine Alexander. What do you want from me to release her?"

Like a grotesque, crawling scavenger that rests upon the beaches of sand, the *Whirlwind* eased onto a sofa and crossed his legs, defiantly looking at Aaron as if he were about to devour him. He knew that Aaron had no fear of him, only fear of what might happen to Jasmine.

Among the trembling and babbling streams of life are secrets that are ill at ease. The *Whirlwind*, had never loved another human being, nor had he ever been loved. Were it not for his lack of a moral compass, one might well have felt sorry for him. Even as a child he had never had a friend, except in his dreams. He had wondered about in life aimless and slow among the rocks of despair, haunted by spectres of woe manufactured by those who controlled his thought patterns and manipulated his will. There had been many a surge and flow to all he did, but he never doubted the righteousness of the cause to which he was devoted. He lived in a mental cavern of the lost that was dark, deep and stained with the blood of the innocents who had suffered his wrath. There had never been tears or remorse for any of the heinous acts he had committed. He was a man with an emptiness of soul that made him an angel of darkness.

The Girl Who Stirred Up The Whirlwind

Just as the *Whirlwind* was about to tell Aaron that there was nothing he could do that would make him release Jasmine, and that they would both fall under his sword, at the top of the stairs appeared Jasmine, her wrists bleeding profusely. She had scrapped the skin off her wrists until she was able to work the bonds loose and escape. The *Whirlwind* went for the pistol in his waistband, while the wiser Wilton scurried into another room, no doubt, to procure a weapon. Aaron sprang up and floored the *Whirlwind* with a swift foot to the groin. The pistol flew across the hallway, and Aaron, with no weapon of his own, felt that he had no time to go after the pistol on the floor. He made a dash for the stairs where Jasmine and he met and missed death by only a hair, as Wilton had returned and was firing a pistol in their direction. One shot actually grazed Aaron's coat jacket.

Aaron and Jasmine never looked back toward their pursuers. They found a window, opened it and leaped the ten feet to the ground. The gate would be locked now by remote, and climbing over the walls would be impossible with the two men in pursuit. Their only hope was to lose themselves in the dense forests around the estate and wait for the opportune moment to fell them. They had no weapons and were on unfamiliar ground. All the advantages were with their pursuers. Aaron said, "I was going to turn the tables on the *Whirlwind*, but I am the one on the run."

The Girl Who Stirred Up The Whirlwind

He stood in disarray, bewilderment and fury.
Never was a man fiercer with purpose.
The Whirlwind armed himself
with more than weapons that spit fire.
He was armed with hatred for Aaron,
as his heart was empty and barren.

He was like a giant bird of prey,
with wings as black as the pits of hell.
He flapped about with intense fury,
coursing a raging storm upon a sea of strife.
His eyes were furious and roaring red.
His deep anger a steely, cold heart fed.

He was an angel of death,
In him cruelty had a human heart,
and evil a human face.
His hatred was forged in iron.
The Whirlwind would be the judge and jury,
He seethed with raging fury.

The two assassins knew Aaron and Jasmine had no weapons, but they also knew that they had the darkness and their cunning, which had served them well previously. Heading out into the darkness, the two men did not take any flashlights, and they carefully wrapped old shirts around their boots to muffle the sounds of their feet. They did not split up, because that would make it easier to get picked off. They were once again in the hunt, and their adrenalin was pumping furiously, as they

J. Wayne Frye
275

both enjoyed the game of cat and mouse. This was more than an attempt to eliminate a woman who might connect them to the assassination of Olaf Palme. It was now a game, a perilous game where the hunter could also become the hunted. It was a most dangerous but exhilarating game.

Jasmine and Aaron made their way stealthily through the brush, straining not to make noise. Aaron had torn his shirt tail and wrapped the cloth around Jasmine's bloody wrists, but they were cut so badly that they had already bled through the material. Still, she uttered not a sound in pain and clung closely to her beloved Aaron, placing all her faith in his ability to get them to safety.

Having no sense of what direction they were headed, Aaron knew that until the morning sun came up, it would be difficult to find the gate, but he knew it was on the east side of the property; consequently, it would be in the direction of the rising sun. He figured they had to avoid capture for about six hours until sunrise, no small task when up against two trained assassins.

As a youth, Aaron had often dreamed of being a mariner, and lived the Coleridge dream of sailing to sea. He would recall those days this night, because he was like a mariner lost in a raging sea of turmoil, fighting against the elements (Wilton and the *Whirlwind*) that were merciless in determination to ravage and destroy.

The Girl Who Stirred Up The Whirlwind

Aaron turned to Jasmine and placed his index finger to his lips, as he sensed something moving their way in the darkness. Complete silence was necessary if they were to avoid detection. Aaron knew that he could kill with his bare hands, but there were two of them, and they would be too smart to separate, so avoidance was safer than confrontation at this point in the pursuit.

Signalling for Jasmine to quietly follow him, they crawled toward a towering pine, and the moon cast a glow in the distance, and they saw their foes for an instance among the brush, but they disappeared in a flash. Suddenly, a thick mist seemed to engulf them and snow started to rapidly fall. It grew bitterly cold, and Aaron wondered if they could survive until morning. He took his coat off and wrapped around Jasmine's shivering body. Could she withstand the cold?

The snow was now piling into little drifts, which would make tracking them easier. They had no weapons, and now the elements had turned against them. Snow was to their left, to their right, in front of them, behind them. It seemed to crack, growl, roar and howl with discontent. In the distance in front of them, the moonlight shone like a spotlight into an area of huge boulders that seemed to lie precariously on a hillside. Then, like a light that was suddenly switched off, the light disappeared as a cloud covered the moon. Still, the fair light had shown Aaron the way, and they stood to flee.

Crouched low and scanning for sight of their pursuers, they safely made their way to the hillside. The ground was cold and slimy, but they huddle on it behind a huge boulder. Grasping Jasmine as tight as he could, Aaron softly whispered, "don't fret. We will make it. I have been in worse spots than this and survived."

Too overwhelmed with cold to speak, all Jasmine could do was give Aaron a determined look. She knew they were in big trouble, and her only hope of survival was by her side.

The death fires were dancing that night, and they could both see the glow of doom, but they could feel no warmth from the fires of destruction – only cold, only the bitter cold that cut through their bodies to the very bones that seemed to be on the verge of cracking. Looking into the darkness, they both knew that death was pursuing them in the land of mist and snow. Their tongues were frozen in silence as dry as any desert drought. Their bodies were withering at the root from the cold that seared their flesh.

It seemed like hours, but was only minutes that weary time had actually passed. Aaron looked into the far distance with a glazed eye of despair. Then, he saw something moving. At first it seemed like just a speck, a tiny piece of undulating mist. It came nearer and nearer, soaring, tacking and veering all about. It bounced up and down.

The Girl Who Stirred Up The Whirlwind

Had the cold overwhelmed him to where he was seeing spectres in the distance? Jasmine turned to look, and she too saw the thing moving toward them. She managed to whisper, "I do not believe in God, but I believe in evil. Is that death coming for us? Dear Aaron, is that spectre in the distance death?"

Aaron had never known fear of another man, but he did fear for his beloved by his side. The stars peeked through the clouds but were not bright. What was this spectre moving toward them in the dead of night? Then, sounds could be heard, feet crunching snow. Yes, it was feet crunching snow.

About 200 feet away, blinking incessantly Aaron saw what had been flashing about. It was a brass button on a coat. There he was, the *Whirlwind*. Aaron grabbed Jasmine by the coat, nudged her up and they climbed upward, the assassin in close pursuit. A single shot shattered the silence, but the bullet ricocheted off a boulder, as Aaron and Jasmine made it over the crest of the hill and scurried down the other side, now out of sight from the evil pursuing them. Aaron wondered to himself, where was Wilton? Why was he not in pursuit with the *Whirlwind*?

Like wanderers on a lonesome road, Aaron and Jasmine ran with dread at their heels. They never turned to look back, because they knew an evil fiend behind them tread.

The Girl Who Stirred Up The Whirlwind

Then, as the two scurried down the hill, there came a sound more frightening than bullets in the silent night. It raised the hairs on Aaron's neck and it penetrated Jasmine's pounding heart. It echoed throughout the dale and it bounded off the rocks. Hounds! Hounds! That was why Wilton was not with the *Whirlwind*. They had hounds, and the hounds were now pursuing Aaron and Jasmine.

At the bottom of the hill, lay death of another kind. The two had run into a swamp. Now, they had to battle snow, cold and the muggy waters of a place that cried of death. There was no end in sight as the two gazed into the distance, knowing that they could not turn back. The only choice, now with the two assassins and the hounds in pursuit was to move forward – forward into the slime and misery.

The two felt like they were walking into their own grave. Yet, their souls were warm and true with love, as Aaron reached and took Jasmine's hand, guiding her into the muck and slime, trying to put distance between them, the assassins and the barking hounds of hell.

Making their way through tangled weeds and beds of reeds, the slime oozed all about them as the snow still swirled about in seemingly sinister delight. Beneath them, the earth appeared to sink as they trudged ever forward.

J. Wayne Frye

The Girl Who Stirred Up The Whirlwind

Oh, and it was not the assassins that preyed on their minds, because a bullet was swift and quick. Ah, but the hounds – the hounds would enjoy ripping their flesh. The sound of the hounds was menacing in the dark.

In the dark dens of the swamp, a desperate Jasmine clung to Aaron. Finding a dry mound, he picked her up and let her lay for a few seconds to catch her breath. Still, he could hear a man's tramp, tramp, tramp in the muck, and the bloodhounds distant barking. The moon again peeped through the clouds, and in the distance Aaron saw waving moss shrouding a pine. Where hardly a foot could pass and only the bravest of hearts would dare, on the quaking turf of the green morass, the two crouched in the tangled mess, gasping for breath. On Aaron alone was the doom of pain. He could not, he would not let his beloved suffer the wrath of the hounds. If need be, he would dispatch her himself to save her the pain.

His whole idea at first was to put distance between himself and the *Whirlwind*; and, to this end, he had plunged along, spurred on in panic caused by devotion to the woman he loved. Now he had gotten a grip on himself, had stopped, and was taking stock of the situation. He saw that straight flight was futile, because he knew not what lay ahead. He was at the mercy of two men who were on familiar terrain. His only hope was surprise.

He thought to himself: "we will give them a distinct trail to follow." And thus, with Jasmine in tow, he tacked off into the trackless wilderness that lay ahead. He executed a series of intricate loops; he doubled on his trail again and again, recalling all he had learned when he was in the army. Soon, they were both exhausted, but he knew that so were the *Whirlwind* and Wilton. Ah, but the hounds. The hounds were animals of boundless energy when in pursuit of prey. There would be no rest from the hounds. Still, it sounded as if there were no more than three or four of them. With a weapon, he might kill two, but that would leave the other one or two to attack Jasmine. He saw several tree branches on a nearby mound. He picked them up, broke them into five pieces, rubbed one end of each piece incessantly against the base of a tree and handed Jasmine two of the sharpest looking ones.

With no emotion, he said, "this is your defence against the hounds. Jab at their eyes. You get them in the eyes and they will flee in disarray. You will easily see their eyes, because they will be like beacons of evil as they hone in on you. Don't be afraid. They can sense your fear, and use it to their advantage. You can do this, Jasmine. I know you can."

Jasmine, her shivering suddenly stopping, as she tightly gripped the sticks, replied in a defiant manner, "you goddamn right I can."

The Girl Who Stirred Up The Whirlwind

A big tree with a thick trunk and outspread branches was a short distance away. Aaron climbed up into the tree, and, stretching out on one of the broad limbs, tried to look in the distance to see if he could distinguish the *Whirlwind's* brass button on his coat in the dim moonlight. There was no sight of him, and the hounds barking seemed to be getting further away, rather than closer.

Then, suddenly in the nearby clearing appeared a spectre of evil. It was coming through the bush in a cautious, defensive manner with a rifle extended from the waist. It was the *Whirlwind*.

He made his way along with intense scrutiny on what lay in front of him. He stopped about 200 metres away from Aaron and Jasmine and surveyed the area by moving his head from left to right, then back and forth again several times.

Jasmine and Aaron held their breathes, fearful that a simple sound might give them a way. The *Whirlwind's* eyes were like bright beacons in the darkness. He was the most cautious man Aaron had ever gone up against.

Suddenly, Jasmine, no longer able to hold her breath, cautiously breathed through her nose. The *Whirlwind's* ears perked up and he scurried behind a nearby tree. He could be faintly heard moving away. Damn, he was a cautious man.

His strides were very deliberate as the sound of the swishing of the muck could be faintly heard as he moved further away. He was a man who took no chances. He sensed he was at a disadvantage, even though he knew Aaron and Jasmine had no weapons.

Aaron let out a huge breath and shared a positive look with Jasmine. Still, they were facing doom. The *Whirlwind* was waiting for Wilton and the hounds to catch up. Then, he would follow the trail through the woods with his uncanny instincts. Hell, the *Whirlwind* was enjoying this. Yeah, this was all part of a grand game to him – a game of cloak and dagger. He was toying with them. He was enjoying going up against Aaron. He had been doing this all his life. He saw Aaron as a menace to the new world order that had been so forcefully touted by that scion of wealth, the first George Bush. New world order, thought Aaron. Yeah, a world where the richest country in the world had 50 million people living in poverty, a country where beggars were arrested for offending the sensibilities of those who had too much and were unwilling to share it with others. A world that was 2/3rd's water, but people still had to pay corporations for water to drink, a world where corporations controlled the food supply. The *Whirlwind* was a man who was blind and deaf to the needs of those who begged for a crumb from the table of plenty. He was a man who defended an intolerable system of servitude with his evil.

The Girl Who Stirred Up The Whirlwind

Signalling Jasmine to follow him, Aaron struck off again into the swamp. As he gripped the branches he had sharpened, his mind was whirling with ideas on how to defeat those in pursuit of them. About five hundred metres from where they had seen the *Whirlwind*, Aaron stopped at a huge dead tree that towered over them. Looking about, he thought that the time in the army had not all been wasted on superfluous brainwashing about the evils of communism. They had also taught him how to kill. Yeah, they never figured he would use the skills to kill an American C.I.A. assassin. Aaron thought to himself, "Well, thanks Sergeant Boxley. Now your training will pay off in a big way."

Beside the dead tree was a small spindly tree that had just recently lost it leaves. Aaron was able to pull it back downward and behind the dead tree. He stood there holding it with both hands, the tension making his muscles flex as he waited for the two men to enter the area, so he would let go of the tree and it would crash against them, hopefully knocking them out. Still, there were the dogs, but that was why Aaron had the sharpened branches. He told Jasmine to go forward in a straight line as fast as she could, and to take her sharpened branches in case she needed to fend off the attacking dogs. She grimaced a bit, but turned and did exactly as instructed, confident that Aaron knew what he was doing. She had unfailing trust in him.

The Girl Who Stirred Up The Whirlwind

Following the trail were three bloodhounds in harnesses with a long leash in the hands of Wilton. Beside Wilton was the *Whirlwind*, whose eyes were constantly scanning the reeds, the bushes, the twigs and the gnarled trees in anticipatory cautiousness. So intent was the *Whirlwind* in his scanning that he missed what was actually in front of him. Aaron let loose the tree, turned and started running, not looking back to see the damage he had done. Both men were not quick enough to avoid the slamming tree, but they did jump aside enough to avoid the full force of the blow, and Wilton, shocked by the sudden turn of events, dropped the leash and the dogs bolted after Aaron. Since all three of the hounds harnesses were tied into one leash, they actually were pulling against one another. Aaron, turning quickly, stabbed them one after the other in the eyes and then swirled around swiftly and rushed to Jasmine's side. Still not looking back to see what had happened to the two assassins, he grabbed her by the arm and off they went into the swamp, hoping against hope that they had stilled the pursuit.

They were not so lucky. Both men staggered and fell from the force of the blow, but neither was seriously injured. Fumbling for their dropped rifles in the muck, they managed to retrieve them, and immediately started the furious pursuit again. Then, in the swamp behind them, Aaron and Jasmine could hear the shouts of a furious *Whirlwind* who came upon the dying hounds.

The Girl Who Stirred Up The Whirlwind

There was an intense, abiding hatred in the *Whirlwind's* voice. "You fuckers are going to die slowly now. I am going to cut off your balls Adams, and make the bitch choke on them. You two are going to woe the day you went up against the *Whirlwind*."

Aaron, never one to underestimate the use of levity in a tense situation, looked at Jasmine as they scurried forward and said, "what are you going to eat for desert sweetheart? What goes good with balls?"

Jasmine smiled and gripped his hand tighter. They continued to run into the darkness, hand-in-hand, bold and unafraid as the ground grew murkier and more coarse. Their feet sank into the ooze. Jasmine began to sink rapidly, almost to her waist in a matter of seconds. Aaron, with a violent effort tore his feet lose and grabbed a nearby tree branch, pulling himself up, and then reached down to Jasmine, who grabbed his forearm. Straining valiantly, Aaron managed to pull her from the ooze and deposited her on a nearby mound. They had stepped into a pool of quicksand.

The frightening sound of the hounds had been stayed, but the silence was almost as terrifying, expecting any second the arrival of the two devils of despair whose sole aim now was to dispatch the two lovers in the most excruciatingly painful way possible.

Aaron, his furtive mind racing through the possibilities of saving Jasmine and himself, looked down at the quicksand and got an idea. The two were familiar with the swamp, no doubt, and they would be aware of the quicksand. Consequently, they would either step to the left or the right of the it. Aaron gambled it would be left, and he told Jasmine to gather as many sharp twigs and branches as possible while he dug a hole with his bare hands.

The soft earth was easy to dig in, and within a few minutes he had a pit about three feet deep. He snapped the twigs and sticks, jabbing the dull end into the ground and making the sharp end stick up slightly below the opening. He put reeds and brush over the opening, and he and Jasmine moved about 200 feet away and waited. It was a crude pit and pretty rudimentary punji sticks since he had no knife to sharpen them, but Aaron had seen just how much damage they could do in Vietnam, no matter how simply made they were. It was one of the most effective weapons used by the Viet Cong in their battle against a superior force with much more firepower. He had seen many of his buddies impaled on the sticks, often pleading to be shot, because they knew that they had been urinated on or spread with human feces to infect the wounds. The likelihood of an excruciatingly painful death was highly probable. According to the USA, these were inhumane, evil contraptions that were the work of a cruel and merciless enemy. Of course, the American claymore mines which sprayed ball-bearings and nails through the air when stepped on were not inhumane. It was sort of like the Bush Administration calling torture the repetitive use of legitimate force, thereby rendering it legal and not torture.

They could hear their pursuers coming by sense as well as muffled sounds. The patting of feet on the soft earth, got louder as the two men had somewhat thrown caution to the wind, so furious they were over the deaths of their hounds. There was a new swiftness to their movement, meaning they would be less careful, and perhaps the pit would be the end of them both.

Aaron and Jasmine could suddenly see the pit better, as the moon came out from behind a cloud and cast an eerie glow down toward the quicksand. It was there that the two men stopped, knowing where the quicksand was. They surveyed all about, but neither man could pick up on the pit opening. Aaron and Jasmine lived a year in a few seconds. Why did they not move to the left and walk into the pit? They just stood there, scanning the area beyond, but unable to see the well-hidden Jasmine and Aaron.

Then, Aaron and Jasmine, hardly breathing for fear of detection, heard a sound that almost made them jump for joy. The twigs and reeds over the pit; they could hear them beginning to crackle.

The Girl Who Stirred Up The Whirlwind

Wilton had moved to the left, and the *Whirlwind* had moved to the right of the quicksand. Suddenly, the pit gave way and the two lovers heard the sharp crackle of the breaking branches. Then came the ear-shattering scream, as Wilton was impaled on several sticks, one penetrating between his legs and surging upwards through the scrotum. He flopped forward from the pain and several sticks plunged into his chest. Now, he was silent.

To the left, the *Whirlwind* stood stoically, watching helplessly as his comrade in deceit and murder disappeared into that deep, dark abyss that awaits all humanity. Now, the *Whirlwind*, for the first time in his life knew fear. Yes, he finally knew what it was like to be the hunted. Aaron had indeed turned the tables on him. The *Whirlwind* thought he was pursuing Aaron, but it was Aaron who was really pursuing him. Should he halt the pursuit and wait for a more opportune time? He had been extremely careful all his life, always aborting a mission at any hint of failure. Yet, his hatred for Aaron was overruling caution. It was now more than just the pursuit of Jasmine to eliminate a person who could connect him to the assassination of Olaf Palme. It was about Aaron Adams, a man who had stood up to the C.I.A. He was a dangerous man if left free to spread the truth about that horrible night 18 years ago. Caution this time was not an option. The *Whirlwind* screamed, "I coming after you asshole. I'm coming!"

The Girl Who Stirred Up The Whirlwind

Aaron signalled for Jasmine to arise and follow him further into the brush. He did not reply to the *Whirlwind*, because he knew silence was more effective than words. He could hear water flowing in the distance, and they kept moving toward the sound. Gradually, the swamp gave way to more solid ground. Then, there it was, a bubbling creek. For a moment, Aaron stopped and seemed in deep thought. He whispered to Jasmine, "I am tired of running. I have him where I want him. I'm going to make a stand. Go over by the creek, just stand there. He will not shot you. He wants to make you suffer. I am going to be behind that gnarly tree," then he picked up a huge branch from the ground and continued, "I will hit him from behind, and we shall end this once and for all."

Jasmine, with complete confidence in Aaron, moved to the edge of the creek and stood, waiting for the W*hirlwind*. The rustling of brush under the now rapidly running *Whirlwind* got louder and louder. And he got nearer and nearer. Suddenly, through a small clearing, there he was. He stopped and stared at Jasmine, his rifle by his side, aimed in her direction. He quickly looked left and then right, knowing that Aaron must be nearby, waiting to pounce on him. He suddenly gave the gun a mighty toss into the creek. "O.K., Adams, let's do this; you and me, one-on-one."

Aaron had to give him credit. He was ready to do battle the old fashioned and honourable way.

The Girl Who Stirred Up The Whirlwind

Aaron stepped out from behind the tree and tossed the stick to the ground. He was going to be just as noble as the *Whirlwind*. Then, the *Whirlwind's* nobility disappeared as quickly as it had appeared. Aaron had given him credit for something he did not possess. There was absolutely no nobility in people like the *Whirlwind*. He genuinely thought all was justified in the fight against those who refused to bow before the altar of greed and self-righteousness promulgated by those who saw no shame in anything they did in the name of patriotism. The *Whirlwind* let a smile creep across his lips, as he reached inside his coat pocket and brought out a revolver. He arrogantly straightened his back and said, "you people are all alike Adams, you think that being noble and playing fair should be the norm. It isn't. The norm is people like me who will use any means available, commit any heinous act, destroy the innocent to get the guilty and turn their backs on chivalrous actions to achieve the greater good that the few know is the best course for all. I am going to kill you slow. Then I am going to rape your bitch girlfriend, cut off her big titties and shove them down her throat until she chokes on them

A blast from behind made the *Whirlwind* lunge forward, dropping his gun as he fell face first onto the ground. Behind him, with his rifle in her hand, that she had retrieved from the creek was the avenging angel of Stockholm, Jasmine Alexander.

The Girl Who Stirred Up The Whirlwind

She walked up behind the *Whirlwind*, the rifle pointing down at him. Breathing heavily, the *Whirlwind* managed to turn his head and see Jasmine standing there. She said very calmly, "you killed my mother. You killed Olaf Palme. You're a fucking disgrace to humanity."

She smiled and pulled the trigger one more time, blowing his brains all over the ground. She dropped the gun and walked over to Aaron, collapsing into his arms.

The two lovers knew that what happened could never be revealed. There would be no way to explain the death of two C.I.A. agents at their hands. They walked out of the forest arm-in-arm and headed for the gate. They would let the truth come out through a newspaper. They thought their ordeal was finally over, but the forces of darkness never rest.

EPILOGUE
SHE TASTED HIM FOR THE LAST TIME

Jasmine sat at the bar by the hotel swimming pool, her long, flowing hair slightly fluttering in the evening breeze. The young man of about 30, with whom she conversed, was obviously enamoured with this striking woman. The long, silk, pink sarong she wore was slit up the left side, and it exposed a shapely, darkly tanned leg that glistened in the soft lights of the outdoor cabaret. Her radiant mischievous smile slightly exposed her glittering white teeth as she was obviously flattered by the attention she was receiving from a young, virile, strikingly handsome man.

As the young man was telling her how beautiful and appealing she was, an older man with a neatly trimmed white beard, obviously in his 60's, meandered up to the bar and placed his hand on her left shoulder. She looked up at the old man with an intense twinkle in her eye and said, "Darling, this young man is trying to seduce me."

The old man said, "well, that isn't unusual, what are you going to do about it?"

The young man, taken aback, could only mutter, "I-I-I," before the older man and Jasmine laughed.

Jasmine, interrupting his stuttering, said, "Don't be so shocked, my husband and I both know sex has nothing to do with love. After all, it is nothing more than a recreational activity. I am very flattered by your attention, but this is the anniversary of our meeting three months ago, and tonight I am going to spend the evening wrapped in the arms of this old man. I hope I see you again before we leave."

Flabbergasted by the extreme candour of the two, the dumbfounded young man could not utter a word as they left arm-in-arm. Leaning slightly against the man as she gripped his left arm tightly, Jasmine whispered, "Aaron, you must know I love you dearly to give up an evening with a young, virile man who probably has a member as hard as Italian granite for a man whose granite is worn, chipped, disintegrated and softened by the ravages of age."

Aaron, knowing that his days were numbered by the ticking clock of mortality, replied, "you can get sex on any street corner, but I can give a lot more than that."

Jasmine leaned her head against his shoulder and gripped him tighter, realizing that she had her whole life by her side. Yet, there was pain in her heart that night. She knew there was something she must do. She desperately wanted to share a final few hours wrapped in his loving arms that had been there for her when she needed them. He was a flawed man like all others, but his flaws never superseded his abiding love and compassion for her. They walked through the hotel lobby and got on the elevator. Alone, as the elevator ascended toward their fifth floor room, Jasmine leaned against his chest, and Aaron wrapped his arms around her, pulling her close as he felt her warmth. This was Aaron's heaven – having her in his arms.

They undressed and bathed together in the large, opulent oval tub, taking their time to gently touch one another and share the intimate moment. Aaron looked at her body and thought how young and supple it was. He found himself titillated when touching it. He thought that if only he could once again get that stiffness that was there so often years ago, perhaps he could make passionate love to her once, just once.

They did not bother to dress. They just dried off and walked leisurely hand-in-hand to the bed, where Jasmine laid down, her radiant, bronzed body shimmering with passion as it always did. The balcony sliding glass door was open and a cool breeze made Jasmine's nipples perky and erect. Aaron stood there gazing at her body, desperately wanting to get an erection so that he could plunge into her warm nest of desire. It did not happen. All he could do was lie on top of her and taste her warm, inviting mouth. They kissed, lingering in ecstasy. Aaron was almost ready to cry, as he surveyed the magnificence before him.

J. Wayne Frye

The Girl Who Stirred Up The Whirlwind

He gently kissed her neck, working his way to her right breast, which he suckled on like a new-born child.

The full moon bathed the room in a soft, subtle light as Aaron worked his way down to Jasmine's navel, kissing, licking and blowing softly on it. He nestled the soft hair that protruded from her lower abdomen and worked his way slowly down to that patch of thick hair that surrounded her love nest. He worked his way to the opening and began to lick, kiss and blow gently as she heaved her pelvis upward to meet his caresses. She was moaning now, and Aaron felt the blood rushing through his body like a river through a gorge. He was hard.

Pushing himself up, he looked down to see if it was actually happening, and there it was. Yes, he was hard for the first time in years. He crawled on top of her and his eyes were twinkling. Their lips met and she felt that stiff member enter her, plunging deep into her soul. She put her hands behind her head, exposing her hairy underarms. Plunging in and out furiously, Aaron uttered exhaustingly, "I love you with all my heart. Before you I only existed. With you, I was born when you kissed me. I have lived a few months while you loved me."

She removed her hands from behind her head, reached up and wrapped her arms around him, pulling him in deeper and deeper as she whispered, "fill me with your essence, I want you inside me forever. You are my life."

Looking into her soft, passionate, undulating brown eyes that sparkled with passion, Aaron exploded like a volcano erupting in primal splendour and glory on some distance island. He emptied every last ounce of his life force deep inside her hot, throbbing womanhood. Exhausted, but proud of his accomplishment, he rolled off her and lay by her side. She reached down to grasp his left hand and got no reaction. He had fallen into a deep slumber from exhaustion. She looked at him and his chest was only slightly raising and lowering. He was at peace. She loved him more than she had even loved Rose. That is why she knew that she had to do that which would forever darken her days and, no doubt, his too. As long as he was with her, he would be a target. The forces of darkness would never let either of them rest. She had no choice, as destiny had forever chained her to a life of wandering and hiding from that day when the evil would finally destroy her and whoever was with her. She had to leave Sweden and her beloved Aaron. She had to protect that which she loved more than herself. Glancing at her clothes piled on the floor, she knew that she must quietly put them on and exit from the life of the man she loved, if she were to keep him alive. She had to protect the man who had captured her heart.

The Girl Who Stirred Up The Whirlwind

She sat up and tears flowed like falling rain, but she did not sob aloud. She sat on the edge of the bed, gazed out at the bright moon and the twinkling stars. She looked down at her hairy mound and saw a white drop of Aaron's essence on it. She reached down with her index finger and picked up the droplet and put it on her lips, rubbing it all about, savouring its feel and taste. She licked her lips and sighed as she tasted him for the last time.

The End

The Girl Who Stirred Up The Whirlwind

**Other Books by J. Wayne Frye Available
From Your Local Bookstore or Amazon.com**

*Fighting for Justice in the Land of Hypocrisy
Worth*

J. Wayne Frye with Jasmine Falling Rain Frye

*Canadian Angels of Mercy:
Nurses in Times of Peril 1885-1918
&
Points of Rebellion: North American
Aboriginals Who Fought for Justice*

**Hockey Lovers Will Enjoy
These J. Wayne Frye Books:**

*How Hockey Saved A Jew From the Holocaust:
The Rudi Ball Story
&
Hockey Mania
And The Mystery of Nancy Running Elk*

J. Wayne Frye

www.ingramcontent.com/pod-product-compliance
Lightning Source LLC
Chambersburg PA
CBHW071255170626
46809CB00001B/229